Acc̲_____ ᴀʟ Cᴀʀᴇᴡ

"Opal Carew is a genius at spinning the most erotic stories by tapping into forbidden fantasies and visiting emotions that literally bring the characters to their knees. A steamy-hot read!"
—*Fresh Fiction* on *Pleasure Bound*

"Carew's book reminds me of a really good box of chocolates that you want to savor, but can't help eating all up in one sitting because it's so decadent and yummy. Feast on this one today!"
—*Night Owl Romance* on *Bliss*

"This romance is emotional, highly erotic, and most definitely a guaranteed keeper—in other words, it was written by Opal Carew!"
—*Reader to Reader* on *Bliss*

"A blazing-hot erotic romp . . . a must-read for lovers of erotic romance. A fabulously fun and stupendously steamy read for a cold winter's night. This one's so hot, you might need to wear oven mitts while you're reading it!"
—*Romance Junkies*

"Fresh, exciting, and extremely sexual, with characters you'll fall in love with. Absolutely fantastic!"
—*Fresh Fiction*

"Carew pulls off another scorcher. . . . She knows how to write a love scene that takes her reader to dizzying heights of pleasure."
—*My Romance Story*

"Opal Carew brings erotic romance to a whole new level. . . . She writes a compelling romance and sets your senses on fire with her love scenes!"
—*Reader to Reader*

ALSO BY OPAL CAREW

His to Possess

Opal Carew

ST. MARTIN'S GRIFFIN
NEW YORK

HIS TO POSSESS. Copyright © 2014 by Opal Carew. All rights reserved. Printed in the United States of America. For information, address St. Martin's Press, 175 Fifth Avenue, New York, N.Y. 10010.

The following chapters in this book were previously published as individual e-books.
His to Possess #1: The Seduction. Copyright © 2013 by Opal Carew.
His to Possess #2: The Morning After. Copyright © 2013 by Opal Carew.
His to Possess #3: Perfect Storm. Copyright © 2013 by Opal Carew.
His to Possess #4: True Lies. Copyright © 2014 by Opal Carew.
His to Possess #5: Entangled. Copyright © 2014 by Opal Carew.
His to Possess #6: Forever. Copyright © 2014 by Opal Carew.

www.stmartins.com

Library of Congress Cataloging-in-Publication Data

Carew, Opal.
    His to Possess / Opal Carew.—First edition.
        p. cm.
    ISBN 978-0-312-67464-9 (trade paperback)
    ISBN 978-1-4668-4102-4 (e-book)
 1. Erotic fiction.   I. Title.
PR9199.4.C367H64 2014
813'.6—dc23

                                    2013048536

St. Martin's Griffin books may be purchased for educational, business, or promotional use. For information on bulk purchases, please contact Macmillan Corporate and Premium Sales Department at 1-800-221-7945, extension 5442, or write specialmarkets@macmillan.com.

First Edition: March 2014

10 9 8 7 6 5 4 3 2 1

To Laurie.
You're the best!

His to Possess

The Seduction

Jessica watched the busy traffic and streams of people passing by the window as she took a last sip of coffee, then set the empty mug on the table. One man crossing the street toward her caught her eye. There was something familiar about his face, but she couldn't get a good look at him to figure out why.

She pulled her wallet from her purse and placed her credit card on the bill the waitress had left on a plastic tray on the table. Eating at this little restaurant a block from her hotel had definitely been a good idea. The food here was much cheaper than at the hotel restaurant and this trip to Philadelphia was already straining her budget. Coming here for the big career fair was worth the risk, though.

The waitress came by and picked up her card. As Jessica waited for her to return, she continued watching the men and women rushing by in business attire, trying to catch sight of the man again.

Self-consciously, she reached behind her head and checked her hair, which was coiled and held up with a clip. She didn't usually wear her long, black hair up, but she felt it looked more professional this way. The same with her smart charcoal gray suit and white blouse. Not her usual attire, since the environment at her cousin Sally's company, where Jessica had last worked, had been pretty casual and everyone who worked there normally wore jeans to the office. Thank heavens for credit cards.

She glanced at her watch, and her stomach churned. She had to get going. The waitress returned with her card and Jessica signed the slip and tucked the receipt into her wallet. As she slipped on her coat, she noticed the man again, this time buying a newspaper from a newsstand just outside. She froze when she realized why this man had drawn her attention.

It was Storm.

This man, in his expensive-looking, tailored suit, his dark hair in a short and stylish cut, was the opposite of the Storm she knew. Her Storm had spiky hair and was typically in comfortable jeans and a skin-tight tank top that showed off his muscles and tattoos, with a black leather jacket at the ready for when he hopped on his big, sleek Harley. He was a guitarist in her brother's rock band, and he wouldn't be caught dead in business attire.

She watched this suited man as he tucked the paper under his arm and started walking down the street. That was definitely Storm's face. She gathered her purse and briefcase from the chair beside her and stood up. What was Storm doing here? And dressed like that?

She hadn't seen him in over a month. Not since the night he'd walked out on her.

Everything had been so good between them before that. Her heartbeat sped up at the memory. It had been better than good. All the women in town had been gaga over him, but he'd only had eyes for her. Hot, incredibly sexy eyes. She almost giggled at the memory. He was so tall, sexy, and macho. He could have had any woman he wanted, but he'd chosen her. He'd always made her melt inside every time he looked at her with that bad boy smile, and those smoldering, love-filled eyes.

At least, she'd thought it had been love, but clearly she'd been wrong. He'd up and left her life as abruptly as he'd entered it six months earlier, leaving her heartbroken and lonely.

She strolled to the door of the restaurant and stepped outside into the cool air. The sky was overcast and she hoped the rain would hold off until she was inside the career fair.

She noticed Storm was now in the crowd of people waiting at the light on the next block. The light turned green and he crossed.

Why was he here in Philadelphia?

Was it possible he'd come here looking for her? Maybe her mom had told him she was here and he'd come looking for her to tell her he couldn't live without her.

But surely Mom wouldn't do that.

It was a far-fetched thought anyway, because right now he and the band should be traveling through California. But she couldn't think of any other reason why Storm would be in Philadelphia. And he *was* walking in the direction of her hotel.

Her heart swelled at the thought that he still loved her. She longed to be in his arms again. His hard, muscular body pressed tight to hers. His big, strong arms around her.

Oh, God, she'd missed him. Dreamt of him night after night, waking up quivering with need.

She glanced at her watch. She could grab a cab to the career fair, which would get her there fairly quickly. That way, a short detour shouldn't make her late. She hurried across the street after him. He turned into a Starbucks. Perfect. She could go in and just casually run into him. No biggie. Just two old friends happening across each other in a new city.

She opened the door and hurried inside, then glanced around and saw him at the counter placing his order.

Her heart fluttered. She knew that if he turned and gave her that heart-melting smile of his, then told her he wanted her back, she'd throw herself into his arms and kiss him like crazy. Then she would probably drag him back to her hotel room.

A smile curled her lips. Why kid herself? If he was here to win her back—and why else would he be here?—she would welcome him with open arms.

She drew back her shoulders and marched toward him.

"Storm," she said as casually as she could manage.

He poured cream into his coffee, then opened a sugar packet, totally ignoring her.

She stepped closer. "Storm."

He glanced toward her and her heart stopped. *Oh, God, that's not Storm.*

Her cheeks heated as she stared at the complete stranger.

A stranger who was every bit as handsome as Storm. Electricity sizzled through her as his piercing blue eyes locked on her. Those eyes were darker than Storm's, but with the same navy ring around the rim. And his dark brown hair, though cut much shorter than Storm's, was the same glossy texture and color. In fact, their features were strikingly similar, which was why she'd mistaken this man for Storm in the first place.

His eyebrows arched. "Excuse me?" he said, in a deep masculine voice.

"Oh, um . . ." She drew in a shaky breath. "I'm sorry. I thought you were someone else."

He smiled. "Are you meeting this someone here?"

"Oh, no. I'm from out of town and I thought . . . you just look like someone I know."

"So you were hoping for a friendly face."

The warmth in his eyes, lit up by that debonair smile of his, stirred something deep inside her. She imagined this man asking her to join him for coffee, then them talking . . . and him inviting her to dinner, and that leading to . . .

She swallowed. "Um, I just wanted to say hello. I mean, to Storm. Not you." Oh, damn, now she sounded rude.

Her heart thumped loudly in her chest and all she could think of was getting out of here. Away from this man's speculative gaze.

This sexy, drop-dead gorgeous man.

"Would you like to join me for a coffee?" he asked.

Panic welled up in her as she realized she was actually considering accepting. Did she really want this stranger to pick her up?

She glanced at her watch. "Sorry, I have to be somewhere. Um . . . good-bye." With that she turned and raced out of the shop, her face still burning.

Dane watched the lovely woman scurry out the door as if she were escaping a predator.

Lightning flashed outside and what had started as a light rain now streamed down the window panes. He liked to walk to the office in the morning, but he drew the line at getting soaked. He picked up his coffee and sat down at one of the tables, then pulled out his cell phone. Outside he could see the lovely stranger trying to hail a cab. He smiled as he watched her timid attempts. Not even stepping off the sidewalk and making a pitiful little hand gesture toward the street. She'd never get a cab that way.

Jessica stuck out her hand as a cab drove past, but it didn't stop. Being from a small town, she wasn't used to hailing cabs, but she'd watched others doing it and it seemed simple enough. Most of the cabs that had driven by over the past few minutes had their top lights off, indicating they were unavailable. This one had its light on, but there were passengers inside, so maybe the driver had forgotten to turn it off. She tried to hail another, but it stopped for someone a little farther down the street. After several more failed attempts, she started to feel invisible.

The rain, which had begun as a drizzle, started coming down harder. Why hadn't she thought to bring an umbrella? Water streamed down her hair.

She tried for another cab, and was pleased to see it pull up, but then a couple pushed past her and hopped inside. She stared at them, her mouth agape at their rudeness.

A black limousine pulled up and the back window glided down.

"Would you like a lift?" asked a familiar male voice. It was the man from the Starbucks.

Should she just climb into a limo with a stranger?

Water dribbled down her forehead and she wiped it away.

"Yes, thank you."

Jessica settled into the leather seat beside the stranger who looked so much like Storm. The limo pulled smoothly into traffic.

"Where are you heading?" he asked.

She pulled the address from her purse and handed it to him.

"Jeff, we'll be dropping the lady at the DoubleTree on Broad Street."

"Yes, sir," the chauffeur said, then closed the smoked glass partition.

This man must be pretty rich with his expensive suit and a chauffeur driving him around. The thought intimidated her a little.

She shifted in the seat, aware that she was dripping water all over the buttery leather seats.

"Thank you again. I really appreciate the ride."

The man beside her smiled. "My pleasure. My name is Dane."

He offered his hand and she grasped it for a handshake.

"I'm Jessica Long."

Heat hummed through her as his fingers closed around hers, then he gently squeezed before he let go. He was so big and masculine. Her hormones pulsed through her, tempting her to lean in a little closer and breathe in the musky male scent of him.

He reached into a compartment beside the seat and handed her a towel. "The rain has played havoc with your hair."

He flipped open a mirror on one of the side panels and she could see her drooping wet hair.

"Oh, no. I look awful."

He smiled. "I wouldn't say that."

She pulled the clip from the back of her head and her hair tumbled over her shoulders. She towel dried it, then pulled a brush out of her purse and ran it through her long, and now only slightly damp, tresses.

"Your hair looks lovely like that."

She glanced at his smiling face and her insides quivered at the heat in his eyes.

"Um . . . thanks. I think it looks more professional up, though."

"You're going to a business meeting, I presume."

"A career fair, actually." She twisted her long hair into a coil, then clipped it up again. She glanced at her reflection in the mirror and tucked in a few loose strands.

"Ah, things too limiting in your current job?"

"I don't have a job right now," she admitted. "In fact, I've been out of work for four months." She glanced at his face, expecting to see disapproval, but he simply waited for her to continue. "I come from a small town and jobs are really limited there."

"Well, you're doing the right thing coming to the city. There'll be a lot of opportunities at the career fair."

She nodded, but the thought of walking into a room with all those people looking for jobs, the employers assessing everyone who stepped into their booth, made her stomach queasy.

"You don't look convinced," he said.

She shook her head. "I'm just nervous because I'm not used to networking and being interviewed. For the past six years I worked for my cousin, Sally, who had her own company developing Web sites. Then she got married and moved to Oregon."

Damn, she was nattering.

"When you're talking to a potential employer, just keep three things in mind."

She gazed at him with a keen focus, ready to soak in his words of wisdom.

"Listen to what the other person has to say. Respond with something positive."

At his pause, she prompted, "And the third thing?"

"Smile. When you do that, your whole face lights up."

She glanced down at her clasped hands self-consciously. "Thank you, but I doubt that will make a difference."

"It will. It makes you memorable, and that gives you an edge. When these people go back to their offices with a whole stack of résumés and a vague memory of the short interviews they had with people, they'll be more inclined to call back someone who stands out, even if that reason is because of a beautiful smile."

She knew he was just trying to make her feel better, but she decided to put his advice into action. "That sounds like great advice. Thank you." Then she smiled.

He chuckled. "I know you don't believe it, but trust me. It'll work."

The limo slowed down and Dane glanced out the window. "We're almost there."

"Thanks for the ride."

The limo pulled to a stop and the driver got out of the car.

"One more thing." He pulled something out of his pocket and handed it to her.

She took what appeared to be a flat stone from his hand.

"It's a tranquility stone. Keep it in your pocket and if you feel yourself getting anxious, rub it between your thumb and finger. It'll help calm your nerves. It'll also remind you to follow my advice."

It was a lovely pale blue with white bands, flat, and completely smooth. And it was still warm from being in his pocket. Close to his body. She stroked her thumb over the surface. It was so . . . comforting.

"I can't take your stone."

He shrugged. "Of course you can."

The driver opened the door.

"Oh, well . . . again, thank you." She slipped the stone in her coat pocket.

The driver held an umbrella over her as she got out of the car.

She turned back and Dane held out her briefcase.

"Jessica, you'll do fine today. I'm sure you'll find a great job."

She nodded and turned away as the driver closed the car door, then walked her to the entrance of the hotel. As she went inside, she realized she should have asked for his card. That was one of the basics of networking. Man, she really was bad at this.

Jessica relaxed into the soft, cushioned booth at the quiet restaurant six blocks from the hotel. She'd spoken to more than two dozen employers today and she was exhausted. She was looking forward to a nice quiet dinner, then going back to her room to recharge before tomorrow. One more harrowing day meeting employers, then she'd be on her way home.

Her fingers stroked over the tranquility stone in her skirt pocket. She was surprised she hadn't worn a hole through it. Dane had been right, it had helped her relax. And she had followed his advice. Listen, make a positive comment, and smile. But she wasn't sure how much good it had done her. After most of the interviews, they just said they'd keep her résumé on file for six months.

Having the stone, and following Dane's advice, had made her think of him all day long. They'd said good-bye this morning and she knew she'd never see him again, but she wished it could be different. It was sweet how he'd offered her a ride, and then given her advice on how to succeed at the career fair.

Her finger stroked over the smooth stone in her hand. It was just a stone, but it had been his. He'd carried it with him. And he'd given it to her. As a gift.

The warmth of the stone against her fingers reminded her of the warmth of his fingers around hers when he'd shaken her hand. There'd been a spark of interest in his warm blue eyes.

The waitress arrived with the wine she'd asked for. Except instead of placing a single glass full of wine in front of her, she placed an empty glass and poured from a blue bottle, then set it on the table.

"I'm sorry, there's been a mistake," Jessica said. "I ordered a glass of the house wine."

"I assure you, this is a much better choice."

At the familiar masculine voice, she glanced up to see Dane standing beside the table smiling at her. She pulled herself up straighter in the chair, her heart racing.

"How did you find me?"

"I wanted to invite you to dinner, so I called the closest hotels to where we met this morning and asked for you. When I found your hotel, you weren't in, so I stopped by the hotel and bribed the concierge for any information he might have about where you went. He remembered you calling down to ask for a recommendation on where to eat." He smiled. "And voilà, here I am."

She smiled. "So you were stalking me." She couldn't believe an important man like Dane would even give her a second thought.

"May I join you for dinner?"

His powerful masculine presence and devastatingly attractive smile dazzled her. She concentrated on keeping her breathing even.

"Well, I can't drink a whole bottle of wine by myself and I'd hate to see it go to waste."

He sat across from her and the waitress produced another wineglass, filled it, and set it in front of Dane.

He sipped it and smiled at her. "Very nice. What do you think?"

She tasted the wine and a subtle flavor of delicate fruits danced across her tongue. She didn't know a lot about wine, but she found this one delightful.

"It's very nice. Thank you."

"My pleasure." He ordered a seafood pasta from the waitress, then turned back to Jessica. "So how did it go?" He picked up the cloth napkin from his plate and unfolded it, then set it on his lap.

"All right. I handed in my résumé to about twenty-five employers. Some just answered general questions and took résumés, but about a dozen actually took time to interview me."

"Good. And did you follow my advice?"

She smiled and nodded. "Yes, thank you. It was very helpful."

"Then I'm sure you'll get some calls."

She wished she was as confident as he was.

The waitress brought their meals and she dug in to her salmon steak. She had barely eaten at lunch and was famished.

"I'm curious about this man you mistook me for this morning," Dane said. "Does he live in Philadelphia?"

"No. Right now, he's probably somewhere in California."

"Then why did you think I might be him?"

She shrugged. "Wishful thinking, I guess."

He offered her the basket of buns on the table and she took one.

"You know, when you first approached me in the coffee shop," he said, "I was hoping you were using an excuse to pick me up." He took a bun for himself and buttered it.

"I would never do that. When I realized you weren't Storm, I was so embarrassed."

He grinned. "I could tell by the way your cheeks turned crimson and then you fled. And I had so hoped you were secretly yearning to tear off my clothes and have your way with me." His eyes glittered with amusement in the candlelight.

She smiled. "Well, if that were true, it was only because I thought you were Storm."

"Then Storm is a very lucky man."

The way he said those words, in his deep, seductive voice, his gaze warm and appreciative, set her pulse racing.

She sipped her wine. This charming, attractive man had a very disturbing effect on her. She wasn't the type to jump into bed with a total stranger, but everything about him made her want to do just that.

"So you said I look a lot like this Storm?"

She gazed at him, taking in his square jaw, classic nose, and vivid blue eyes. The two men shared the same classic good looks and imposing presence, but up close, the resemblance wasn't as similar as she'd thought. If she was honest with herself, she'd have to wonder if her lingering feelings for Storm were making her see him in every handsome man she saw. A kind of wishful thinking.

"I don't know. You seem a bit older and more mature." She smiled. "Maybe it's the suit."

"So the question is, do you like older men?"

Her smile broadened. "Well, I suppose I could be convinced."

He sipped his wine and stared at her intensely. "That sounds like a challenge . . . and I accept."

And he wasn't kidding. All through dinner he was the most charming man she'd ever been with. He made her feel like the most beautiful, captivating woman in the world. That and the effect of his strong male presence had her practically panting for him by dessert.

The waitress poured their coffee as Jessica took a bite of her caramel crème brûlée.

"Why don't you tell me a little about Storm? Were you two involved?"

She swallowed a sip of coffee, trying to tamp down the painful memories his words brought up. She was tempted to change the subject, but she really hadn't talked to anyone about how much it hurt when Storm walked out of her life. Maybe talking about it would help.

"Yes. We were in love. At least, I was in love with him. I thought he returned my feelings, but a month ago he just decided to walk out of my life."

"Do you still love him?"

She drew in a deep breath, then pursed her lips. She missed him. Every day and every night. He'd been a sensational lover and, despite the bad boy persona, oh, so tender. She'd really believed he returned her love. She'd felt special with him. But he was probably like that with every woman he was with. He was sensitive and considerate. Very hard not to fall in love with.

But if he didn't return her love, how could she love him?

"No, I don't still love him." Even if that wasn't true, she was working to make it so. She had to.

"I'm glad, because I wouldn't want to steal you away from another man."

Her gaze jerked to his. "Steal me?"

He reached across the table and took her hand, then raised it to his lips. "That's right. When I take you back to my place."

Her back stiffened and she hesitated. She shouldn't be surprised. It's not like they hadn't been shamelessly flirting all through dinner, but it had all seemed unreal. They were just sharing dinner.

Now it had become all too real.

She'd never had a one-night stand. Her chest tightened at the thought of having sex with a stranger. Especially this handsome, determined, sexy stranger. He was way out of her league.

But the feel of his lips playing over the back of her hand sent a shimmer of heat through her. Then when he turned her hand and pressed his lips to her palm, she melted.

"I know you're considering saying no. But don't."

She stared into his mesmerizing blue eyes and felt her anxiety dissipate. She wanted to be with him.

But she was not comfortable going to his apartment.

She drew her hand from his seductive lips and shook her head. "I'm not going to your place."

He raised an eyebrow. "You're not?"

"No." She smiled. "But you can come to mine."

Jessica slid her key card into the slot then pushed open the door to her room. She had slipped off her coat on the elevator ride and now hung it in the closet along with her suit jacket. Once she stepped further inside, however, and saw the bed dominating the room, the heat that had been building inside her seeped away. Her heart thundering, she turned to face the virtual stranger behind her and tell him this was a big mistake.

"You aren't going to tell me you've changed your mind, are

you?" He stood far too close, and it sent her senses reeling. Part of her wanted to run, yet another part wanted him even closer.

He stroked her cheek. The gentle touch sent shimmers through her. She gazed at him, captivated by the intensity of his eyes. Compelling. Inviting. And reminding her far too much of Storm.

Her heart clenched. She really couldn't do this.

"I'm sorry, I'm not sure we should—"

Before she could finish the sentence, he swept her into his arms and kissed her, his lips moving on hers with firm authority.

Being enveloped in his big, muscular arms, held tight against his solid chest, sent her heart racing. His tongue glided along the seam of her mouth and without thinking, she opened. He slipped inside, invading her with gentle strokes.

When he finally released her lips, she stepped back, needing a little distance between them.

"I have a theory." He stepped toward her and she took another step back.

"What's that?" Her words came out breathless.

"I think the reason you're nervous being with me right now is the same reason you're having trouble in your job search. Because you're uneasy around authority figures."

"I don't think that's true." But the words sounded uncertain even to her.

He took another step forward, and she stepped back again.

She hadn't realized how tall he was, and his shoulders were so broad. She felt a little intimidated, but then he took her hand and brought it to his mouth. Tingles danced along her arm and down her back at the feel of his lips delicately caressing her palm.

"I want to help you be comfortable with someone of authority taking charge." He smiled. "In fact, I'd like to show

you that giving up control to someone else can be both stimulating . . ."—his mouth shifted and at the delicate play of his lips
on her inner wrist, her insides quivered—"and pleasurable."

When he stepped forward this time, her backward step
landed her against the wall.

"So, I'm going to take charge and you'll do exactly as I say."

"I don't think—"

His mouth captured hers again and her heart rate leapt.
When he released her lips, she gazed into his inscrutable blue
eyes in a daze.

"That's good. I don't want you to think. I want you to just
do as I tell you." His quiet tone was calming and persuasive.

Oh, God, this was sexy.

"But the choice is yours," he continued. "I can leave now,
or I can stay and we'll let this play out."

She gazed up at him with wide eyes, knowing she did not
want him to leave.

At her nod, he smiled. "Good."

He stripped off his suit jacket and tossed it aside, then took
her hand and guided it to his chest. "Now unbutton my shirt."

She could feel the solid muscles under the fabric. She swallowed at her deep desire to feel his naked flesh under her fingertips. Her resistance melted away and she released the buttons
one by one, her throat going dry as she watched his tanned,
sculpted flesh slowly revealed.

After she released the last button, he stripped off his shirt
and tossed it onto his jacket on the floor.

He reached behind her head and unfastened the clip holding her long black hair in place. It tumbled around her shoulders and he stroked his fingers through it, then tucked it behind
her ear. At the gentle touch, shivers raced along her spine.

His fingertips slid along her neck, down the V of her neckline, and then he released her top button. Then the next. At the feel of his fingers lightly brushing her skin, heat flashed through her.

Cool air caressed her skin as her blouse fell open. He drew it from her shoulders and it slipped down her arms. She sucked in a deep breath as she watched him gaze at her lace-clad breasts with admiration.

Then his fingers curled around her head and he drew her forward. As his lips approached, anticipation burned through her. She breathed in his spicy male scent, mesmerized by his compelling blue eyes filled with desire.

His mouth brushed hers and her knees went weak. His lips were coaxing at first, then demanding. He slid his tongue into her mouth and boldly explored. She sighed, stroking his tongue with hers as she melted against his hot, hard chest.

He stroked her back, then she felt the elastic of her bra loosen. He eased back, then guided her bra straps off her shoulders. The cups clung to her breasts for an instant, then the garment fell away.

Her cheeks heated at being half naked in front of him.

He brushed his thumb over her nipple and it blossomed into a tight bud. Wild sensations rippled through her. He brushed the other nub and it hardened, too.

"Take off your skirt," he murmured.

She reached behind her and unfastened the button, then drew down the zipper. As he watched, a glint in his eyes, she pushed her skirt down her hips, then to the floor. She picked it up and he took it from her hand and tossed it on top of his clothes.

"Now the pantyhose."

She wished she'd worn stockings and a garter belt, but she'd had no idea tonight would turn into a sexual tryst. She kicked off her high-heeled pumps and stripped off her pantyhose, tossing them onto the growing heap of discarded clothing, then stood before him in only her tiny panties.

He caressed her breast, sending electricity sparking through her. Her nipple thrust forward, pressing shamelessly into his palm.

Then his mouth swooped down on hers and his hard body pressed her against the wall. He pinned her wrists over her head with one hand as he continued to plunder her lips. Her whole body thrummed with need. At the feel of his thick shaft pressed tight against her belly, a small moan escaped her lips.

His gaze locked on hers. "I think you like a powerful man taking control."

His free hand glided down her arm, then across her stomach. The cadence of her heart beat accelerated.

"I . . . um . . ." She did, but she wasn't comfortable admitting it.

His possessive fingers moved over the crotch of her panties, then dipped under the fabric. She arched against him, her wrists straining against his grip, then sucked in a breath as he stroked over her slick folds and found the wetness there.

His deep blue eyes gleamed. "There's my answer."

She longed for him to slide his fingers inside her.

He smiled and drew his fingers from her panties. She held back a groan, wanting him to touch her there again.

He released her wrists and she watched him sink downward. She lowered her hands from above her head.

"No, keep them up."

His words, firm and authoritative, sent shivers through her.

Without even thinking, she raised her hands again, keeping them above her head as if he still held them.

He stroked a finger over the top of her lace panties. "Very pretty. Would you like me to touch you here again?"

She shivered with need. "Yes."

His warm fingers were so near where she wanted them to be. He lightly dragged his fingertip along the elastic, then pulled it down slightly. Anticipation quivered through her.

Then he stopped again and she stifled a groan of frustration.

"Touch me again," she pleaded.

His smile broadened and he tucked his fingers in the elastic of her panties and drew them down. Slowly. His gaze remained locked on the front of the tiny lace garment as he eased it lower, guiding it down her hips. Her breathing seemed louder as he exposed her, bit by bit, his eyes darkening with desire. Then her panties glided down her legs and off.

He stroked down her stomach, then over the neatly trimmed hair framing her intimate flesh.

"Nice. I like this."

Pleasure washed through her at his approval. Then he leaned forward and licked her. She moaned at the intense pleasure of his tongue sweeping over her. He slid his fingers between her thighs and stroked her as his tongue found her clit. He nudged it lightly, sending intense heat winding through her. His fingers stroked along her slit, then one found its way inside, gliding along her slick passage. Then another slid inside.

Her head dropped back against the wall. Yes, that's what she wanted.

"So beautiful." His fingers slipped out and he drew her folds open and stared.

She shifted, uncomfortable with his intense scrutiny, yet wanting it all the same.

He stroked her with a single fingertip. She arched forward, wanting more.

"Are you willing to do anything I say?"

"Yes, yes. Anything you want. Just don't stop."

His eyes darkened. "Tell me exactly what you want me to do."

Breathing became difficult and her heart hammered in her chest. "I want you to thrust your fingers into me. Stroke me until I come."

His finger jerked into her and she sucked in a breath at the sudden, and deliriously pleasurable, sensation.

A second finger slid inside and he stroked her. With his other hand, he parted her folds, exposing her clit, then he eased forward and licked it. Vibrant sensations shimmered through her. His tongue quivered over her sensitive nub, then he sucked lightly.

"Oh, God, yes."

She slumped back against the wall, her hands still over her head, as he licked and sucked her clit. At the same time, his fingers began to move inside her, in and out. She clenched around them, riding the rising pleasure.

His sucking turned to licking again, and the pumping of his fingers slowed. She arched forward, encouraging him to continue. He resumed sucking her button, his fingers plunging into her again, ramping up the waning pleasure, but then he slowed again.

"Oh, please don't stop," she whimpered.

He stood. "You agreed to do anything I want." He took her hand and drew her toward the bed, then sat down and positioned her in front of him. "And right now, I want to do this."

He leaned forward and his lips brushed her nipple. She sucked in a deep breath as his tongue brushed over her nub, then swirled around it. Then her nipple felt cold as he moved to her other one and drew it into his mouth, warming it with his swirling tongue. When he sucked, she gasped, then threaded her fingers through his hair and held his head against her. He lapped his tongue over her, then sucked deeper.

He drew her onto his lap, her knees on either side of his thighs, then sucked her other nipple again. Her heart thundered in her chest and she could feel her insides melting. She ached for him. She slid her hands over his naked shoulders, so broad and strong.

She could feel the fine wool of his pants brushing her intimate folds, then he drew her closer and the bulge in his pants pressed against her.

It was big. And growing bigger. She wanted him to take off his pants. She wanted to see his cock. To hold it.

She wanted it to glide inside her and fill her so full she would burst into orgasm.

Oh, man, she had it bad.

She stroked down his chest. The skin was satiny and pulled taut over the big, well-developed muscles.

Her fingers slid down his sculpted abs, but when she reached his pants and started to unfasten the button, he grasped her hands and drew them away.

"I didn't say you could do that."

"But I want to see you."

He grinned, then took her hand and placed it over the bulge, then squeezed her fingers around it.

Oh, God, it was huge.

"Tell me you want to see my cock."

She licked her suddenly dry lips. "I want to see your cock."

He chuckled, a deep rumbling from his chest.

"Good. If I told you to suck it right now, would you?"

She squeezed him again, loving the feel of the hot, hard shaft in her hand. What did it look like naked? How would it feel in her hand? In her mouth?

She nodded.

"Good girl."

He guided her to her feet and stood up, then released the buckle of his elegant leather belt. She watched as he drew down the zipper, unbuttoned his pants, and let them fall to the floor. Next, he tucked his thumbs under the waistband of his dark gray boxers and pushed those down, too. When he stood up, her gaze locked on his swollen erection. It stood up firm and proud, curving slightly toward his body. The shaft was long and covered with thick veins. It swelled to a large mushroom-shaped tip.

She reached for it, but he captured her hand.

"Not yet."

She dragged her gaze from the delightful cock to his face.

He sat down on the bed. "Now kneel down in front of me."

She obeyed, staring at the big shaft in front of her, eagerly awaiting his next instruction.

She was actually finding the whole situation incredibly arousing. And fun, too. She liked behaving differently than she normally did. Acting out a role. It was like she was someone else entirely.

"Now wrap your hand around my cock and stroke it."

She reached forward and touched the big cock. The skin was smooth as silk. And hot. She wrapped her fingers around it and stroked.

The bulbous tip was now purple and she could feel the veins pulsing along the side of the shaft. She wanted to lean forward and take it in her mouth, but he hadn't given her permission yet. She continued to stroke him, satisfaction growing at the quickened pace of his breathing.

"Oh, yes. That's good. Now I want you to suck me. I want you to make me come."

She leaned forward and licked the tip of him. The flesh was smooth under her tongue. She had to open wide to fit the big, plum-size tip into her mouth. As she swallowed him, he rewarded her with a groan.

His fingers coiled in her hair and he drew her head forward. She loved the feel of his cock filling her mouth and gliding deeper.

"That's right. Take as much of me as you can."

He was so big that she could get only halfway down. She wanted to go deeper—to give him more pleasure—so she relaxed her throat and went a little farther. He was deeper than she'd ever taken any man.

"Yes. That's great."

She drew back and surged deep again.

He groaned as she took him in and out, squeezing him in her mouth as she did. His fingers clutched her head and she could feel his body growing tense.

She stroked over his hairless balls, then cupped them in her palm. She caressed and fondled them as she continued to pump him in and out of her mouth.

His breathing was erratic. She sucked him, squeezing hard as her hand stroked his scrotum. She pumped her other hand along the exposed part of his shaft, determined to take him all the way.

But he coiled his fingers in her hair and drew her head away from his cock. "Stop," he said in a commanding tone.

"But I thought you wanted me to make you come."

"Don't argue. Just do as you're told. Now sit on the end of the bed, your legs open."

Hesitantly gazing at his no-nonsense expression, she stood up.

"Now." His commanding tone sent her scurrying to the end of the bed. She sat down with her knees apart. Anticipation rippled through her.

His intense blue gaze remained locked on her as he approached, then he knelt in front of her. His fingers stroked along her folds, then he parted them and his gaze shifted to her slick flesh.

"Oh, yes. You're very ready."

He leaned toward her, and when she felt his tongue rasp over her clit, she groaned and lay back on the bed, her eyelids drifting closed. Her fingers coiled in his wavy hair, but he glided upward, lightly kissing her stomach as he moved. Then she felt his lips wrap around her nipple. She clutched him to her chest as he suckled sweetly. Her insides fluttered with anticipation. His fingers found her slit and teased it, then slid inside. She clenched around them.

His tongue returned to her clit, sending ripples of delight through her. He licked, then sucked lightly.

"Oh, God, yes."

Pleasure washed through her as his fingers moved inside her, stroking her. She moaned and arched against him, trembling as an orgasm began to swell within her. Then he drew away and she groaned.

She glanced up and saw him rolling a condom over his

engorged cock, then seconds later he was back. He slid her higher on the bed and prowled over her, then his hot, hard flesh nudged her opening. She gasped as his massive cockhead slid inside. His enormous shaft moved deeper, stretching her with his tremendous girth, gliding on forever as he filled her.

Then he stilled, his big body over hers, holding most of his weight on his arms, as they both sucked in air.

"You're so big. I can hardly believe you're all the way inside me."

He chuckled and kissed her lightly. Then he began to move. Drawing out slowly, then gliding back in. Stroking her sensitive passage.

Ramping up her pleasure.

His solid flesh slid in and out, over and over again, thrilling her with each stroke. She grasped his broad, muscular shoulders, arching against him. She squeezed him and the intense pleasure of his rock-hard shaft moving inside her sent her senses reeling.

Wild sensations tingled through her and she gasped as he drove deeper still.

He pumped faster and her breathing accelerated.

"Tell me you're going to come." His words rasped against her ear.

She nodded, barely able to catch her breath.

"I want to hear you say it."

"I'm going to . . ." She moaned as pleasure swelled within her. He thrust faster. "Oh, God, I'm going to come."

"Yes. Come for me, baby."

An orgasm blasted through her. "Oh . . . Yes . . . I'm coming." She gasped, then wailed long and loud.

He thrust deep and hard, then jerked against her and groaned. She clung to his shoulders as he catapulted her orgasm to a new level. She sucked in a breath, then continued to moan as she shot to heaven.

Slowly, she returned to earth and the warmth of his body over hers. He rolled to his side, taking her with him, then wrapped his arm around her waist and drew her close.

She rested her head against his solid chest, listening to the steady beat of his heart. Part of her wanted to scoot off to the bathroom and collect herself. Another part wanted to stay right here, all cozy and warm. If she left, he would probably gather up his clothes and leave. She wouldn't even get to see him dress. He'd give her a quick good-bye kiss and be gone. Never to be seen again.

That's how one-night stands worked, right?

And that's what she wanted, right?

He stroked her hair. It felt so sweet and tender.

She glanced at the clock. Eleven thirty.

"Are you tired?" he asked.

"Um, yes. I have an early morning."

Unfortunately, he would probably take that as his cue to leave.

"Of course." But instead of grabbing his clothes and pulling them on, he reached for the bedside lamp and turned it out, then enveloped her in his embrace.

Her head settled against his chest again, the steady thumping of his heart against her ear, and she decided she really liked this. Being close to him. Hearing his heartbeat.

She'd missed having a man in her bed. Being close and cozy. Feeling loved.

Well, maybe not loved, but cared for.

His breathing slowed. She closed her eyes and lost herself in the warmth of his arms.

He was an interesting man. Domineering but completely focused on her pleasure. Teasing and authoritative all at once. She mused at how sexy it had been. She never would have thought she'd be okay being ordered around by a man, but it had been a major turn-on.

And being with him had been nothing like being with Storm whose lovemaking was more tender and solicitous. In fact, she thought with satisfaction, Storm hadn't even entered her mind until now. Maybe she really was starting to get over him.

Jessica woke up and opened her eyes. It was still dark. And a man's arms were around her. She glanced toward him. Although she couldn't really see his features in the dark, she remembered Dane's face. So much like Storm's.

Oh, man, she couldn't believe she'd actually had sex with this man she hardly knew. And the things they'd done. The way she'd behaved, allowing him to order her around. Embarrassment spiked through her.

She glanced at the clock on the bedside table and realized it was five a.m. She wouldn't get back to sleep now, so she'd spend the next hour just lying here, stressing about having to face him when he woke up. *That* would be really embarrassing.

She glanced at the clock again. It would take her about forty-five minutes to shower and get dressed, fix her hair and makeup, then finish packing the few things she had into her overnight bag. That meant by the time she checked out and had the front desk lock away her overnight bag for safekeeping while she was at the career fair, it would be six and she'd have time for a leisurely breakfast where she could prepare herself for the day ahead.

Slipping away now would mean no muss, no fuss. And he'd probably be just as happy to avoid awkward morning-after conversations.

She'd be tired today, but she wasn't going to sleep any more, anyway. She might as well do something useful.

She slipped from the bed, being careful not to waken Dane. When she returned from the bathroom, dressed and ready to go, he was still sleeping. She tossed her makeup bag and toiletries in her case along with yesterday's clothes, and quietly zipped it closed. She grabbed some stationery from the desk and wrote a quick note for Dane, then headed out the door.

Dane woke up to an empty bed. He glanced around and saw a note sitting on the dresser. Pushing aside the covers, he shoved his hair from his face, then strolled over and picked up the note.

Last night had been delightful. Jessica had resisted being commanded at first, but clearly she enjoyed it once they got going. In fact, it had turned her on immensely.

He grinned. It had been fun coaxing her into submission. He would love the opportunity to pursue more with her. To ease her into a full Dom-sub relationship.

He read the note, telling him that she'd wanted to get an early start on breakfast and to prepare for the career fair.

He snorted. Right. She had definitely fled. Just like she had from the Starbucks.

She went on to assure him that she'd paid for the room and all he had to do was leave the keycard behind when he left.

A woman who left a note and fled in the middle of the night—from her own hotel room—definitely had issues. Whether they were with him, with the domination, or with getting over her ex, he didn't know.

But he was willing to take the time to figure it out. He just needed to find a way to see her again.

Jessica sighed as she sat down with the paper coffee cup in her hand. The noise of the hustle and bustle in the big ballroom where the career fair was taking place washed over her. She had been networking like crazy and had talked with representatives from a few companies which offered positions that she felt would be well suited to her, but after the interviews she didn't feel that prospects were good. They wanted experience that directly related to what they were doing, and seemed disinclined to take on an inexperienced but enthusiastic employee to train because, frankly, with the job market the way it was, they didn't have to. There were lots of people with the exact experience they were looking for in search of a job.

Her experience was just too general. She stroked her finger over the smooth stone in her pocket.

"Do you mind if I sit with you?"

Jessica glanced up at the female voice. A pretty woman with upswept hair and wearing a tailored suit—the basic uniform of the day for everyone here—stood by the table with a coffee in her hand. There were a few empty tables around, but Jessica knew she should take every opportunity she could to network.

"Not at all."

The woman placed her coffee and small clutch purse on the table and sat down. Jessica noticed her badge with the blue band, indicating she was an employer.

"My name's Melanie Taylor." Melanie held out her hand and Jessica shook it.

"Hi. I'm Jessica Long."

Jessica sipped her coffee, wondering how many more employer booths she could squeeze in before the fair ended, two hours from now. To be honest, though, she'd be happy to just keep sitting here and veg until the whole thing was over. If it weren't for the fact she had to justify her travel costs to get here, she'd leave right now.

"You look pretty discouraged. The hunt not going well?" Melanie asked.

Jessica glanced at her table companion. "No, not really. Every employer I've talked to wants specific experience I don't have. I don't know how to break into something new and what I was doing before is so general that no one is really interested."

Melanie nodded. "I know what you mean. Have you talked to anyone at Ranier?"

Below Melanie's name on her badge were the words Ranier Industries, so that was the company she represented.

"Yes, they were one of the first companies I handed my résumé to, but the lines were so long I didn't get a chance to talk to anyone. They look like a great place to work."

"We're a growing company and we have fabulous benefits."

"That's great." Jessica found herself wearing her positive smile—the same smile she'd plastered on her face for the past two days—but she doubted she'd hear from them, since so many people were handing in their résumés and they probably all had way more relevant experience than she did.

She stroked the stone in her pocket.

"Oh, honey," Melanie said, "I can see your eyes glazing over and that smile is pathetic." At Jessica's frown, Melanie smiled warmly. "I'm sorry, I'm not criticizing. I totally sympathize. I'm not with Human Resources—I'm just helping out at the booth today because, as you saw, they're swamped—but I feel for you, and all the others that come by. It's tough out there."

"I've been out of work for four months. I'm probably going to have to give up my apartment and move in with my parents." She hated having to admit that. A grown woman shouldn't have to live with her parents.

"Oh, you poor thing. I just had my roommate move out a month ago and I haven't been able to replace her, so I'm feeling the pinch, but I sure wouldn't want to have to move in with my mom. I love her dearly and all but, whoa, that's too close quarters for me."

Melanie glanced at her watch. "Look, my break is almost over, but come on back to the booth with me. I'll get you in to talk to Stephanie in Human Resources. You can give her a new copy of your résumé and have a bit of a talk with her. She's really nice." She smiled warmly. "And I'll put in a good word for you." She stood up and gathered her things.

"Thank you, I really appreciate it." Jessica stood up and grabbed her purse and briefcase.

"You look stunned."

"Well, we don't even know each other. I'm not sure why you'd be willing to go out on a limb for me."

She followed Melanie through the crowd.

"You remind me of myself two years ago when I was standing in your shoes, so trust me, I know how much it sucks to be unemployed."

They arrived at the Ranier booth and Melanie smiled brightly. "And if you want some company for dinner, come by the booth later."

"I'd like that, but my flight leaves at seven, so I have to head to the airport as soon as this is over."

"Of course." Melanie pulled out a card and handed it to Jessica. "Well, if you do get a callback for an interview in town, or wind up living here, give me a call. I could show you around the city."

Jessica took the card and tucked it in her purse. "Thanks."

It was nice to know that if she got the opportunity to move to the city, she'd know at least one person.

"Now, let's go find Stephanie."

A week later, back in her apartment in Bakersfield, Jessica stacked her DVDs in the cardboard box sitting on her dining room table. There should be enough room for her CDs in the same box. A stack of bills sat on the table beside the box. She hadn't heard back from any of the employers from the career fair yet. It was a little early, but either way, she'd need to move out of this apartment. Either she'd be moving in with Mom and Dad, or she'd be moving to Philadelphia. She sighed. The former seemed the most likely.

The phone rang and she walked to the living room to pick it up.

"Ms. Long, please."

"Speaking," Jessica said.

"Hi. This is Stephanie Reynolds. I work in Human Resources at Ranier Industries."

Jessica's heart jolted into high gear.

"Yes, Ms. Reynolds. How are you?"

"Fine. I'm calling because we'd like to have you come in for a second interview. Would that be possible?"

"Um, yes, of course." Jessica wrote down the details. When she hung up the phone, she couldn't stop smiling.

Maybe she wouldn't have to move in with her parents after all.

Jessica pushed open the glass door of the tall office tower and walked across the lobby, Melanie alongside her. The clacking of their high heels on the marble floor blended into the sounds made by dozens of other people heading to their jobs in the huge building.

Excitement skittered through her at the thought of starting her brand new job.

"Human Resources is on the eighth floor," Melanie said as they stepped into the elevator. "They'll process you then bring you up to the executive floor. If you have any questions, feel free to call me. You wrote down my extension, right?" Her eyes glittered with excitement.

"Yes, I've got it." Jessica grinned. "I think you're just as nervous as I am." Other people crowded into the elevator around them as Melanie pressed the button to floor eight and floor thirty-six.

"Maybe a little, but I know you'll do fine."

Jessica couldn't believe her luck at having fallen in with Melanie. Melanie had arranged for her to talk to Stephanie Reynolds at the career fair, which had led to a second interview. The company had even paid her expenses to come back to Philadelphia. They'd put her up in a hotel, and Melanie had shown her around the city after the interview. Since they'd hit it off so well, Melanie had invited her to stay for the weekend so she could get a better feel for the city. They'd had such a great time together that when Jessica had received the job offer, Melanie had suggested she take over her ex-roommate's old bedroom.

The past four weeks had been a whirlwind of activity and excitement. She'd be lying to herself if she didn't admit that part of that excitement was knowing she and Dane were living in the same city now, and while the odds of them bumping into each other on the street weren't very high, stranger things had happened. Still, she had other things on her mind, like her glamorous new job.

Now, here she was, on day one, her heart beating quickly in nervous excitement.

The elevator door opened on the eighth floor.

"Good luck. I'll see you later," Melanie said.

The door closed and Jessica glanced around, then headed to the reception desk. "Hi. It's my first day here. I'm supposed to see Ms. Reynolds."

The receptionist was a lovely young blonde in a white satin blouse, with soft pink lipstick and a bright smile. "Welcome. I'm Gina. Stephanie's office is the second on the left down that hall. Go ahead in."

"Thanks." A moment later, she tapped on Stephanie's open door.

Stephanie chatted to her a bit about benefits and company policies, then sent her to the reception area to fill out a pile of forms—for payroll, insurance benefits, taxes, et cetera. An hour later, she finished the last one and walked back to Reception and handed Gina the folder of paperwork.

"Great. Stephanie asked me to take you up to your new office once you're done." Gina stood up and led Jessica to the elevator. Butterflies danced through her stomach as she realized that in a few moments she would be at her new desk and would be meeting her new boss.

The ride up the elevator seemed too fast and suddenly the doors opened to a new floor. The décor was a notch up from the Human Resources offices. Actually, several notches up. The chairs in the waiting area were of rich, warm brown leather and the carpets were plush. The view from the floor-to-ceiling windows along one wall gave a spectacular view of the city below.

Gina led her across the large reception area. There were several closed doors, all rich red, cherry wood.

Melanie sat at an elegant desk in the corner. She smiled as soon as she saw Jessica.

"Hi, Melanie. Is he in?" Gina asked.

"Yes, go ahead in."

The butterflies in Jessica's stomach became more agitated. She was working for a high-level executive?

Gina tapped on the door and a deep muffled voice inside said, "Come in."

Gina pushed open the door and stepped inside, Jessica on her heels. "Mr. Ranier, this is Jessica Long your new assistant."

Jessica was in awe, gazing around at the lush office with its rich mahogany wood bookshelves, leather chairs, and expensive-looking artwork on the walls.

"Good morning, Miss Long."

At the familiar voice, Jessica's gaze jolted to the man sitting behind the impressive desk by the huge window overlooking the city. Her stomach tightened.

There sat the man she'd had a torrid one-night stand with. Her cheeks burned at the memory. Oh, God, he couldn't be her new boss.

The Morning After

"Have a seat, Miss Long. That'll be all, Gina."

"Yes, sir." Gina left the office, closing the door behind her.

Jessica sat down in one of the leather chairs facing his desk, her pulse racing. Dane continued to view his computer screen.

Her hand slipped into her pocket and stroked the tranquility stone she always kept with her. Ever since he'd given it to her, she'd found she'd used it for comfort in times of stress.

The leather was soft and supple and the chair extremely comfortable. The brisk scent of his cologne filled her nostrils and memories of that night wafted through her mind. A quiver raced down her spine to think she'd been in bed with such a rich and powerful man.

He came from an entirely different world than she. He not only controlled a huge corporation, he controlled people's jobs. Their lives.

And all she could think about was the need in his eyes as she'd wrapped her hand around his massive cock. Her gaze slid to his lips and she couldn't help remembering his tongue nuzzling her most intimate parts.

Her heart thundered in her chest. From both embarrassment and . . . God, because she wanted to do it all again.

But now he was her boss. He was so intimidating in his expensive suit, sitting behind his big desk in this high-class, executive office.

She ran her hand along the armrest, thinking of kid leather which reminded her of . . . Oh, God, she had to stop thinking about . . . *that*.

He flicked the computer mouse, then his gaze fell on her and her stomach clenched.

She saw no reaction in his eyes. Was it possible he didn't recognize her?

The night they'd spent together was over a month ago and maybe he did that kind of thing all the time. Maybe she just wasn't that memorable.

But wouldn't he have remembered her name when the company decided to hire her? That process had started only a couple of weeks later. Or maybe Human Resources handled all that.

He raised an eyebrow. "Is there a problem?"

She realized she was clutching the armrests of the chair tightly.

"Um, no. Just first-day jitters, sir."

The "sir" had just slipped out. He was her new boss, after all.

His lips turned up in a smile. "I like it when you call me sir."

At the twinkle in his eye, she knew he definitely remembered her.

"So this is awkward, and strangely coincidental," she said.

"Oh, it's not a coincidence. When you told me you were at the career fair, I told my staff to watch for your résumé. When they hadn't received it by the end of Saturday, I had my secretary, Melanie, go help out at the booth. I told her to watch out for you and persuade you to submit your résumé."

Melanie knew about this?

"Why didn't you just tell me who you were?" She asked.

"It was clear you were already intimidated by me. I would never have had a shot with you if you knew I was a potential employer. You would have been too nervous around me."

Her head was spinning. "So you didn't tell me you might hire me, because you wanted to sleep with me?" Her stomach churned as the implications of the situation slowly sank in. "So was that night a job interview?"

His eyes darkened like storm clouds. "Of course not."

But she barely heard him. She'd been looking forward to this job. She *needed* this job. Now she found out it was just some rich playboy's way of getting her back into his bed.

"I'm not sure I can accept your job offer," she said.

Her heart sank at the thought of packing up all her stuff and moving back to Bakersfield. And the cost. If she walked out on this job, she'd have to pay back the company for her moving expenses.

"Don't be ridiculous. Of course you'll keep the job."

She really didn't want to turn it down, but how could she stay?

She sucked in a deep breath. "I'm not going to have sex with you in the office."

"Good. That would be highly inappropriate." There was a glitter of amusement in his piercing blue eyes. "And contrary to what you might believe, I do not base my business decisions on a great lay. I hired you because I thought you would be an asset to my company." He leaned forward. "Is that clear?"

She nodded, willing herself to keep breathing under the force of his scrutiny.

"Yes, sir."

"Good. Now go and get us both a coffee—I like one sugar—and we'll discuss the job."

Jessica escaped Dane's office and glanced around. Melanie was away from her desk and there was no one else to ask where to get coffee, so she scouted around the floor until she found a small kitchen with a coffeemaker. She grabbed one of the burgundy mugs from a tray on the counter and filled it with coffee, then poured in one packet of sugar. She didn't get herself a cup because her heart was already beating frantically. Caffeine would only make it worse.

She walked back into his office with the mug in her hand, but he was on the phone. He nodded at her as she put the coffee down in front of him.

"Hold on a second," he said into the phone, then covered the mouthpiece and glanced at her. "This might take a while. It's after eleven, so take an early lunch and we'll talk this afternoon."

She nodded and picked up her purse and briefcase and hurried out the door.

"Hey, how's it going?" Melanie was at her desk again, glancing at Jessica over her computer screen.

"Um . . . Mr. Ranier said to go to lunch now. He got busy with a phone call so wants to talk again this afternoon."

"Oh, I assumed he'd take you to lunch today, but now we can go together." Melanie opened her desk drawer and pulled out her purse, then glanced at Jessica and hesitated. "Did you want to go to lunch together?"

"Yes, of course. I'd love to."

"Okay. You just look uncertain."

Jessica shook her head and strode to the elevator, wanting to avoid further discussion about her state of mind.

"How are things going so far?" Melanie asked as the doors closed behind them.

"Fine."

Jessica's lips compressed, but the doors opened and another person joined them in the elevator. They rode the rest of the way in silence. When they stepped onto the street, the warm spring breeze blew several loose strands of Jessica's hair into her face and she brushed them aside.

Melanie's shoulder-length dark blonde hair fluttered along the collar of her dove gray suit. She wore a light turquoise and white print blouse today and her tailored jacket accentuated her slim figure. She was a little shorter than Jessica, but the heels she wore today put them at the same height.

"I know you're on a budget, so we could go to this great little diner around the corner," Melanie suggested.

"Sounds good."

She walked with Melanie down the block and they turned right at the light. A few minutes later, they sat at a window booth in the modest diner, while the waitress filled their glasses with ice water.

"So is there something wrong?" Melanie asked, concern in her emerald green eyes.

Jessica shook her head, her stomach still churning. "I don't know. I have some doubts about this job."

What could she possibly say to Melanie? That she thought she only got the job because she'd slept with the boss?

"Are you concerned you can't manage it?" Melanie asked. "Because I'm positive you can."

"I'm not really sure what he expects of me yet. We were supposed to talk about it before he got that call."

"If you're worried about working for Dane Ranier, don't be. He likes things done his way, but he'll take the time to ensure you know what that is. He's patient and fair. As far as bosses go, he's a gem."

"I . . . uh . . . met him before today."

Melanie sipped her water. "Yeah, I know."

Jessica's gaze darted to her new friend's face. "You do?"

"Yeah, he told me. He gave you a ride to the job fair when it started to rain in the morning. I thought that was so nice of him. In fact, he asked me to check for your résumé, assuming you'd drop it off at our booth and when you didn't, he asked me to go to the job fair to find you the next day."

"So that wasn't really a chance meeting between us," said Jessica, even though she already knew that.

"No. I felt a bit guilty about not mentioning it, but I really liked the fact he wanted to help you out and I liked being a part of it. He told me if I just explained the situation to you, that you would probably be uncomfortable. That made sense." She gazed at Jessica with wide eyes. "You aren't mad at me, are you? I just wanted to help."

"No, I'm not mad. I'm just wondering . . . why did he go to so much trouble to help me?"

Melanie frowned. "You don't think he was trying to hit on you, do you? Because if he wanted to do that, he wouldn't actually hire you. He'd just offer the possibility of a job, then talk you into sleeping with him. And by 'he' I mean most men, not Dane Ranier. A Ranier man wouldn't have to trick a woman into his bed."

Something about Melanie's tone and her faraway expression drew Jessica's attention.

"Are you attracted to Mr. Ranier?"

Melanie's cheeks tinged pink. "Well, not *that* Mr. Ranier."

Her eyebrows arched. "What do you mean not *that* Mr. Ranier?"

"Your boss, Dane Ranier, has a brother. Rafe. He's the other big office on the floor. I work for both of them."

"And . . . ?"

Melanie shrugged and her cheeks tinged a deep rose. "I've always had a bit of a crush on Rafe Ranier." She toyed with the napkin on the table in front of her. "But I would never act on it. I love this job, and I wouldn't want to jeopardize it. An office romance is a tricky business, especially with someone who runs the company." She raised her gaze to Jessica again. "And that's why I know you don't need to worry about Dane Ranier as your boss. Neither brother has ever made a move on one of their employees."

Was it true? Had Dane Ranier had his fun with her and now she'd be strictly off limits? The thought was encouraging and at the same time . . . disappointing.

Jessica picked up the ringing phone from her desk.

"He's back," Melanie said from the other end. "He wants you to come to his office."

"Thanks."

She saved the document she'd been working on and grabbed a pen and spiral pad from her desk so she could take notes. Melanie had shown her where the office supplies were and given her some materials to read until Dane—Mr. Ranier—could talk to her.

She left her office, which was situated beside her boss' office, and glanced at Melanie who was sitting at her desk a few yards away.

"When he's expecting you, just go right in," Melanie said.

Jessica opened his office door and went inside. He glanced up from his computer and stood, then gestured toward a sitting area by one of the large windows. There were two easy chairs facing a low, round table. In another part of the office, there was a high table surrounded by chairs where he might hold more formal meetings, but this spot was clearly meant for more relaxed conversations.

She sat down and set the pad and pen on the table, within easy reach.

"The job you've been hired for is to be my personal assistant," he said.

Had he put ever so slight an emphasis on *personal*? But after the conversation with Melanie, she realized she was being a little crazy. Why would a wealthy businessman like Dane Ranier hire her just to get sex? With his looks and confident demeanor, he could have any woman he set his mind on, without need of offering her employment, or anything else for that matter. He oozed masculinity. All he'd have to do is smile and women would drop to their knees.

She should know. She had.

"How is that different from what Melanie does for you?" she asked.

"Melanie is my secretary. You are my personal assistant, so you'll be doing more personal things for me."

A tingle danced along her spine as she remembered some of the very personal things she'd done for him that night. Damn it, she thought she'd avoided the whole morning-after awkwardness by slipping out of the hotel early, but it had returned with a vengeance. Her gaze flicked to his but she ensured her expression remained neutral.

This morning, Dane had been shocked to discover that Jessica actually thought he'd hired her just so he could have sex with her. When she'd said she wouldn't take the job because of her anxiety about it, he knew they had a problem they needed to deal with. But that hadn't been the time. He'd decided she'd needed a little time to calm down and think about it, so he'd sent her away.

Sure, he'd love to continue a physical relationship with her, but she clearly wasn't comfortable with that.

He sighed. "Jessica, it seems we have an issue."

"We do?" Her eyes widened slightly.

"When I say you need to do personal things for me, I'm not talking about you dropping to your knees and unzipping my pants." Though at the thought of her kneeling in front of him, her fingers brushing against the fabric covering his shaft, it began to swell. "I'm talking about you picking up my dry cleaning, sometimes getting me coffee, ensuring I have everything I need when I head to a meeting."

Her cheeks tinged pink, but the rest of her expression was unreadable.

"And occasionally you may have to work after hours. I have projects outside the office that I need help with and that's also part of your job as my assistant. I don't want to have you quivering in fear of being seduced every time I ask you to work late." He raised an eyebrow. "Is that understood?"

She nodded, but he wasn't sure she was convinced. They both knew she really needed this job, so despite her earlier claim that maybe she couldn't accept the position, he was sure she would cling to it even if she had doubts about his intentions.

"Jessica, we had sex. It was intense and amazing. And I would love to do it again. But that won't happen unless *you* want it to happen. In that, you are totally in control."

Her gaze flicked to his, then down to her notebook.

"But in everything else, I'm the boss. Got it?"

Again, she nodded.

He stood up and walked to the front of his desk, then turned around. "Good, now come over here."

Her eyes widened, but she stood up and took a step forward, leaving six feet between them.

"Keep walking until I tell you to stop."

She continued forward slowly, her hands clenching into balls at her sides as she approached. He waited until she was two feet from him before he told her to stop. He was a good eight inches taller than her, towering over her as their bodies infringed on the usual comfort margin of personal space. He watched her cheeks tinge a deep rose and she stared at his tie rather than meeting his gaze.

The closeness of her body, and the sweet scent of orange blossoms from her hair, sent his senses reeling. He wanted to drag her into his arms and claim that soft, pink mouth of hers. To feel her soft breasts crushed against his chest again.

But he didn't.

He smiled. "You see. I'm not ripping off your clothes. We can work in the same office. We can sit side-by-side."

He wanted to reach for her chin and tip it up, so she would look at him, but as confident as his words were, he was afraid touching her would be his undoing.

"Look at me, Jessica."

She raised her gaze to his. He could see it. The heat in her big green eyes. And that heat set his blood simmering. He wanted so badly to stroke her cheek. To drag her body against his and storm her mouth.

Instead, he reined in those feelings with an iron will.

"We can even stand facing each other like this without me throwing you onto that couch and having my way with you." He paused, letting that sink in. "Nothing is going to happen unless you want it to." When she didn't say anything, he said, "Do you understand?"

"Yes, sir."

Oh, God, when she called him sir he wanted to take total control of her, and order her to do some *very* personal things.

"Good. Now for the next week or two, you'll need to learn about what we do here. You'll be working closely with Melanie. She knows what I expect of you and will explain your duties in detail. In a few days, I'll have you accompany me to a few meetings. I assume Melanie has already given you some reading material."

"Yes, sir."

"Good. That should keep you busy for the rest of the day."

"Yes, Mr. Ranier." She turned and headed for the door.

His gaze fell to the delightful sway of her hips as she walked. When she reached for the doorknob, he said, "Jessica."

She turned to face him.

"If you do change your mind, I'll be only too happy to continue what we started that night."

He was sure he saw heat flicker in her eyes before her gaze darted away and she opened the door and escaped.

Damn it, why had he said that? The whole point of this

conversation had been to calm her down, not to deliver an invitation to party.

As he sat down at his desk, he knew the reason was because he wanted her. Badly. She'd really gotten under his skin and despite the fact he'd told himself he could handle keeping the relationship between them strictly professional—and he could— he was quickly discovering how excruciatingly difficult that would be.

Jessica escaped to her office, her cheeks still warm from her encounter with Dane. When he'd ordered her to stand in front of him, so close she could feel the heat of his body, she could barely keep her breathing in check. She'd wanted him to pull her into his arms and kiss her. To ravish her lips, then throw her down on the couch and take her.

He'd calmly pointed out how he could stand so close to her yet not tear off her clothes, which should have made her happy, but instead it had instilled in her a deep desire for him to do just that.

But she knew that was just her raging hormones. Of course she wouldn't initiate sex with him. It would make it too difficult to work with him.

She rested her chin on her hand and gazed out the window at the city below. But a girl could dream.

After a few moments, she sighed and opened one of the thick binders Melanie had given her. She started reading, familiarizing herself with the organizational structure of Ranier Industries.

Over the next couple of days she spent her time at the office reading and talking to Melanie about her duties. A big part of her job was to keep Dane organized, including maintaining his calendar to coordinate both his business schedule and personal schedule.

Today, she was to start accompanying him to meetings and, as soon as she was up to speed, it would be her job to ensure that he was briefed on what he needed to know for any meeting or appointment he had, to keep at hand all the materials he would need when going into any meeting, to track what went on once there, and to follow up on any action items that arose.

She found it all a bit daunting, but Melanie assured her that Dane was reasonable and would give her plenty of time to learn.

Her phone rang and she picked it up.

"Jessica, come into my office," Dane said on the line.

"Yes, sir." She rose and hurried toward his office.

Her hand slipped into her jacket pocket and she stroked the flat, soothing stone as she opened the door and entered his office. Instead of sitting at his desk, he was at the round meeting table with his laptop open.

He glanced up as she walked toward the table.

"Sit down." He gestured to the chair beside him. "I want to go over the agenda for this afternoon's meeting."

She rolled the chair closer beside him so she would be able to see the screen, quivering as she remembered when he'd made her stand so close to him the other day, the heat of attraction simmering between them. She sat down, intensely conscious of his big, masculine presence beside her. Her thumb continued to stroke the stone in her pocket.

As he walked through his talking points for the meeting, she tried to calm her unsteady physical reaction to him. He was her boss. She had to be able to sit beside him without wanting to fling herself into his arms.

But he was so masculine. So sexy. If they just had sex again, maybe that would get rid of all this pent-up desire and allow them to move forward. But she knew that was just her libido talking.

"Jessica?"

She locked gazes with him and flushed when she realized she hadn't been paying attention.

"I'm sorry, sir, I missed that last bit."

Dane had been going over the agenda with her, trying to ignore the simmering heat inside him at her closeness, but then he'd realized her attention had drifted off. Now her cheeks tinged a deep rose, a response he was getting used to.

Clearly, she was having just as much trouble concentrating when they were close as he was. And it didn't help that she kept calling him sir. He didn't tell her to stop, because he felt it would help keep a professional distance between them, but damn it, it also turned him on.

"Okay, just give it a read over on your own to see if you have any questions."

He leaned back in his chair and watched her as she scanned the document on the screen.

He hoped that this intense craving for her would diminish over time. He knew he could wait it out. On the other hand, if she ever decided to give in to the heat simmering between them, he knew they could find a way to make it work. And if they allowed themselves that release, then the rest of the time in the office together could be more relaxed.

But, damn, he wanted to sweep her into his arms right now and plunder that sweet mouth of hers.

She shifted her gaze from the screen to him. "It's all clear, but I'll go over the documents you reference so I have the background."

"Good. We'll meet back here at 1 P.M."

She nodded and stood up to leave. She pulled her hand out of her pocket and something fell to the floor. He leaned down and picked it up.

"This is the stone I gave you when we first met," he said.

It was still warm from being close to her body.

"Yes. Did you want it back?"

He chuckled. "No, of course not. I'm just surprised you still have it."

He handed it to her and her delicate fingers brushed against his skin as she took it from him.

"I . . . like it. It's very calming."

She slipped it in her pocket again and headed out the door.

He couldn't stop smiling at the knowledge that she valued the simple stone he had given her.

He'd originally intended to give the stone to his brother, because the blue-lace agate—light blue with white streaks—reminded him of the summer sky at the cottage they'd gone to one summer as kids, where they'd skipped stones on the lake. They'd been close that summer, probably more so because there were no other kids around, but whatever the reason, he treasured those memories. He'd wanted to remind Rafe of that time, in hopes they could get past the issues between them and move forward. Unfortunately, Rafe had up and left before Dane could give it to him.

Jessica knew Dane had walked into the room even before he said anything. She and Melanie were sitting in the cafeteria, enjoying coffee and muffins during their afternoon break. Even in such a big room, Dane's authoritative aura filled the space. Only a few other employees were taking their break at this time and several glanced up at his arrival.

"There you are." He walked to their table. "I'm afraid I'll have to cut your break short."

Did he want to talk to Melanie or her? She tried to ignore the quiver of excitement that danced along her spine every time he got close.

"Is there a problem with the presentation?" Melanie asked.

Jessica had covered Melanie's basic duties this morning because Dane had sent Melanie to the Marketing Department for a few hours to help them put together a quick presentation for this afternoon. Jessica knew everyone was quite anxious about it, so Melanie must be worried something had gone wrong.

"Not at all. I'm told you did an excellent job, as usual."

Melanie smiled, clearly pleased at his approval.

"Jessica, I need you back upstairs."

She stood up, and reached for the empty tray on the table so she could dispose of her cup and the plate with her half-eaten muffin.

"Don't worry, I'll handle that," Melanie said.

Jessica grabbed her purse and followed Dane out the door of the cafeteria to the elevators. They stepped inside and the doors closed behind them.

His masculine presence filled the small space, and his closeness made her skin prickle in awareness.

"It's about that call you took for me this morning from Brenhart and Saunders."

From what she had learned about the business so far, Jessica knew Ranier Industries had been in talks with Brenhart and Saunders to form a partnership to develop a lighter, more efficient battery for electric cars so the vehicles could travel longer on a single charge. This was a new direction for Ranier and she knew the project was very important to Dane.

"It turns out what I thought was just a meeting with their board is actually a banquet to honor their founder. I need to arrive in a tux and I need you by my side."

"Me?"

"I'll have the opportunity to make a lot of inside contacts, and to talk with some of the senior staff on the development team directly. You can track the contacts and their information and take any notes I need."

"Of course." Clearly, she'd be working late tonight. He had warned her that would happen on occasion. It wasn't like she had anything going on this evening. "What time?"

Since this was a formal affair, she'd have to leave early to get ready, and that meant soon. She wondered if the one little black dress she had would do. It wasn't long or elegant, but maybe Melanie could loan her some jewelry or a nice shawl to dress it up.

"My driver will pick us up here at six." He glanced at his watch. "That gives us two hours."

"Oh, well, I'll have to rush home to get changed. Maybe I should go directly to the event."

"No time. I need you to go pick up my tux at the dry cleaners before they close. I'll arrange a dress for you." The elevator door opened and she followed his brisk pace back to his office. "It should be here by the time you get back."

"I don't understand. How will you get me a dress?"

He gestured her into the office and closed the door behind him, then sat down at his laptop sitting on the meeting table and opened a window. "Here she is, Roberto."

She sat down and stared at the attractive man with black hair and deep, brown eyes staring back at her from the screen. "Good to meet you, Ms. Long. What are your measurements?"

"I beg your pardon?"

"If I'm going to pick out a dress for you, I need to know the size."

"Oh, I'm an eight."

He laughed, dismissing her words. "If you don't have your exact measurements, just tell me your bra size. I'll stay away from anything fitted at the waist and hips." He held a pen and small notebook in his hand. "So . . . ?"

"You want my bra size?"

She was very conscious of Dane sitting in the chair right beside her. She couldn't help remembering when she'd stripped her bra off in front of him, then how he'd gazed at her naked breasts with heat simmering in his eyes.

"It's . . . um . . . 34C."

Her cheeks flamed as he wrote down the information. It was just very unsettling sitting in a business office with two men discussing her bra size.

He also asked her shoe size and various preferences in dress color and shoe style. She swore if he asked her weight, she'd walk away.

"Now stand up and turn around. Make sure I can see you in the camera."

She stood up, feeling a little ridiculous, and started to turn.

"Wait. Take your jacket off first. I want to get an idea of your body type."

She shed her jacket and turned around, then sat down again.

"Good, now lean in close to the camera." He narrowed his eyes as he examined her face. "Nice bone structure. Your eyes are a lovely shade of green." He jotted more things in his note-book then disappeared from the screen.

She glanced at Dane. "Wouldn't it just be easier for me to go home?"

"Roberto is my personal shopper. He's at one of the most exclusive women's stores in the city right now. Don't worry."

Roberto appeared again. "I have two dresses here I think would be perfect." He held up a pale blue one with a high-waisted bodice that glittered with beads and sequins. "It all de-pends on what it looks like against your skin tone. I can't tell for sure with this computer monitor. I think the safer choice would be this one." He held up a lovely black dress in a silky fabric. It looked so rich and elegant. "Okay, I can tell by your expression that this is the one. I'll have them send it right over."

Jessica happily escaped to the street, on her way to pick up Dane's tuxedo. It had cooled off a bit since this morning, so she pulled her jacket tighter around her. She walked the couple of blocks to the dry cleaners, paid for the suit with the company credit card Dane had given her, then quickly walked back to the office.

The lobby was empty except for the security staff at the desk, and when she arrived on the executive floor, Melanie was gone. Dane must have told her Jessica would be working late. She walked to Dane's office and went in. The lovely black dress Roberto had shown her was draped over one of the leather chairs. She carefully laid Dane's tux on the couch, care-ful not to wrinkle it, then lifted the clear plastic that was cov-ering the dress and ran her hand over the silky fabric.

"There you are."

She turned around and her eyes widened as she saw Dane standing in the center of the office wearing only a towel. His thick hair was damp and his face was freshly shaven. Seeing his broad, naked chest and breathing in his musky aftershave triggered memories of the two of them entwined in an intimate embrace. She sucked in a breath, not wanting to go there. To remember how their naked bodies had arched together, his hot, hard masculinity and authoritative attitude overwhelming her with the desire to do things she'd never done before.

He walked toward her and she held her breath. Was he going to sweep her into his arms? If he consumed her lips in a breathless kiss, she knew she would not be able to resist him. Not once her hands came in contact with his chest. It would be too much. She would succumb.

But he stepped right past her to the tuxedo lying on the couch. He tore back the plastic and pulled out the hanger with the white shirt.

"Good. I couldn't remember if I had sent in a shirt with it." He tossed the shirt on the back of the couch and walked to a cupboard near his desk, then retrieved a pair of boxers and some socks from a drawer inside.

Then he dropped his towel. Her gaze dropped to his big, dangling cock, even though she tried to stop it. Oh, God, she couldn't help remembering it big and hard. And so long.

He pulled on his boxers, then sat down on the chair to pull on the socks.

"Aren't you going to get changed?" he asked.

"Um . . ." A little rattled, she snatched up the dress and glanced around, then started for the door.

"Where are you going?"

"The ladies' room."

"We don't have time."

"But . . . I can't change here."

"Why not? I've seen you totally naked. Seeing a little lingerie is no big deal."

Her heart lurched. "It's a big deal to me."

He chuckled. "All right. Use my private bathroom then."

Of course. She carried the dress to the open door behind him, then slipped inside.

"Wait."

She stopped and turned toward him again.

He picked up a small bag from his desk and lifted something out of it, then held it up. A strapless black bra.

"Roberto sent this. The straps on the dress are pretty skinny."

She stared at the spaghetti straps and knew her current bra just wouldn't work. She walked toward him and held out her hand. When he gave her the bra, the brush of his fingers on her skin sent quivers through her. He still wore just his boxers, his beautifully sculpted chest bare.

It would be so easy to acquiesce to the demands of her body and stroke the contours of his chest, surrendering to the raging attraction between them.

She closed her fingers around the bra. "Thanks."

She turned and walked back to the bathroom, trying to ignore the sight of his rippling muscles as he pulled on his shirt.

She closed the door behind her. The steamy air was filled with the scent of his soap. She hung the dress on the hook on the back of the door and slid off her suit jacket. As she began to unfasten the buttons of her blouse, she couldn't help but think of the sight of him when he'd dropped the towel, revealing his sexy, naked body.

She slid her blouse from her shoulders and laid it neatly on the counter. She unzipped her skirt and dropped it to the floor, only then realizing that she'd worn a thong today because this skirt was a bitch when it came to showing panty lines. If she had changed in the other room, he would have gotten an eyeful of her naked ass.

She unhooked her bra and tugged it off, then put on the black bra, which was cut low and pushed her breasts high. She remembered his handsome, teasing face when he'd suggested she change in his office.

There was no doubt what that would have led to. Excitement quivered through her at the thought.

So who said you couldn't have sex with your boss?

She sucked in a breath. *Your common sense. That's who.*

She swept up the filmy plastic covering the dress and freed it from the hanger, anxious to cover herself before she lost all common sense and opened the door to give in to their attraction.

She dove into the dress and pulled up the zipper, then smoothed down the fabric.

She glanced at the silky, flowing garment. It made her feel like a princess. She turned to face the full length mirror. The dress suited her figure perfectly. The deep neckline revealed the soft swell of her breasts then cascaded in a fluid line to the floor. It made her look soft and feminine. And sexy.

A knock sounded at the door. "Come in," she said.

The door opened and there stood Dane, devastatingly handsome in his tuxedo.

His eyes glimmered as his gaze swept down her body. "You look sensational in that."

He walked into the room and stepped behind her. His powerful presence sent her senses off kilter. He stood so close, gazing at her in the mirror. It felt incredibly . . . intimate.

Her breath caught as his fingers brushed along the back of

her neck, but then she realized he was just fastening the hook at the top of the zipper.

"I think your hair would look nice down." He unfastened the barrette at the back of her head, and the mass of glossy black hair tumbled down. He gently arranged it over her shoulders.

"Beautiful." The approving glint in his eyes pleased her.

They stood like that for a moment, their gazes locked in the reflective glass of the mirror. Her heart thumped loudly and she longed for him to touch her.

But then he stepped back. "We really need to go."

Moments later, they hurried out the front door of the building to the waiting limousine.

Dane couldn't take his eyes off Jessica as they sat in the large ballroom that shimmered with soft light from the candles on the table and the light reflected from the crystals on the dimmed chandeliers above. The waiter refilled their wine glasses as they enjoyed their lobster bisque.

She had done very well keeping up with him while he'd networked before dinner, as he'd struck up conversations with the development staff, the marketing people, and the other senior staff of Brenhart and Saunders. The whole time, he'd never seen her jot anything down, yet when he'd questioned her about a couple of points he wanted to ensure he remembered, she had the information right at hand. He was sure she had a notebook in that small evening bag which Roberto had sent over with the dress, but in keeping with the social feel of the evening, she was doing an excellent job of being discreet with her note-taking.

He'd gleaned a lot of useful information over cocktails, and now it was time to relax and enjoy the evening. Especially with such a lovely companion by his side. She looked absolutely stunning in that dress. The accessories Roberto had included really enhanced the elegance. From the lovely oval ruby surrounded by diamonds that hung around her neck, glittering in the candlelight, right down to the red-bottomed black stiletto heels. Even the black evening bag glittered.

But what he really loved was how the dress hugged her breasts, dipping low between them to reveal a delightful amount of rounded flesh. He sipped his wine, thinking how much he would love to sweep her away and take her back to his apartment, then slip first one thin strap, then the other, off her shoulders to reveal even more of those luscious breasts.

He remembered those soft breasts filling his hands. The feel of the hard nipples against his tongue. Heat rushed through him at the memory. He wanted to see them again now. To touch and worship them.

But that was not to be.

The waiter took their empty soup bowls and placed the main course in front of each of them. The two seats beside Dane were empty and the development people on the other side of Jessica were talking amongst themselves about some design issue.

He turned to Jessica. "Are you enjoying your dinner?"

It was a delectable cut of prime rib, with roast potatoes and asparagus.

"Delicious."

"And are you enjoying living in Philadelphia so far?"

"Yes, I really like the city. I miss my family, of course, but I enjoy sharing an apartment with Melanie. She's been showing me around, so it's been a lot easier to transition than it would have been."

"Good."

"She's also teaching me a lot about the company, but there's one thing I'm curious about."

"What's that?"

"Well, she said the other executive office on our floor is your brother's, but I never see him. She hasn't said much about it, but I got the impression he's moved somewhere. If that's true, are you going to bring someone else in, or convert the office to another purpose?"

He grinned. "Are you looking for a promotion already?"

She looked startled then laughed when she realized he was kidding. "No, of course not. I just thought maybe you hadn't had time to think about it and maybe I could help with it."

He sipped his wine. "No, we'll be keeping that office available for my brother. It's not generally known, but my brother is going through a rebellious phase." He tipped his head. "Actually, he's been in a rebellious phase since he was a child, but about a year ago—six months after our father died—he decided he needed to get away and find himself. You see, he never wanted to be part of this company, I think more because he didn't get along with our father and didn't want to be part of his legacy, rather than because of any real aversion to running the business. He didn't like how Dad ran things and, I think, when I took over, he felt I was too much like our father and he decided to rebel against me. When I insisted he take a more active role in the company, he decided to walk away entirely."

She glanced at him with a warmth and concern in her eyes. "Have you seen him or talked to him in the last year?"

He shook his head. "I have no idea where he is or what he's doing, but he's always wanted to travel so he's probably doing something like hiking around Asia."

"Are you worried about him?"

He was, but he wouldn't admit it. "He can take care of himself. He can live quite comfortably, on what he's earned with this company and the generous inheritance from Dad, for a long time."

"Do you miss him?"

A typical female question.

"I don't miss his brooding or his constant disapproval of my methods."

She nodded. "In other words, you wouldn't admit it if you did." She finished her last bite of prime rib then put down her fork. "Clearly from the fact you're keeping his office, you're hoping he'll come back. The question is, what will you do when he does? Will you listen to his ideas and try to incorporate them into your plans for the company?"

Irritation spiked through him. "Don't you think you're overstepping your bounds?" he said in a stern voice.

Her lips compressed and she looked properly contrite. "I'm sorry, sir. You're right. It's none of my business."

Instantly, he missed the warmth in her eyes. The connection they'd been sharing that went beyond the boss-employee relationship. Maybe they couldn't act on the sexual attraction between them, but he didn't want to lose the closeness they'd established over dinner.

She had only been trying to help, but he wasn't used to anyone poking their nose in his family business. On the other hand, he hadn't been doing a great job keeping a good relationship with his brother and he truly wanted him back.

"I'm sorry. I'm not used to opening up about my family relationships. I shouldn't have snapped at you."

He didn't go on to tell her that this business with Brenhart and Saunders was exactly the kind of thing Rafe would want them to pursue.

Her eyes filled with understanding and she placed her

hand on his. Instantly, a spark of awareness sizzled through him. He saw it in her eyes, too, and she shifted her hand away and wrapped her fingers around the stem of her wine glass, then lifted it to her lips. He couldn't help but watch as she sipped the burgundy liquid. Her lips glistened as she ran her tongue around them and he longed to lean forward and taste them. To slip his tongue inside her silky, warm mouth, then to kiss her while she melted into his arms.

A waiter came by and collected their dinner plates, replacing them with martini glasses filled with chocolate mousse.

"Sometimes it helps to talks about things," she said. "Why don't you tell me a story about you and your brother growing up? How did you get along?"

He smiled. "Well, when I turned eight years old, Rafe was six, and he decided he wanted to get me something for my birthday. Our parents always arranged a gift from brother-to-brother on these occasions, but Rafe was adamant that he would arrange his own gift. Something he got himself. So on my birthday, he handed me a small box that he'd wrapped himself. There was tape everywhere and not all of the box was covered, but he was proud of his accomplishment. When I opened it up, inside was a gold watch. Just like the one my father had, that he knew I had always been fascinated with."

"Where did he get a gold watch?"

"That's the thing. It was my Dad's. At that age, Rafe didn't really understand the idea of ownership. He just knew I loved that watch, and Dad barely wore that one since he had several, so on the morning of my birthday Rafe retrieved it from my Dad's dressing room, wrapped it up, and presented it to me."

She smiled, her green eyes glittering in the soft light of the candles. "That's sweet."

She was right. Even at eight years old, Dane had been touched
by his brother's generosity and desire to make him happy. He
had hated the fact that his father had only seen a child who
needed a lesson in ownership and had beaten him with a belt.
Their mother had not stood up for Rafe because she would never
disagree with their father.

"But enough about me. Let's delve into your past, shall
we?"

"What do you want to know?"

"Why don't you tell me about this ex of yours. You said
he's incredibly handsome?" he said with a grin.

She laughed. "Yes, he's confident and handsome like you.
But in every other way, he's totally different."

"How so?"

"For one, I could never imagine him in a business suit. He
rode into Bakersfield—the little town I grew up in—on a big
Harley, wearing torn jeans and a leather jacket. He's tall, broad
shouldered, and totally ripped." She grinned. "Okay in that way
he's just like you, but his muscles are covered with tattoos, at least
over his arms, shoulders, and back. And he plays guitar in a rock
band."

"So that's the kind of guy you like? A free-wheeling musician?"

"Not necessarily. He just . . ." She shrugged. "I don't
know . . ."

"Swept you off your feet?"

"Yeah, I guess so."

"So why did you think he loved you?"

"I didn't say that."

"No, but your eyes did."

She drew in a deep breath. "He always looked at me like

I was something special, and even though the other girls in town fawned over him, he only seemed interested in me."

"I can understand that."

She gazed at him uncertainly. "Thank you. You know, that's another way you two are alike. He was very charming, too."

Dane wondered how this biker guitarist could just dump her like yesterday's garbage. Some guys just didn't understand a good thing when they had it.

"But I guess what really convinced me he was in love with me . . ." Her gaze flicked to his. "Because you're right, I did think that . . . was when he got this tattoo."

"Don't tell me he got your name tattooed across his chest?"

"No, it was on his shoulder, and it wasn't my name. In fact, it was really sweet. You see, I had a framed picture of a leopard moth in my room, which he asked me about. I told him that when I was a kid, I was always a perfectionist, and one time a teacher gave us a list of ten butterflies and moths that we had to draw as a science project. She wanted them from a specific book in the school library, but there were only five copies and everyone kept checking them out. By the time I got a copy, with only a few days left before the deadline, I realized that the picture of the leopard moth had been torn out of the book. I drew all the others, but I was in tears because I didn't know what to do about the tenth picture.

"The next evening, my mom showed up with the picture I needed. She'd taken the afternoon off work and driven all the way to Garnersville to the big library there and found the book, then photocopied the page and brought it home to me. I got an A on the project and that picture became a symbol of how much my mom would do to support me and how she would always be there for me. When Storm chose to have a leopard moth tattoo, I foolishly thought he was telling me he would always be there for me, too."

She gazed at her wine glass and the sadness in her eyes tore at Dane's heart. How could the guy have been that callous?

She shrugged. "Now I realize that it was probably just a badge of sorts. Like a notch on his bed to represent another conquest."

"You know you're better off without him."

Her lips curled up slightly. "So people keep telling me."

A waiter came by and cleared away their dessert plates and coffee cups. Music began playing and a few couples wandered onto the dance floor.

"Let's dance," he said.

She glanced at him. "Really? But I thought we were here on business."

"That doesn't mean we can't relax and enjoy ourselves."

Looking a little skeptical, she rose with him and he led her to the floor. As soon as he swept her into his arms, he realized his mistake. He was far too aware of her soft, warm body close to his. He longed to pull her closer, and feel her breasts crushed against him, to capture her full lips and plunder her delectable mouth.

He had to concentrate so as not to allow his body to harden noticeably. He had a lot of self-control, but why was he making things so difficult for himself? As much as he wanted this woman, she'd made it clear she didn't want to have an intimate relationship with him.

As soon as the song ended, he led her from the floor.

"I think it's time we call it a night."

Jessica wasn't sure quite what had happened. First, Dane had led her to the dance floor and drew her close, sending her hormones revving, then as soon as the song ended, he'd dragged her out to get their coats, and before she knew it they were in his limo heading home.

At least, she assumed he was taking her to her apartment. Surely he hadn't gotten the wrong idea and thought she wanted to go back to his place. They had talked about personal things and then when they were on the dance floor, he could probably see the desire in her eyes.

She couldn't help it. He was a sexy, debonair man. Strong and masculine. Charming. And when he wanted to be, which was most of the time, authoritative. In a way that made her want to succumb to his power. Tonight she'd seen a softer side of him, but that sense of authority and power that she found so devastatingly sexy were ever present.

She glanced at the streets they passed and even with her sketchy knowledge of Philadelphia, she soon realized they were heading out of the city, and she knew he lived right downtown, very near where she'd first seen him on the street.

They didn't talk much on the ride, but when they pulled up in front of her building and she turned to the car door, he rested his hand on her arm.

"Jessica, I enjoyed our evening together. It was good to talk about Rafe. It's been a long time."

She smiled. "I enjoyed tonight, too."

Then her gaze caught his and she sat, mesmerized, as he leaned toward her. His lips brushed hers lightly at first then he deepened the kiss. She couldn't help it. She melted against him. His arms came around her, holding her tighter to his body. His persuasive lips moved on hers with passion, filling her with longing.

She wanted him. She knew it. She'd always known it.

But they couldn't.

He seemed to sense her withdrawal and he released her. She stared into his intense blue eyes, so filled with desire.

"I . . . uh . . . have a roommate," she stammered. But, of course, he already knew that.

He smiled and stroked her cheek with one finger, sending a tremor through her.

"Jessica, if I'd wanted you in my bed this evening, you'd already be there."

He gestured to the chauffeur and the man hopped out of the car and opened her door. Dane followed her out of the car and walked her to the entrance of her apartment. Once there, he waited while she unlocked the door and pulled it open, then he took her hand and kissed it, his lips brushing her skin lightly, sending shimmering awareness through her.

"Just remember. If you ever change your mind about pursuing something more than a boss-employee relationship, all you have to do is say the word."

At that, he held the door open until she was inside, then he turned and disappeared into his black limousine. She watched it drive away, wishing she'd thrown caution to the wind and leapt back into the car with him.

Why did he have to say that?

Jessica lay in bed staring at the ceiling. She had decided when she'd first found out that Dane owned Ranier Industries that there would be no hanky-panky between them. They worked together. He was her boss.

But spending the evening together getting to know one another had torn away the business veneer she had used to shield herself from his intense magnetism. He wasn't just a business man. He had a brother he cared about. Whom he missed. She'd seen a glimpse of the emotion in his eyes, even though he'd done a heroic job shielding it from her. It made him more human to her. A man with feelings. Vulnerabilities.

She closed her eyes and tried to forget that kiss in the limo. She'd been so sure he wanted to come up here and take her, just like he'd taken her that one night they were together. And she'd wanted him to, despite her lame protest.

She closed her eyes and tried to fall asleep, but she tossed and turned all night, haunted by the memory of that one night she'd spent with Dane. She ached for him. When she finally fell asleep, she was plagued by dreams of their naked bodies entwined, his powerful hands gliding over her skin, his muscular body crushing her to the bed while he thrust into her again and again. She woke up, drenched with sweat, the sheets twisted around her legs, wishing she could ease her yearning.

As she showered, scrubbing her skin with her loofah sponge, she wondered how she would get through the day. Now that he'd reawakened the intense attraction between them, she didn't know how she could ignore it.

She towel dried her hair, then put on her makeup and dressed. Over breakfast, Melanie asked how the evening had gone, and Jessica told her a few details about the event and Dane's networking, but said nothing about the dance or, heaven forbid, the kiss. She knew it sounded pretty dry, so soon the conversation turned to the latest nail polish trends, a particular passion of Melanie's. She followed all kinds of blogs and tended to be a bit of an addict when it came to her nails.

When they finally arrived at work, Jessica actually found herself getting nervous about seeing Dane again.

It didn't help that, as soon as she got to her desk, she saw a note in his distinctive handwriting, telling her to come to his office.

Jessica tapped on the door to Dane's office, then opened it and stepped inside. Rather than sitting at his desk reading his e-mail, he was in one of the armchairs by the window.

"You wanted to see me?"

"Join me." He gestured to the chair across the small, low table in front of him.

She crossed the office and sat down, her gaze never quite meeting his.

"Coffee?" he asked.

She noticed a thermos of coffee on the table and two cups, one already filled with steaming black coffee.

"No. Thank you."

He leaned back in his chair. "I wanted to talk to you about last night."

"Did I do okay? I got all the contact names and information. I'll enter it all in the computer this morning."

"You did fine. That's not what I'm talking about."

Her gaze drifted to his, then flicked away from his scrutiny.

"I'm talking about the kiss. I was worried that it might cause some tension between us. And I see it has."

"No, it's all right. I don't have a problem with it. We'll just forget about it."

"Can you?"

Her gaze shifted to his again.

"I . . . uh . . ."

"Because I can't."

She blinked.

"I'm not saying that it needs to affect our work. And I will

still respect your decision to avoid an intimate relationship between us." He leaned forward, his intense blue eyes boring into
her. "If that's still what you want."

"I . . . of course, that's still what I want."

He raised an eyebrow. "You're sure?"

She nodded.

At his continued scrutiny, her stomach tightened. Why did
this have to be so difficult?

"All right." He stood up.

Reluctantly, she stood up, too. She slowly turned and walked
toward the door.

They would go back to the way things had been. Boss and
assistant. She would find a way to ignore the galloping hormones
that plagued her every time she got near him. Or thought about
him. Or heard his name.

She realized her steps were slowing as she neared the door.
She stopped and turned around.

"Dane . . . I mean, Mr. Ranier, I . . ."

"Yes, what is it, Jessica?"

"No, it's nothing. I'm sorry." She headed toward the door
again.

"Jessica, come back."

At his command, she turned and returned to stand in front
of his desk, where he was now sitting.

"What was it you were going to say?"

She wasn't sure exactly, just that . . .

"I'm not sure if it's still what I want."

He stood up and walked toward her, his gaze never leaving
hers.

As he approached, her body began to tingle. Excitement
quivered through her.

He brushed her cheek with his fingertips, the merest whisper of a touch. And still he held her captive with his gaze.

"What *do* you want?" he asked.

Gazing deep into his eyes, she could barely think straight, let alone find her voice.

"I . . ." Oh, God, what was she doing? "Want . . ." She tried to stop . . . knew it was a bad idea . . . but she couldn't help herself. "You."

The last word—the incriminating, no-turning-back admission—was a throaty whisper. A smile spread across his face and he tipped up her chin. Those blue eyes of his gleamed with desire as his face approached hers. Her eyelids fluttered closed as their lips touched.

The kiss was gentle at first, then passion flared between them as their tongues clashed.

His arms pulled her close to his body, crushing her breasts, swollen from need, against his solid chest.

"And I want you," he proclaimed. "I suggest we take the day off and spend it in my bedroom."

"No, that's not a good idea." She summoned the strength of will to draw away from him a little, but he didn't release her from his arms.

"I think it's a great idea." He smiled and kissed her, a light brush of lips this time. "But if you'd rather, I'll take you out to dinner tonight. Candlelight and wine in an elegant restaurant. A stunning view of the city. *Then* back to my place." He adjusted his tie. "But I'll warn you now, I intend to make it an early dinner."

She shook her head, her eyes wide. "No."

Why was she panicking? She wanted to be with him. Could barely keep herself from tearing his clothes off right now.

"You've refused going back to my place twice. What is it you want, Jessica?" His eyes glittered. "It seems you're having trouble making up your mind."

"It's just so complicated. I just got out of a romantic relationship and I'm not ready for something like that again. But I'd be lying if I told you that I didn't find you . . . extremely distracting. So if we're going to do this, I want it to be a physical relationship only."

He raised his eyebrows. "I see. So there will be no romantic entanglements, no relationship demands."

She nodded. "But I don't want our personal involvement to get in the way of business. And I would prefer that no one know about it."

He slid his arms around her again and drew her close. "All right. I agree with those conditions."

As his lips captured hers, her heart thundered in her chest.

"Since you insist we don't let our affair interfere with work, we'll have to go to my 10:30 meeting."

"Oh." She drew in a deep breath. Her body was aching for him, and she longed for him to take control of her. To order her to please him.

Clearly, however, that would have to wait. They would have to leave in fifteen minutes.

"I'll go gather my things."

But when she attempted to slip from his arms, he merely tightened his hold.

"I didn't say you could go yet."

That commanding tone of his sent her nerve endings fluttering.

"But you said—"

"I said there was little time. So you'd better be quick."

Her eyes widened.

"I want you to fuck me. Right now." He nuzzled her ear, his swollen shaft pressing against her belly. "Right here in the office. The walls are soundproof so no one will hear when I make you scream."

At her hesitation, he said, "It's not a request." He captured her mouth in a commanding, passionate kiss. His tongue swept inside and her knees went weak. "Fuck me," he said softly against her lips.

His commanding tone dug deep inside her and she couldn't control herself.

"Yes, sir," she said in a shaky voice, her hands trembling with the need to wrap themselves around his shaft.

She unzipped his pants, and then reached inside. Oh, God, he was hard as rock. She drew him out of the confines of the fabric and gazed down at the big, plum-shape head, longing to take it in her mouth. She started to lean down but he stopped her with a hand on her shoulder. "That's not the part of you I want to fuck. Spread your legs for me."

She pulled up her skirt and opened her legs.

His fingers glided through her long hair. "Very good," he murmured as his hand slid inside her pantyhose, tugged them to her knees and then tugged the crotch of her panties to one side. He pressed his hard cockhead to her damp folds, and slowly slid into her slick core.

She almost gasped as his massive cock glided inside her. Filling her so deeply. Once he was fully immersed, he grasped her hips and held her tight against him, turning her until she pressed back against the desk. His lips nuzzled her temple.

Oh, God, she couldn't believe she was standing in his executive office, pinned between him and his desk as his cock impaled her. If anyone walked in . . .

But they wouldn't. No one would walk into Dane Ranier's office without his permission.

Still, if someone knocked and Dane delayed before he answered—

"Don't think." His breath brushed across her ear. "Just fuck me."

His hands on her hips guided her back, then forward again. His considerable girth stretched and caressed her passage as they moved.

He tucked his hands under her ass, pulling her tighter against him. His long cock pushed even deeper inside her as he lifted her from her feet. She pulled one leg out of the pantyhose and wrapped her legs around him as he set her on the desk. He drew back, then drove forward with a powerful thrust, filling her with every considerable inch of his cock.

"Oh, God," she whimpered. Pleasure swelled within her as he pumped into her body. Her erratic breathing sounded like whimpers. She nuzzled his clean-shaven neck, loving the brisk smell of his cologne.

He pressed his hand to her lower back and thrust deep. She sucked in air as her whole body vibrated with need. He drove deep again and she clung to his shoulders, feeling the joyful sensations dance through her.

Just when she was about to soar over the edge, he stopped his movements.

"Please don't stop," she whimpered.

"Do you want me to keep fucking you? After you've done so much to tease and torment me since you got here. I think I should make you suffer."

She couldn't imagine him stopping. She was so close. She wanted him so badly. She nearly cried when she felt him withdraw from her completely.

"Yes, please, sir. Keep fucking me."

An amused smile spread across his face, and he drew his hips back and thrust hard. Her insides melted. Tingles danced across her skin.

"I'll reserve your punishment for another time," he said, then spiraled his shaft inside her, driving her pleasure to a new level. "You're lucky your sweet little pussy feels so good, otherwise I'd have no problem leaving you empty and aching."

He continued to drive into her. He spiraled again and she moaned as pleasure rippled through her.

He thrust faster. Deeper.

"Oh, fuck," he ground out.

She felt liquid heat erupt inside her. She gasped, then plummeted over the edge right along with him. He continued to fill her—in and out—as she rode the wave, her moans filling the office.

Slowly, the orgasm waned and she felt herself drifting back to earth. Her head rested against the lapel of his jacket, his heartbeat thumping against her ear. As her heart rate slowly returned to normal, she became conscious of the complete inappropriateness of the situation. Here she was, sitting on his desk, her skirt pulled up, his big cock deep inside her.

Twitching. Oh, God, he was getting hard again.

"Well, if that's what I have to look forward to in the office," he said, "I may decide never to go home."

Jessica sat in the limo beside Dane as they traveled to his meeting with Dan Johansson, the senior partner of an architecture firm he was thinking of hiring to design a new manufacturing facility on the outskirts of the city. As they drove, she reviewed the notes she'd taken about the questions he wanted to ensure were answered during the meeting.

When they arrived, she spent her time during the meeting jotting down notes and providing Dane with information when he requested it. But mainly, she kept her mind firmly *off* what had happened in his office this morning.

She didn't regret it. Not one bit. And even though a part of her wanted to resist his sexual dominance, she enjoyed it more than she could have ever imagined. So now she just needed to figure out how to get used to their new relationship.

Dane stood and shook Mr. Johansson's hand. "Thank you. My assistant will get back to you if I have any further questions."

Jessica stood up and followed him from the office back to the limo, then settled in beside him. The driver pulled into traffic.

"That went well. Can you have that information put together for our Planning Department this afternoon?"

"Yes, sir."

He smiled. "You know, it drives me crazy when you call me sir."

Her gaze darted to him. "Should I stop?"

"Not at all. I love it."

She smiled. "So I shouldn't start calling you Dane?"

"No. Definitely sir. Or Mr. Ranier."

"Even when we're . . ."—her cheeks heated—"having sex?"

"*Especially* when we're having sex."

This was definitely going to take some getting used to. Every time she called him sir in the office, there would be a thrill of excitement pulsing through her.

Going to the office was definitely going to be a whole new experience from now on.

When Jessica returned to her office, Melanie had already left for lunch, since the meeting outside the office had gone long. Dane had a lunch appointment, but she was relieved not to have the choice of eating lunch with him. Their relationship was about work and sex. Nothing more.

She grabbed a sandwich at a deli nearby and ate at her desk. She was actually glad not to sit with Melanie today. Her new secret would probably be written all over her face. It wouldn't be so awkward on the trip home, because they didn't get into deep discussions on the bus. They usually talked about non-work-related topics like weekend plans, the new guy Melanie was seeing, or affordable fashion boutiques that Jessica should check out.

When they got home, Melanie found that her latest online nail polish order had arrived and she went off to ooh and aah over them, then to try a new ombre manicure she'd been talking about doing. Jessica always liked all the interesting colors and textured polishes Melanie found, and the creative manicures she tried. She knew Melanie would come and show her the results later in the evening. But for now, she was relieved to be left to her own devices.

After she changed into her jeans and walked back into the living room, she noticed the light blinking on the answering machine and pushed the button to listen to the message.

"Jessica, sweetie? It's Mom." Jessica smiled. Mom always felt she had to identify herself. "I guess you're not home yet. Can you call me right away? Well, not right away, I mean, it's not an emergency or anything, just as soon as you can."

Jessica dialed the phone and her mother picked up.

"Hi, Mom. I got your message."

"Oh, sweetie, hi. It's so nice to hear your voice. We miss you, you know."

Jessica smiled. "I know, Mom. I miss you and Dad, too."

They chatted for a few minutes about her dad and how work was going, and about Mom's latest quilting project. But something in her mother's tone seemed off.

"Is something wrong, Mom? You seem distracted. Are you and Dad okay?"

"Oh, no, sweetie. We're fine. I just know you're doing so well at your new job, and you sound so happy. I don't want to upset you."

She sat forward in her chair. "Well it's too late. Now you've really got me worried. Is it a health concern?"

"Oh, no, nothing like that. Sweetie, I know how hurt you were when Storm walked out on you to go on tour. I know you were in love with him and it broke your heart. But he came to see me and . . . he told me he wants to talk to you." Her mother hesitated. "Jess, I think he's still in love with you. He wants to find you."

"Oh, Mom, you didn't give him my number, did you?"

"Of course not. I wouldn't do that, but . . ."

Jessica gritted her teeth at her mother's hesitation.

"Unfortunately, your dad did."

Jessica's stomach clenched.

"And, honey, I'm pretty sure Storm's coming to find you."

Perfect Storm

Jessica gripped the phone tightly, her other hand balling into a fist.

Damn it! She had just gotten over Storm, or at least gotten to a point where she didn't ache inside every time she thought about him. And a big part of that was because Dane was such a major distraction.

Her hand slipped into her jeans pocket and she stroked the flat stone Dane had given her.

But Dane was more than just a distraction. When he hadn't even known her, he'd helped her out, given her advice and confidence. He'd given her a job.

"Mom, did Dad give him my address, too? Or tell him where I work?"

"No, not your address, but where you work? Um, I'm not sure."

"Oh, Mom." Jessica put her face in her palm. "Why would he do that?"

"Sweetie, you know he really likes Storm, and he'd love to

have him as a son-in-law. I'm sure he thought that you would be happy to see him. He just wants you to be happy. And so do I."

"I know, Mom."

"You know, I was just wondering. Would it be such a bad thing if he found you?"

Her mother had always liked Storm. Well, of course she did. Mom wanted her to be happy, and she'd never been happier than during her time with Storm.

When she still thought he loved her.

Did he still love her? Even in spite of all he'd done, her heart leapt at the thought.

But all Mom had said was that she *thought* Storm still loved her. That could so easily be wishful thinking on her part. When Storm had walked out on Jessica, she knew that her mother had been in almost as much pain as she had been. Because that's how mothers were with their kids. They wanted to protect them and make things right. Her mother would have given anything to make things right again so Jessica would be happy.

So Mom was probably only seeing what she wanted to see. Storm likely didn't want to come here to find her at all. Probably the only reason Storm wanted to talk to her was because he had left something behind that he wanted back. For instance, she remembered finding a copy of one of the demo CDs he'd made of him playing with the band. She remembered when she'd noticed the plain white CD, labeled with a black Sharpie, sitting on her dresser. It included the song he'd written for her. She'd played it over and over again, her only tangible link to him and the love they'd shared. Remembering the way he'd played it for her in the nude. They'd both been lying entwined on his bed after making love when he'd stood up, retrieved his guitar and begun playing a song so heartbreakingly tender it had brought tears to her eyes. But as the reality hit her that he really had walked away from her, and their love, she'd tucked it away in a drawer, like any dream that was destined never to come true.

He probably only wanted to retrieve that CD.

"I really don't want to see him. I have a new life here."

"I know, but . . . are you sure? Because if he wants you back, then maybe you could work things out."

"Even if he does want me back, which I doubt, *I* don't want *him* back. "

"But if you still love him . . ."

"I'll get over it. Mom, please don't worry about me. I can take care of myself."

Mom sighed. "I know that, sweetie. And you know I'd do anything in the world to make things better for you. I'm really sorry about this."

Jessica smiled. "It'll be okay, Mom. I know Dad's heart was in the right place." She held the phone with both hands, wishing Mom was here right now so she could give her a big hug. "I love you. And I miss you."

"Me, too, sweetie."

A few minutes after she hung up the phone, Melanie walked into the living room.

"Was that your Mom on the phone?"

Jessica nodded.

"Hey, is everything okay?" The concern in Melanie's voice jarred Jessica from her thoughts.

She shrugged. "Mom said that my ex is back in Bakersfield and he asked her for my number."

Melanie's eyebrows arched. "And . . . ?"

Jessica had told her about Storm and how much she'd loved

him. How he'd left her and how difficult it had been to get over him. How difficult it still was.

"My father gave it to him."

Melanie's eyebrows arched. "Did he give him your address, too?"

"No, thankfully, but now I'll be on pins and needles wondering if and when he'll call." She hugged her knees and gazed at Melanie. "I love my father but sometimes he just doesn't get it."

Melanie nodded, a thoughtful look on her face. "Did he give you our home number or your cell?"

"I'm not sure. Probably my cell."

Melanie smiled. "Okay, if it's our home number, we can just screen the calls. For your cell, here's what we're going to do. First we'll add a blocking app to your phone for any calls or texts he sends you that shoots unknown numbers straight to voicemail. Then we're going to forget he even exists. You know I got my new nail polish, right? How about I do your nails with this great new color I think you'll love, add a bit of glitz, then we'll hit the town?"

At her pursed lips, Melanie held up a bottle of rich burgundy nail polish in one hand and the real gold leaf flake topcoat she had been raving about for weeks in the other, and then tilted them back and forth.

"Come on. You know you want to."

Jessica grinned. She did love the color of polish Melanie had picked out, and she would love to see what those delicate gold flakes looked like over the top of it.

She laughed. "Okay. It's a deal."

Ten minutes later, Melanie had finished applying the burgundy polish to Jessica's nails, and she sat on the couch sipping a glass of wine while waiting for them to dry.

"You know, I think what would help you right now would be to find a hot guy and get laid."

Jessica couldn't help laughing. "I think you're absolutely right."

She just wouldn't tell her friend that she'd already found the hot guy, but she'd have to wait until Monday—at the office—to get laid. Again.

Midmorning on Monday, Jessica sat by Melanie's desk with a notebook on her lap as she asked questions about the various subsidiaries under Ranier Industries' control.

The elevator doors opened and Dane stepped out. At once, awareness rippled through Jessica, but she continued to write down the most recent answer Melanie had provided.

"Good morning, Melanie. Jessica. I hope you had a nice weekend."

"Very nice, thank you, Mr. Ranier," Melanie answered as he walked by her desk, only a foot from Jessica.

His gaze fell on Jessica and heat washed through her.

"Yes, very nice," she said.

Usually he threw out this kind of small talk as he continued on to his office, so there was only time for a quick response before he was gone, but Melanie jumped in.

"And you, Mr. Ranier?" Melanie asked.

"Fine. A little socializing, a lot of work. The usual."

Jessica wondered if the socializing included a woman. Surprised at the rise in what seemed suspiciously like jealousy, she admonished herself.

"Jessica, as soon as you're finished here, join me in my office."

She closed her notebook. "I think we're done now. I was

just asking Melanie some questions about the company's infra-structure."

He nodded and continued to his office, leaving the door open behind him. She stood up.

"I'm going to go grab him a coffee. Want one?" she asked Melanie.

"Sure, thanks."

Jessica left her stuff on Melanie's desk while she poured three coffees, then dropped one off at Melanie's desk, picked up her notebook and pen, and continued to Dane's office.

She placed the mugs on Dane's desk, then went back and closed the door.

"Thanks." He picked up the mug took a sip, and moved to the sitting area by the window. She sat across from him.

"I wanted to talk about last Friday. You've had the weekend to think about things, and I just want to ensure you're still okay with what happened between us."

He was offering her the chance to return their relationship to business only.

"Yes. I'm fine with it."

Fine with it? Now there was a glowing recommendation of what they'd done. *Way to show your enthusiasm.*

His blue eyes watched her, assessing her expression.

"No regrets?"

She shook her head. "None."

"Good." He leaned toward her and smiled. "With our new arrangement, I will periodically set down rules or assign you tasks of a more personal nature." He raised an eyebrow. "Understood?"

"Yes, Mr. Ranier."

His smile broadened, revealing his even white teeth.

"Very good. Now come over here."

She stood up, her insides quivering in anticipation. She'd been longing for his touch all weekend. Dreaming of their bodies entwined, his massive erection sliding into her. Melanie had tried to set her up with one of her male friends on Friday night, but even though Jessica's desire for a man thrummed through her the only man who she'd be satisfied with was Dane.

She stepped in front of him, wondering if he would stroke her breasts. Or ask her to strip down in front of him. Or to kneel down and unzip his pants, then reach inside . . .

"Turn around," he instructed.

As soon as she'd turned around, her back to him, he ran his hand along her hip, then over her ass. His fingertip plucked at the elastic of her panties through the fabric of her skirt.

"Are you wearing pantyhose or stockings?"

"Pantyhose," she said.

"Turn around again."

She turned back to face him and his gaze fell on her crotch area. She felt heat well inside her.

"From now on, when you're at work, I want you to wear a garter belt and stockings. And instead of these bikini panties, you will wear a thong. Over the garter belt, not under it."

So they would be easier to take off while leaving on the stockings.

Her vagina clenched. God, she wished he would touch her.

"Yes, sir. Should I go home at lunch and change?"

He chuckled. "No, tomorrow will be fine."

He stood up, placing his body intimately close to hers. If she leaned forward a hair, her breasts would brush his chest. She gazed up at him, wondering if he would kiss her. At the gleam in his eyes, she was sure he would and she raised her chin in anticipation.

He leaned a little closer, his eyes twinkling. "It's time to go back to work."

Surprised, she drew in a breath and took a step back. "Yes, sir."

She retrieved her notebook and pen from his desk, and then headed out the door. When she got to her own office, she sat down and sucked in air. Damn, now she was hot and horny with no outlet in sight.

She remembered that she had left her mug in his office. She could go back and get it and, while she was there, make it clear she wanted him. But if she did that, she would get nowhere. Dane enjoyed being in control. When they made love again, it would be because it was his idea, not hers.

For some reason, that made it all the hotter.

When lunch time rolled around, Jessica told Melanie she had some errands to run and instead of eating with her friend, she headed to a little lingerie shop around the corner. When she returned, she had on a sexy, dark red garter belt, stockings, and a very tiny matching thong under her skirt. She also wore the matching bra, and had even bought new shoes in the same color. Very sexy shoes with stiletto heels.

"Aren't you afraid you'll fall off those things and break your neck?" Melanie teased when she walked into the office.

Jessica grinned. "I couldn't resist them. They're so pretty."

"They are very nice. And they certainly add pizzazz to your black suit." Melanie glanced up from the shoes. "They're not your usual style." She grinned. "When a woman buys shoes that sexy, I have to wonder if there's a man she's hoping to attract. Anyone I know?"

Jessica felt her cheeks heat. "No. I just really liked them."

"Okay, I didn't mean to embarrass you. But Jerrod really

liked you Friday and you didn't seem interested. I never thought it might be because you had someone else in mind."

Jessica escaped to her desk. She did *not* want Melanie to figure out she was attracted to Dane.

Dane returned to his office around three o'clock. It wasn't appropriate to take Jessica to all his meetings and he was glad he hadn't this afternoon. This morning, he'd had to rein himself in because after touching her sexy round ass, when she'd lifted her pert little chin, clearly expecting him to kiss her, desire had rushed through him. He'd wanted to drag her into his arms and plunge into that sweet little mouth of hers, then strip off her clothes and fuck her for hours.

But he didn't want to overwhelm her with constant sex, and if he allowed himself to have her anytime he felt the desire, that's what would happen. He'd be fucking her nonstop.

He sat down at his desk and opened his e-mail. Jessica had already marked forty messages as "handled," and flagged a handful that required his personal attention.

A knock sounded on his open door and he glanced up to see Jessica standing in the doorway. Instantly, he noticed the sexy spiked heels she wore.

"Come in."

She closed the door behind her and he watched the delightful sway of her hips as she walked toward the desk. Those shoes were new since this morning and, if he had to guess, he'd bet she wore a few other new things, too.

"I see you went shopping."

She glanced down at her feet. "Yes." She gazed at him uncertainly. "Are they okay? I mean, you don't think they're too . . . uh—"

"Sexy for the office?"

Someone must have teased her about them already, because there was nothing wrong with the shoes. They were extremely sexy—any high heels were because of the way they accentuated a woman's ass—but Gina in Human Resources wore more flamboyant shoes than that.

But he knew Jessica had bought those shoes to entice him and he wasn't going to let her off the hook too easily.

He stood up and walked around his desk. "Come over here. Let me have a closer look."

She walked toward him, then stopped. The shoes gave her extra height, so the crown of her head now reached his eye level.

"Turn around so I can see the heels."

She turned around. The heels were slim and tall. Definitely very sexy. But where his gaze lingered was on her backside. Pushed up and out by her changed posture, it looked even firmer and rounder than usual. His hand itched to stroke her alluring ass.

He leaned closer and murmured near her ear, "Are you trying to entice me?"

"No, sir."

But the smile in her voice told him the truth.

"Did you buy anything else while you were out at lunch?"

"Yes, sir."

He couldn't drag his gaze from her body. The barely perceptible bump of panty lines was gone. His groin tightened as he realized the fabric of her skirt brushed against her naked ass. And rather than pantyhose, the stockings covering her legs would end a few inches below her panties, leaving a strip of bare thigh.

His hand fell to her hip, then glided along her rear. His cock swelled.

"What did you buy?" When she started a stuttered response, he said, "Never mind."

He cupped her ass with his hand and squeezed, then reached down and lifted her skirt. As he slid his hand up the back of her leg, his fingertip brushed against a garter, then he felt bare skin. He could hear her draw in a breath. Then he stroked the curve of her delightful, naked flesh.

"Very nice. Let me see your new purchases."

He forced himself to step back, then watched avidly as she unzipped her skirt, then eased the waistband over her hips and let it drop to the floor.

Her white blouse covered her to the tops of her thighs, but the band of naked flesh above her stockings was visible, and the red lace garters matched her shoes. Before he had a chance to command it, she unbuttoned her blouse and opened it.

"The bra is new, too," she explained as she dropped the white silk garment to the floor.

He stared at her breasts, hiked high in the sexy lace bra, her white mounds spilling over the top of the cups. Then his gaze dropped to her panties, framed by the garter belt and stockings. It was a tiny strip of cloth that barely covered her pussy.

Then she turned around, revealing her completely bare ass, and leaned over to pick up her blouse and skirt. As she was leaning over, her ass swaying in the air, he could barely stop himself from lurching forward and driving his hard, aching cock into her.

Then she stood up and placed her clothing on the guest chair.

"Get over here," he growled as he unzipped his pants.

He pulled her to him and kissed her, hard. His tongue surged into her as his hand slid down her silky, flat stomach, then found her panties. He thrust into her mouth again as he tugged aside the crotch. His cockhead felt the warmth of her flesh as he pushed it forward, then her moist heat surrounded him. She was completely ready for him.

"Oh, God, you feel so good around me."

Then, with his hand flat on her back, he tugged her forward, driving deep inside her.

The sound of her moan sent his erection twitching. She wrapped her fingers over his shoulders, steadying herself.

He drew back and thrust again. It was like heaven inside her tight, hot passage. He wanted to be deeper, so he lifted her in his arms and moved toward the wall. When she wrapped her legs around his hips and squeezed him inside her, he groaned. He pushed her against the wall and drove deeper still.

"Oh, yes."

He nuzzled her long, elegant neck, then leaned down and kissed the swell of her breast. Still deep inside her, he pushed up one cup, revealing her swollen nipple. He licked it, then took it in his mouth. She moaned again as he teased the hard bud with his tongue, then he suckled.

His body demanded release, so he started to move inside her again, pulling back then driving forward. He released her nipple, needing to give full attention to the demands of his body. And hers. She liked his mouth on her breast, but her whimper told him she needed more. He thrust his cock into her again and again, driving her hard against the wall each time.

Her breathing accelerated and she moaned as she clung to him.

"Are you close?" he murmured into her ear. He knew the answer, but loved to hear her admit it.

"Yes, sir."

Fuck. He drove deeper, grinding her to the wall.

"You know what I want to hear."

He drew out, then glided forward slowly, torturing her.

"Yes, Mr. Ranier." Her breathless voice sent his blood boiling.

He drove into her and kept on thrusting. Faster and faster.

She sucked in a breath, then whimpered.

"Oh, sir . . ." She gasped, then stiffened. "I'm . . . going . . . to . . ." Her words came out between thrusts.

She threw her head back. "Come." Then she wailed loudly.

His cock throbbed, then he felt liquid fire stream through him as he erupted into her hot, sweet body.

They both gulped in air as he held her pinned to the wall.

Finally, he drew back slowly, ensuring she was steady on her feet. He grinned at her, stroking back a few strands of hair that had escaped her barrette.

"Maybe next time, we should figure out how to work in a little foreplay."

On Friday night, Jessica was sitting on the couch reading a magazine when Melanie breezed into the room in the brand new dress she'd bought at lunch. They'd spotted it in the window of a shop they'd passed on the way to the deli where they'd gone to eat. Melanie had been taken by it, so Jessica had suggested they stop in the store on the way back to the office. As soon as she'd tried it on, Melanie had fallen in love with it.

"That dress really does look great on you," Jessica said. With its bright splashes of color and glittery trim, it was quite different from the conservative attire she wore to the office.

Melanie beamed. "Thank you. I feel like a million bucks in it." She pulled on her coat and then picked up her purse. "Are you sure you don't want to join us?"

"No, I don't really feel like partying tonight."

"You know Jerrod's going to be there. He really likes you, you know. I thought you were at least a little interested."

Jerrod was tall, attractive, and interesting to talk to, but he was no Dane.

"He's a great guy, but I really don't want to get into a romantic relationship right now."

"I know, it's too soon, but that doesn't mean you can't go out with the guy. Even sleep with him. *Especially* sleep with him. I think it would do you a world of good."

"Don't worry, I'm doing fine."

"You do seem pretty relaxed for someone who hasn't gotten laid in months." Melanie pursed her lips. "In fact, maybe too relaxed." She sat down on the couch beside her. "If I didn't know better, I'd think you were seeing someone."

"I told you, I don't want—"

"A romantic entanglement. I know. But that doesn't mean you aren't getting some." Her eyes narrowed. "Is it someone at work?"

"Melanie . . ." But she could feel her cheeks tinge red.

"Because that's a really bad idea. A really, really bad idea. Tell me you're not."

Jessica tried to utter the lie, but she couldn't get her mouth to cooperate. So she said nothing.

"Oh, honey, no. Who is it?" Then she waved her hands. "No, I don't want to know. Is that what you're doing when you're running those errands at lunch?"

There were three times Jessica hadn't gone to lunch with Melanie. Once because Melanie was busy, once because Jessica had some banking to do, and once was when she'd gone out shopping for the garter belt and shoes. Her cheeks burned hotter.

"Okay, it's none of my business. I just think it's a really bad idea to get involved with someone at work. And if Mr. Ranier found out, he would probably be livid. You remember I mentioned that I had a little crush on Mr. Ranier's brother, Rafe?"

Jessica nodded.

"Well, it was more than a crush. I kind of fell in love with him." Melanie waved her finger at Jessica. "And that stays between us."

Jessica nodded. "Of course."

"But I never acted on it, even though every day I wanted to throw myself at him and tear off his clothes."

"Melanie . . ."

"I know, I said it was none of my business." She frowned. "And I'm not judging. Getting laid is a great idea. I just don't want to see you get into a tough situation. If the guy is more senior than you, it could lead to all kinds of trouble if it ends badly. And let's face it, it's going to end. Especially if there's only sex between you."

"Thanks, Melanie. I'll keep that in mind."

"Okay. That's all I'll say about it then."

"Mel, I'm sorry about you and your boss."

Melanie nodded. "And it kills me that he's gone. Before he left, even though I knew we could never be together, at least I could see him every day."

Melanie's wide green eyes turned to Jessica and the depth of pain and vulnerability there astonished her.

"I miss him so much."

Jessica nodded, then pursed her lips. "I tell you what. If you can wait a few minutes, I'll run and change."

A smile crept across Melanie's face, driving away the sorrow. "That's great. I'll wait right here."

———

That night, Melanie's words marched through Jessica's brain.

And let's face it, it's going to end. Especially if there's only sex be-tween you.

She was right, of course. It would end. Then what would happen to her job?

But everything she knew about Dane told her he would do right by her. He would ensure she had a new job somewhere in the company, she was sure of it. And people changed jobs all the time. She wouldn't expect to stay in this position forever, even though she loved working for Dane. And she would miss working with Melanie if that happened.

But all that was a long way off. She'd just started this relation-ship with Dane and was determined to enjoy it while it lasted.

And enjoy it she was. Every afternoon they had sex in his office and it was always fast and furious. They had yet to work out having anything more than minimal foreplay, because they were always so intensely turned on by the time they started. He was so freaking sexy. And there was something about being in an office. She was sure they would explore other scenarios. But right now the relationship was still new and intense. Not that it would ever stop being intense with Dane. But she remembered the long, thorough lovemaking they'd enjoyed that first time.

Her body ached at the memory.

No matter what happened in the future, this time with Dane was definitely worth it.

Jessica sat down at the table in the little café. She and Dane had been at a meeting on the outskirts of the city until late morn-ing and had another across town at one o'clock, so he had sug-gested they grab lunch out.

This was the first time he'd taken her to lunch and, in fact, the first time they'd been together in a social setting since the dinner event she'd accompanied him to. It felt a little awkward as she watched him over her water glass while he checked his phone messages. Should she review his e-mails while they waited for lunch?

She opened her purse, which sat on the chair beside her, and pulled out her tablet.

"You aren't thinking of working, are you?" he asked as he slipped his phone into his jacket pocket.

"Well, I wasn't sure."

"Relax. It's lunchtime."

The waitress arrived with a basket of freshly baked bread and took their order. Dane recommended she try the soup as an appetizer. The waitress returned a few moments later with two steaming bowls.

Jessica tasted it and glanced at Dane. "This is the best clam chowder I've ever had."

He smiled. "I wouldn't steer you wrong."

She tipped her head and smiled. It was true. Everything he'd advised her to do had worked out amazingly well. Her finger brushed against the stone in her jacket pocket.

"You know, I really appreciate the advice you gave me when we first met. It really helped build my confidence when I was at the career fair."

She drew the light blue stone from her pocket and laid it on the table. "I still carry the stone you gave me."

He casually picked it up and gazed at it.

"And I've never really thanked you for hiring me," she continued.

"You're doing an excellent job." He stroked the stone with his thumb. "You know, I originally got this for my brother, Rafe.

Our mother taught us about crystals and Tarot cards and other crazy stuff like that when we were kids. Our dad thought it was all hogwash, and it didn't much interest me, but Rafe was fascinated by all her quirky ideas. Once Dad died and the problems got worse between Rafe and me, I bought this for Rafe, to show him I respected his beliefs, even if they were different from mine."

"That's really nice."

He placed the stone back on the table in front of her. "But he left before I had a chance to give it to him."

She would have thought he'd want to keep it as a reminder of his brother, but maybe it had become too painful.

Trying to lighten the mood, she smiled. "So you're telling me you never believed in any of the things you told me about the stone?"

"On the contrary. It is soothing when you rub it. And that calms your nerves. Right?"

"True."

"That doesn't mean I believe the stone has any healing powers."

She slipped the stone back into her pocket as the waitress took away their soup bowls and placed a plate of pasta in front of her and a steak in front of Dane.

"You said after your dad died, the problems got worse between you and your brother." She knew she was treading on sensitive ground, but she really wanted to know more about this man. "What kind of problems were you having?"

"Typical things between brothers."

She poked her fork into the long strands of fettuccine on her plate. "I'm sorry, I didn't mean to pry."

He gazed at her solemnly for a long moment, then sighed. "You know what? It felt good to talk about it the other day, so why not now? Let me tell you what happened that destroyed our relationship."

He leaned back in his chair. "About two weeks before his senior prom, Rafe skipped class to spend some time with a girl he wanted to ask to the prom. He was caught and our father, who valued hard work and a sense of responsibility above all else, berated my brother and then grounded him for a month."

"Including the prom?" she asked.

He nodded. "I was home from college at the time. I tried to change Dad's mind, but he wouldn't budge. There was already a huge rift between Rafe and Dad and if Rafe missed such a memorable event in a person's life, he would resent Dad forever. So, I decided to help. I knew if I suggested to Rafe that he slip away to the prom, he'd reject the plan. I tended to fall in line with what Dad wanted, so Rafe didn't trust my opinions. He accused me of trying to control things and would often do the opposite of what I'd suggest."

"So what did you do?"

"I had Rafe's best friend tell him to sneak out the back on prom night and meet him down the street. I had one of the servants ready to cover for Rafe if our dad went looking for him, and I arranged to pick up Rafe's date and deliver her to the prom."

"Wouldn't it have been easier to just have Rafe and his friend pick her up?"

"Easier, and smarter as it turns out. But there was a part of me that wanted him to know that he could depend on me."

She smiled. "I can understand that." She could just imagine Dane beaming with pride as he presented the young woman to Rafe. But the purpose of this story was how the rift between the brothers had started. "So what went wrong?"

"Rafe's date—I don't even remember her name—is what

went wrong. Years earlier, in high school, I had dated her sister and it turns out she'd had a crush on me. Wishful thinking convinced her that I returned her feelings and this had all been a ploy for me to hook up with her."

"So she kissed you, and that's when your brother turned up."

"It wasn't just a kiss, it was a full body assault. When Rafe arrived, her arms were around me and her tongue was halfway down my throat."

Jessica couldn't help but laugh at his description.

"Of course, Rafe didn't believe it was innocent on my part, and his date insisted I had made the first move."

"Leaving your brother believing you were stealing his girlfriend. That is so unfair."

"True, but clearly our problems were deeper than that one incident; otherwise Rafe would have believed me."

He sipped his water as he glanced at her almost empty plate. "I've been sharing a lot of my past with you. Now it's your turn."

"Okay." She finished her last bite of food and pushed her plate aside. Dane had been doing most of the talking, so his plate was still almost full. "Since you shared a painful memory with me, I'll share one with you. I already told you about my ex-boyfriend Storm."

"The musician."

She nodded. "We had been living together for almost five months." Memories of his big, naked, tattooed body stretched out beside her in bed sent goose bumps along her flesh. It had been exciting to be with someone like him. And it was devastating when he'd left.

"Then one day I came home from work and he was sitting on the couch waiting for me. Said he was going on tour in

California with the band. When I asked him when he'd be back, he shrugged and said he wasn't sure he'd be back, that he was a drifter and had been in one place too long. Of course, I was devastated. All he said then was, 'Hey, you knew this was just a casual thing. But maybe if I do come back and you're still free, we can hook up again.'"

The awful pain stirred in her gut again. "Then he picked up his pack and walked out."

Dane shook his head. "The guy sounds like a total jerk to me."

She stared out the window at the street outside. "Yeah, I guess." She gazed at him. "But the thing is, Storm had never seemed like a jerk before. He had always been caring and attentive. And I was so sure he loved me just as much as I loved him. That's why the whole thing blindsided me."

Dane reached out and covered her hand with his, and even with thoughts of Storm filling her head, awareness of Dane crept through her body.

"I'm sorry that happened to you. You deserve better."

She pushed aside the painful memories and smiled. "Well, I have better now. I have a great job." Her smile turned to a grin. "And this interesting relationship with you."

"Since you've brought up our interesting relationship . . . Remember when I told you I would occasionally give you new rules or assign you special tasks?"

At his words, she became intensely aware of the satin lining of her skirt against her naked backside, and one of the garters holding up her stockings pressing into her lower thigh. "Yes, I remember."

"Well, I have a task in mind."

————

Jessica couldn't believe she was doing this. She'd waited until Melanie was away from her desk to sneak into Dane's office and now she stood beside his desk, waiting.

He had an appointment in a few minutes with Mr. Lane from Human Resources about a new benefits plan for the employees. The door to the office was open and she heard the elevator bell ring, then the doors open. Melanie greeted Mr. Lane and told him Dane would be along shortly.

At lunch yesterday, Dane had challenged her with the task of doing something to surprise and excite him. She glanced at her watch. He should be returning from his two o'clock any second now. She heard the elevator again and Melanie greeted Dane.

That was her cue. She ducked under Dane's desk. She heard Dane talking to Mr. Lane and his voice grew louder as they approached. Her heart thundered as they came into his office.

She didn't want to startle Dane when he pulled out his chair, because then her presence would be given away to Mr. Lane, so she sent him the text she had ready to go on her phone. He received texts only from Melanie and herself, and they sent only time-sensitive messages, so she knew he'd check it right away. She heard his phone beep, signaling that it had received her text.

"Take a seat, Jerry."

A second later, he stepped behind the desk and pulled out his chair. He dropped a piece of paper and leaned down to pick it up, then peered at her, his eyebrows arched questioningly. She grinned at him.

Her text had told him she was under the desk and it was part of his surprise. If he chose to end it now, he might whisk Mr. Lane away briefly, then order her away. Possibly exile her to his private bathroom to wait out the meeting if she couldn't sneak past Melanie.

Dane sat down in his chair, facing Jerry Lane, well aware of Jessica crouched on the floor in front of him, hidden by his desk. Jerry had no idea what was going on.

Her soft hand stroked over his crotch while Dane opened the file folder she had left on his desk in preparation for this meeting. His cock swelled as she stroked over the fabric of his pants. He glanced at the report in front of him which summarized Jerry's recommendations. It was hard to concentrate with her soft little hand gliding over his hard flesh, her fingers wrapped around him as best she could while he was still contained in his clothing.

As Jerry began to discuss the first point in his report, Dane felt her fingers slide down the length of him, releasing his zipper. As Jerry talked about the benefits of extending the number of sick days allowed to employees, Dane stiffened at the feel of Jessica's fingers slipping into his pants and wrapping around his erection.

He drew in a slow breath as she drew his shaft from its confines. He asked Jerry a question about how many sick days he recommended for each employee per year and if it should differ based on seniority, even though he vaguely remembered seeing the answer in the report.

It was hard to concentrate with the soft fingers gripping him firmly and stroking his length.

Jerry gave him an answer and he nodded, but had no idea what the man had said. Then he felt dampness on the end of his cock as her warm tongue licked his tip.

Oh, fuck, that felt good. Then her lips wrapped around him and she took him in her mouth.

"Is something wrong?" Jerry asked.

Dane's gaze jerked to Jerry, who stared at him with concerned gray eyes. Damn, had he made a sound, or did he just look dazed?

"Sorry, just a little distracted." Fuck, actually majorly distracted as Jessica swirled her tongue over his cockhead. He drummed his fingers on the desk, pretending to examine the report. Jessica drew back from his hard flesh, which gave him a moment to breathe.

"Please continue," he said to Jerry, but Jessica seemed to take his words as a command and wrapped her lips around him again.

Jerry moved on to the next point and Dane steeled his will to stay calm as Jessica slid forward on his cock, taking him deep into her warmth. Then she drew back and glided deep again. He clenched his stomach as he resisted the urge to moan at the exquisite pleasure. Then she sucked, and a noise escaped his throat. He glanced up at Jerry.

What must the man think with Dane sitting here, his hands clenched into fists, his face probably flushed?

He coughed. "Sorry, I think something I ate at lunch must not agree with me."

As her warm mouth moved up and down his cock, her tongue stroked his shaft. He shifted in his chair.

"Maybe I should take one of those sick days we're talking about."

"Would you like to reschedule?" Jerry asked.

Dane's automatic reaction was to say no—he could control his response to her delightful touch—but her fingertips grazed his hairless balls as she sucked again and he found himself nodding.

"Good idea. Talk to Melanie on the way out to set up a time tomorrow."

Jessica caressed his balls, then wrapped her hand around his shaft and stroked as she continued to suck his bulbous tip.

Jerry nodded. "Anything I can get you?"

"What?" Dane's gaze jerked from his closed fist to see Jerry standing in front of his desk. "Oh, no. Thanks."

He gritted his teeth as the man walked the length of the office and then, finally, opened the door and exited. As soon as the door was closed, he slumped back in his chair. His eyes closed as she pumped him with her hand. His groin ached with the need to release, but not yet.

He grabbed her wrists as he rolled his chair back, and pulled her forward and into his arms. His cock dropped from her mouth into the cool air. He captured her lips and plunged his tongue into her mouth.

"What the hell were you doing distracting me like that?" He grinned at her. "I should punish you right now." He cupped her head and pulled her to him again so he could ravage her mouth.

As soon as he released her, she stood up and walked to the window behind his desk. She drew up her skirt and bent forward, then rested her hands on the window ledge, presenting her perfect, naked ass to him. His office was high enough that no one could see her from another building, but right now, he didn't really care if they could.

He stroked over her smooth, round flesh, then drew back and smacked. Her skin flushed a soft rose color. He smacked again, and at her small gasp, he wanted to keep on smacking, but his cock ached painfully.

"If I wasn't so fucking close, I'd continue this. You were a very bad girl."

"Yes, sir."

He stared at her delightful ass in front of him and he stroked his thumbs over it, then pulled her thong down and drew apart the flesh to reveal her folds which glistened in the light. "I've been very patient with you, but I can't tolerate this kind of thing. I need to teach you a lesson."

He pressed his hard cockhead to her slick opening, intending to glide into her slowly, but as soon as he started to press into her hot, moist flesh, he couldn't help himself. He grasped her hips and drove forward until he filled her to the hilt.

He twitched inside her and she groaned. He couldn't resist giving her delightful backside another hard whack. "Do you like this?"

"Yes, sir." The need in her voice sent his hormones soaring.

"We can't have that," he said, with an edge to his voice, and then he gave in to temptation and smacked her ass again.

His cell beeped in his pocket, but he was damned if he would check a text now. Whatever it was, Melanie would deal with it.

He drew back and thrust forward again. Her smooth passage, so hot and wet, hugged his cock in a tight embrace. Then she squeezed her intimate muscles around him and he groaned at the exquisite sensation.

He drew back and thrust forward. Filling her so deep. Then he thrust again. She moaned.

His office door opened. "I'm sorry, Mr. Ranier," Melanie said, "Mr. Lane was concerned so I thought I should . . ."

Jessica stiffened in front of him. Dane didn't glance behind him, but Melanie hesitated as she seemed to realize what was going on.

"Oh, my God, I'm sorry."

He heard the door close behind her.

He felt Jessica start to pull away, but he tightened his grip on her hips. "You stay right here." He thrust again, driving deep into her. He reached around and found her clit and teased it with his fingertips.

"Does that feel good?" he asked.

She groaned and pushed back against him. "Oh, yes, sir."

He was so close, but he wanted her to come first. He stroked her clit a couple more times, until she was gasping. He corkscrewed inside her, then began to thrust in steady strokes. She moaned as he filled her again and again. She squeezed him and he felt her body tense. Then she gasped and began to wail.

Watching her reflection in the glass, he could see the euphoric expression on her face as she catapulted to heaven. He pumped deep, the spasms of her passage massaging him, until his groin tightened and he shot inside her with steady spurts of liquid pleasure. Ecstasy consumed him until he collapsed against her folded body, holding her tight against him.

Finally, still sucking in air, he drew her to her feet and continued to hold her.

"That was incredible, but I see I'll have to be careful what *tasks* I assign you in the future."

He grinned as she turned to face him, but she gazed up at him uncertainly, as if she was worried she'd done something wrong. He kissed her, loving her soft, sweet mouth against his.

"Don't worry. That was perfect." He nuzzled her neck. "In fact, I love your creativity."

"What about . . ." Her cheeks turned deep red. "Melanie came in."

"I know. Don't worry. She couldn't see you. My body blocked her view. She probably couldn't even tell there was a woman here."

"You really think she thought you were alone?"

He couldn't help grinning at the thought that Melanie

might have thought he'd been masturbating in front of the window. But Jessica had been making sounds, and Melanie would definitely have heard them.

"No. But there's no way she could tell it was you."

"What are you going to say to her about it?"

He smiled. "Absolutely nothing. And she won't ask."

Jessica sat on the couch in Dane's office while he walked outside to send Melanie on an errand. How he could face her only moments after her catching him having sex in his office, she didn't know. But then Dane was used to being in control and no one questioning him. Especially his staff.

A moment later, he reappeared.

"The coast is clear," he said.

She stood up and smoothed her skirt, then walked to the door. She peered out to ensure no one, let alone Melanie, was outside the office, then she strode quickly to her office. Even before she sat down, her cell phone beeped. She pulled it from her pocket as she sat down and checked the display.

I could really use a coffee. Want to join me in the lobby?—Melanie

Jessica drew in a deep breath, then typed in her response.

Sure. Be right down.—Jessica

She collected her purse from the drawer and walked to the elevator. Melanie was waiting for her in the lobby. It was a warm day today, so they didn't need their coats.

She forced her mouth into a smile and waved as she walked toward her friend. "You decided to enjoy the sunshine?"

Melanie just nodded. "I can use the fresh air. Starbucks okay?"

"Sure." She followed Melanie out the glass door and they strolled two blocks down to the Starbucks they often went to in the afternoon.

Once they bought their coffees, they sat down at a table by the window. Jessica's stomach clenched. She wasn't sure what to say or, worse, what Melanie was going to say. Did Melanie know she was the woman in Dane's office? Would she confront her about it?

Melanie stared at her coffee cup, and the anxiety on her face made Jessica realize that Melanie was just as uncomfortable about this as she was.

"Um . . . is something up?" Jessica asked, finally breaking the silence.

Melanie glanced at her, then back to her cup, nodding.

She waited, but the silence continued.

"Do you want to tell me about it?"

"Yes, but . . . no."

"No?" Jessica's nerves frayed. Oh, damn, she must know.

"I mean . . . I shouldn't."

Shouldn't?

"Why not?"

"It's . . . about Mr. Ranier."

A wave of relief washed through her.

"And someone else," Melanie continued.

She tensed. "Who?"

Melanie shook her head. "I don't know. All I know is, I walked into his office . . ." She clenched her hands into fists. "Oh, damn, I really shouldn't tell you. He trusts me. But . . . you are his assistant. You should know what you might be walking into."

"Please, just tell me. I promise it won't go any further."

Melanie nodded. "Okay." She drew in a deep breath. "He had that meeting with Mr. Lane from Human Resources." She glanced at Jessica as if for reassurance that she should continue.

"Yes."

"Well, Mr. Lane left Mr. Rainer's office after about fifteen minutes and said he needed to reschedule the meeting. He said that Mr. Ranier was feeling sick. After he left, I texted Mr. Ranier to see if he needed anything, but he didn't answer." She leaned forward. "He always responds, so I got worried. What if he was really sick? What if he'd passed out or something? I knew he was in there alone—at least, I *thought* he was—so I broke his most basic rule and walked into his office." She stared at Jessica with haunted eyes. "I was just concerned about him."

"And he wasn't in there alone after all?"

"That's right. He was with a woman and . . ." She leaned in closer and lowered her voice. "They were doing it."

Jessica bit her lower lip. "Oh, my God. Did you see who it was?"

Melanie shook her head. "No, all I saw was a little of her backside, but I'm sure it's someone who works at the company."

Relief surged through her.

"You poor thing. That must have been really embarrassing."

"It was. That's why I needed to get out of the office. I'm not even sure how to face him." Her hands clenched into fists, her pink-polished nails digging into her flesh. "Oh, damn, I wish I hadn't walked into his office. He's going to be so angry about that." She stared at Jessica. "Do you think he'll fire me?"

"Oh, no, Melanie. I'm sure he won't. Don't you think he's just as embarrassed as you are?"

She stared at Jessica in amazement. "Really? You've met the man. Do you actually think he's even capable of embarrassment?" She shook her head, toying with the plastic lid on her coffee. "No, moments later he walked out calm as you please and sent me on an errand, no doubt so he could sneak the slut out of his office."

Jessica's stomach clenched. "Is it really fair to call her a slut?"

Melanie's head jerked up and her eyes narrowed. Then they widened.

"Oh, my God, it wasn't you, was it?"

Jessica's gaze jerked away from her friend's. Oh, damn. Why couldn't she have kept her mouth shut?

"Was it?" her friend prodded.

No matter how much she wished otherwise, she couldn't lie to Melanie. But she couldn't say the words either. She just gazed at her friend with a guilty expression.

"Oh, Jessica. That's a really bad idea."

"I know. You already told me what you think of office liaisons." She couldn't bring herself to say office *romances* because that's not what she and Dane had.

"But Mr. Ranier? Oh, Jessica."

"Melanie, look, it's not the same as with you and Rafe. I'm not in love with him. And I made it clear that I don't want anything more than a physical relationship."

Melanie shook her head. "I can't believe he would go along with this. Having sex with someone who works for him. It's *such* a bad idea."

She wrapped her hands around her coffee cup. "Well, I didn't work with him the first time we did it."

Melanie jerked her head to stare at Jessica with wide eyes. "What?"

"You remember he gave me a ride when I came here for the job fair?"

"Don't tell me you had sex in his limo?"

"No, we wound up having dinner together that night and we hit it off. That led to us going to my room together." She shrugged. "I'd never had a one-night stand before, but I was really attracted to him."

"So it must have been a total shock when you found out he was your boss."

She remembered those heart-pounding, stomach-fluttering moments when she'd first walked into her new boss' office only to see Dane sitting there.

"The biggest shock of my life. I almost walked away."

"Your instincts were right on, but,"—Melanie bit her lip— "I'm glad you didn't turn down the job." She shook her head. "So this has been going on since you got here?"

"No." She really didn't want Melanie to think that. "When I told him I couldn't work for him . . . because, you see, I was worried he'd hired me because of the sex, you know?"—and she didn't want Melanie to think that was true—"he said he really wanted me to work here and that we could keep a business-only relationship if that's what I wanted."

The look of disappointment in Melanie's eyes faded a little. "I hope you're not worried that you don't deserve this job, or that you were hired for the wrong reason. You are exceptionally qualified for this position, and you're doing an excellent job."

"Thank you. That means a lot to me."

"Obviously the agreement between you fell apart." A grin spread across Melanie's face. "So he was that good that you barely lasted a couple of weeks?"

"Well, he does excel at everything he does."

Melanie laughed. It started out as a chuckle, but quickly grew into full-blown laughter. "I can't believe that was *your* butt I saw in there. And with Mr. Ranier! *So* awkward!"

Jessica couldn't help laughing herself. "Well if anyone was

going to walk in on us and see my butt, I'm glad it was you. And you don't have to worry about Dane . . . I mean Mr. Ranier . . . talking to you about coming into his office. When I asked him about it, he said he wasn't going to say anything."

Melanie smiled. "Well, I guess there are some advantages to being a friend of the boss' girlfriend."

"No, not his girlfriend. I don't want a romantic relationship. It's just a physical thing between us." It made her uncomfortable admitting that out loud to someone.

"Well, you're a grown woman and you can make your own decisions. I just hope you know what you're doing."

Jessica smiled sadly at her new friend. "I hope so too."

Jessica glanced at Melanie's empty desk as she walked toward Dane's open door. She must be off on an errand. She slipped into Dane's office, carrying a stack of folders. Dane was at a late lunch, and she wanted to ensure that he had all the information he needed to review for this afternoon.

She set the folders on his desk, and then turned to the wooden filing cabinet behind it. She was sure she'd seen some useful background material on the electric car battery design in there last week. She crouched down to open the bottom drawer and started scanning through it.

"Hello, excuse me, miss."

Her heart stopped cold at the familiar male voice. She glanced around and almost toppled over at the sight of Storm standing in the doorway, big as life. But instead of wearing faded jeans and a T-shirt, he wore a tailored suit, and his normally spiky hairstyle was combed down smooth.

Her heart thundered in her chest as she stood up. "What are you doing here?"

Oh, God, how had he found out where she worked?

"Jess?" He strode across the large office and before she could react, he'd pulled her into his arms. "I can't believe you're here."

She knew she should pull away, but the feel of his strong, familiar arms around her numbed her wits. It felt so good.

His lips found hers and she melted against him.

She couldn't believe she was in Storm's arms again. She'd missed him so much.

Longed for him.

Been so lonely without him.

But, damn it, the bastard had walked out on her without a word of remorse.

She pressed her hands against his chest and pushed until he eased away. He gazed down at her, his sky blue eyes glittering with happiness.

"Why are you here?" she demanded.

"I was hoping to find you. I can't believe my luck finding you so quickly. What are you doing here?"

"I work for Ranier Industries. I'm Mr. Ranier's personal assistant."

He smiled. "You're kidding." Then his smile faded. "But you don't know . . ."

His words trailed off.

"Know what?"

He shook his head. "It doesn't matter right now. All that matters is that I found you." He captured her lips again and her heart stammered as a turmoil of emotions swirled through her.

She wanted to be happy he was here, to believe that they could rebuild what they'd lost . . . but she couldn't. He'd caused her too much pain. How could she trust him again?

And what about her relationship with Dane? She didn't

want it to end for something that might fizzle out the first time Storm decided he didn't want to be tied down again.

She pushed on his chest. He released her lips, but his arms stayed firm around her.

"Let me go," she said with gritted teeth.

"I suggest you do what the lady requests."

Her gaze shot to the doorway where Dane stood, his arms crossed. She blanched. Just what she needed. Her boss—and lover—catching her in his office in a clinch with her old flame.

Storm's arms loosened around her and he turned around.

"Hello, Dane."

Dane's gaze jerked to Storm's face and his eyes widened in surprise.

"Rafe?"

A numbness crawled through Jessica as she heard the name Dane called Storm, but she couldn't quite conceive of what it meant. She glanced from one man to the other.

The embarrassment and concern at having been caught in Storm's arms was replaced by shock as a shiver raced down her spine.

It couldn't be.

She'd been mistaken when she'd thought Dane was Storm the first time she'd seen him. But now seeing them side-by-side . . . She sucked in a breath. Their features were indeed similar, especially with Storm dressed as he was in an expensive suit with his dark hair combed back.

Astonishment coiled through her. "Oh, my God," she murmured.

With eyes wide in astonishment, she turned to Storm.

"You're Rafe Ranier!"

True Lies

As Jessica fled the office, the elevator doors opened. She raced toward them, her heart pounding, trying not to look at Melanie as Melanie exited the elevator.

"Jessica?"

But she just continued into the small space and jabbed the Close button, hoping to escape Melanie and her inevitable questions, but Melanie turned and slipped back onto the elevator before the doors closed.

Jessica swiped an errant tear from her eye, hoping her friend didn't notice. Was it a tear of anger? Pain? Or just a result of her heightened emotions after getting such a shock?

"Jessica, what's wrong?"

Her tight throat and clenched jaw ached. She shook her head, wishing Melanie hadn't decided to follow her.

"Did something happen between you and Mr. Ranier?"

Mr. Ranier. Mr. *Rafe* Ranier.

"You could say that."

"Oh, Jessica, I was worried this would happen."

Jessica's head jerked toward Melanie. "You did?" But how could Melanie have known about . . .

"Having an affair with your boss is bound to cause complications," Melanie continued.

Jessica met her friend's concerned gaze. Of course she'd naturally think it had something to do with Dane and their sexual relationship.

"This isn't about Dane and me."

Confusion washed across Melanie's face. "But you said—"

She shook her head. "This is about Storm."

"The guy who broke your heart?"

Jessica nodded. "He's here."

"In Philadelphia?"

"Here in the *building*. He walked in while I was in Dane's office organizing the folders he'll need this afternoon."

Melanie frowned. "But why would your ex-boyfriend walk into Mr. Ranier's office? How did he know you were here?"

"That's the thing. He didn't. You see—"

She stopped cold. As she'd been gazing into Melanie's wide green eyes, she suddenly remembered that Melanie had told Jessica that she was in love with her old boss, and . . .

Oh, God, how could she tell Melanie that Rafe, the man she loved, was in love with Jessica?

Luckily, she was saved by the bell as the elevator came to a stop and the doors opened.

"Melanie, I'm going home. I'll take a sick day, or a day without pay. I don't care. I just have to get out of here."

At that, she fled the elevator, leaving a confused Melanie behind.

———

Dane crossed his arms and stared at his brother. He was thrilled to have him back and had all kinds of questions storming through his brain, but that was tempered by one overriding issue.

"How do I justify not slugging you for manhandling my assistant?"

"I wasn't manhandling her."

"I come in here and find her in your arms and then she runs out of here, clearly upset."

It wasn't like Rafe to treat a woman with disrespect, and definitely not to hit on one of their employees, let alone aggressively try to seduce her. But his brother had been gone for almost a year. Dane had no idea how he might have changed.

"Jess and I know each other. Over the past year, I spent eight months in a town called Bakersfield. I met her there and we dated."

Understanding smacked Dane in the face.

"You were the guitarist with the leather jacket and the motorcycle?"

Rafe's eyebrows arched. "She told you about me?"

Dane tipped his head. "Yeah, well, you did break her heart."

Damn it. His brother was in love with the woman Dane was having a rampant affair with. And she used to be in love with him. And maybe she still was.

But Rafe had walked away, hurting her deeply.

Just like he'd done to Dane.

Rafe dropped into a chair. "I know. It was the stupidest thing I've ever done."

"That's saying a lot, given you walked away from this kind of success to be a rock musician."

"Damn it, Dane. You sound just like Dad."

Dane sighed. "Right. Sorry."

What the hell was he doing? Rafe had come back, giving Dane the chance to mend their relationship and move forward. He had to keep a tight rein on his words.

"Mr. Ranier?" Melanie walked into the office and Dane realized Jessica had left the door open when she'd fled. "I wanted to tell you—"

Her eyes widened as her gaze shot to Rafe.

"Mr. Ranier, you're back."

Rafe smiled, revealing the straight, white teeth their father had paid thousands in orthodontia to ensure. "Melanie, you used to call me Rafe."

Although the employees all called Dane Mr. Ranier, since he liked to keep a level of discipline in the office, Rafe had the staff that worked closest with him call him by his first name. It did make things simpler when they were in a meeting with Melanie, so she wasn't calling them both Mr. Ranier.

She nodded. "Rafe," she said quietly.

The softness in her eyes when she gazed at Rafe hit Dane in the gut. How could the man look at her and not realize she had feelings for him? Sometimes his brother could be an idiot.

She turned back to Dane. "Mr. Ranier, I just wanted to let you know that Jessica has left for the day, since she's not feeling well. Your two o'clock appointment will be here in a few minutes. Would you like me to have someone fill in for me at my desk so I can take over Jessica's duties during the meeting?"

Dane glanced at his watch.

"Take your meeting, Dane," Rafe said. "You and I can catch up later. I just stopped by to let you know I'm back, and now I'm headed to my apartment. I trust you didn't sell it on me?"

"It's still the way you left it. You can thank Melanie for that. I had her arrange to keep it cleaned and maintained while you were gone. She even has someone come in and water your plants."

While Dane lived in a residence at the Ritz-Carlton, where he didn't have to worry about any kind of upkeep or meal preparation, Rafe had bought a penthouse apartment.

Rafe turned to Melanie and smiled. "Thanks."

The poor woman nearly melted into a puddle at his charming smile. His idiot brother really was blind not to see the effect he had on her.

Dane walked to his desk and skimmed through the small pile of folders that Jessica must have brought in.

"It looks like I have everything I need, Melanie. I can get by without Jessica."

Melanie nodded. "Yes, Mr. Ranier."

She turned and left the office.

"Are you free this evening?" Rafe asked.

"I'll make sure I am," said Dane. "I've got a dinner meeting, but meet me at my place at eight. We'll have drinks."

Rafe smiled. "I'm looking forward to it."

Before Rafe turned to walk away, Dane saw the truth of those words in Rafe's eyes.

Maybe there was hope for them yet.

The elevator doors opened onto the executive floor and Melanie stepped off.

"Hey, there you are."

She glanced around to see Rafe sitting in one of the chairs by the large windows. He stood up and walked toward her. Her heart fluttered as he drew closer.

"I thought we might grab a coffee before I head back to my apartment."

"Um, I'd really like to, but I shouldn't leave my desk again."

"Don't worry. I arranged for someone to come and answer the phone."

She smiled. "Oh, thank you." Damn, she sounded like a dope. She drew in a deep breath, willing herself to stay calm and collected.

A few minutes later, they settled at a nice table by the window of a café just a few doors down the street from the office. They ordered two coffees and the waitress brought them in big, colorful mugs.

She couldn't believe she was sitting across the small table from Rafe. Her heart fluttered as she took in the sexy sight of him in his black linen suit paired with a black T-shirt, probably made of Egyptian cotton. She longed to reach out and stroke the soft, fine woven fabric, imagining the feel of his hard, muscled chest beneath her fingertips.

It wasn't his usual elegant business style, but he'd only sported that look to stay in line with his father's wishes. He was really pushing the limits coming to the office in such relatively casual attire, but he hadn't quite crossed a line Dane would take exception to.

His dark hair was longer than he used to wear it, but combed back, and she noticed small diamond studs in his ears. This whole new bad boy look had her heart palpitating.

"It hasn't been the same around here without you," she said.

His sky blue eyes locked on her, and he smiled, stealing her breath away. "I missed you, too, Melanie. Especially those wild nails of yours." He glanced at her fingers, wrapped around her coffee cup. "But I see you've toned them down. Probably Dane's doing. Did he read you the riot act and tell you to go more conservative in the office?"

She glanced at her fingernails. She was wearing a duo-chrome polish that flashed from peach to gold in the sunlight streaming in the window, but looked mostly peach in the office lighting. It was as far as she would push it at work, but when Rafe had been here, he'd been fine with her typically daring choices, like a rich teal holographic, sparkly purple, or black with flashy green and royal blue flakes.

When she was younger, her parents had stifled her creative urge, insisting she take more practical courses in college than art. She knew it was because they were concerned about her finding a stable, secure job, but that didn't change the fact she had to leave her passion for color and design behind. But Rafe had encouraged her to be herself. That was one of the things she had loved about him from the start.

"He never actually said anything," she said, "but I noticed his disapproving glances at my hands from time to time, so I finally backed off to pale, more neutral colors."

So her nails, like her life, had simply become more beige after Rafe had left.

He shook his head. "That's Dane alright. It's too bad you caved."

She straightened a little in her chair. "That's easy for you to say. You're his brother. You don't have to worry about your job."

"True." He sipped his coffee. "And I wasn't criticizing. I just hate to see him riding roughshod over everyone. I always loved the way you expressed yourself." He smiled again, sending tremors through her. "I admired that about you."

"Well, maybe now that you're back, I'll go a bit wild again."

A frisson of excitement rushed through her as she realized maybe she didn't mean just wild nail polish. Now that she was near Rafe again . . . she felt this intense yearning to be folded into his arms and devoured by his lips . . . maybe she would let him know how she felt about him.

Maybe, like Jessica, she would allow herself to take a chance and experience what she'd only dreamed about.

"Good for you. I highly recommend it." He smiled. "And don't worry about Dane's disapproving glances. We'll just ignore them."

Her eyes widened. Had he read her thoughts? Did he mean he and she should . . . ?

But it was just his usual charming, although quite devastating, smile. There was nothing in his sexy blue eyes that showed any interest in her as a woman.

None at all.

Just as well. She probably didn't have it in her. Taking chances wasn't her thing.

Not like Jessica, who'd jumped into her relationship with Mr. Ranier with both feet. Not like Rafe, who'd walked away from his life for a year, searching for happiness.

"Why are you here?" she asked.

He tipped his head. "Why? Don't you want me back?" he teased.

"No, I just wondered. You told me you wanted to live life your way. Not by your father's rules. Or your brother's. What changed?"

He shrugged. "I went out and lived my dream. Took to the open road on a motorcycle. Joined a rock band. Played in front of enthusiastic crowds." He gazed at her. "I found complete freedom."

His already incredible sexiness level rocketed to new heights. She quivered at the thought of him wearing a black leather jacket, mounting a motorcycle, then her climbing on behind him and wrapping her arms around his muscular torso. She drew in a breath, still wanting an answer to her question.

"But . . . ?"

His eyebrows arched. "Why do you think there's a 'but'? Why don't you just think that I did it and now it's time to return to my old life?"

She shrugged. "Why would you? You never liked working in a big company like this. You've got enough money to live your life without financial worries. Why would you come back?"

He smiled. "Would you believe me if I said it was because I missed you?"

Her insides trembled, wishing so very much that it was true. But she knew it wasn't.

She shook her head. "Sorry, no. I think it's because you missed your brother, and you want to work things out."

She hoped that was part of it. She knew Mr. Ranier had missed his brother and she'd love to see the two of them get past their differences. She wanted to see Rafe happy.

And she really hoped he was going to stay.

"You know, I don't want to let the cat out of the bag, but he's changed things around here. For the better. I really think he's missed you and he's trying to take the company in a direction that you would approve of."

Rafe snorted. "I'll believe that when I see it."

She nodded. "Okay, why *did* you come back then?"

He sighed deeply. "It has to do with a woman."

"Oh?" Her heart skipped a beat. Could it be . . . ?

He leaned forward and heat simmered through her. "I know you won't believe this but . . ."

"What?" she asked breathlessly.

"The woman is Jessica."

Her shoulders stiffened. "Jessica?" She shook her head in disbelief. "But . . . you've only just met her." But as soon as she'd said the words, she realized it wasn't true.

"That's just it. I met her during my travels. Pretty crazy, right? I was living in this small town—"

"Bakersfield?"

He gazed at her in surprise. "That's right. You know where Jessica is from?"

She nodded. "We're roommates. We've gotten to know each other pretty well."

"Well, I met her in Bakersfield and I fell in love with her."

She sucked in a breath. "Oh, God, you're Storm."

Damn it, how lucky could one woman be? Jessica had had an affair with both of the devastatingly handsome Ranier brothers.

"She told you about me. That's a good sign."

"She told me you broke her heart."

"I know. And I'm going to talk to her about that. Make it right." His long, masculine fingers wrapped snugly around the bright orange, yellow, and white patterned mug in front of him. "Because when I was away from her, I realized that I'd been a complete jackass and thrown away the best thing that ever happened to me. Then I tried to get in touch with her and she was gone. She'd moved away without a trace. When I realized I'd lost her for good, I died inside." His haunted gaze locked on her. "I found out she'd moved to Philly, but I had no idea where. So I came home. Partly in hopes I'd be able to find her, but also because I needed to be around people who know me and care about me. Even if one of those people is a brother I don't get along with. He's family and that's what I needed."

She wondered if he considered her one of the people who cared about him. She was only his secretary, but over the time she'd worked for him, they had developed a closeness of sorts.

Then a smile chased away the sadness in his eyes.

"How crazy is it that when I come home, she's right here." He beamed at her. "It's got to be fate, right?"

Melanie forced a smile, wishing with all her heart that he would feel about her how he obviously felt about Jessica.

She kept the smile pasted on her face even though all she wanted to do was sob. She nodded cheerfully. "You're right. It must be fate."

When Rafe stepped into Dane's living room, he noticed Dane's eyebrow arch when he saw Rafe's faded blue jeans and T-shirt. Or was it because of the tattoos flowing down his arms? Well, hell, he wasn't going to wear a suit all the time.

"Problem?" he asked as he walked into the lavish living room and sprawled on the couch.

"The tattoos aren't really what one would expect of an executive of a big firm like Ranier Industries."

Rafe shrugged. "Maybe I don't like being what people expect."

Dane's brow rose again. "Maybe?"

"Are you really going to play it like Dad would have?"

Dane placed a drink in front of Rafe, then settled into the armchair facing him.

"Of course not. You know I'm not Dad. And I never agreed with the way he treated you."

"But you never stopped it." As soon as the words escaped Rafe's mouth he regretted them. He leaned forward, his hands folded. "I'm sorry. It wasn't up to you to fix things. I should have stood up to the man years ago."

"How could you? He had all the power. Even if you'd tried to walk away from the family, he wouldn't have allowed it."

Rafe laughed without humor. "True. He may not have wanted me for a son, but he wouldn't allow the world to see his failure."

Dane swirled his glass, the ice cubes tinkling against the side. He was clearly unable to refute his brother's words.

"Well, he's gone now and I want you here." He locked gazes with Rafe. "Not because I want to force you into a life you don't want, but because you're my brother and you're important to me."

Rafe just nodded, but his heart swelled at his brother's admission. Dane had always been the tough older brother, but Rafe had always sought Dane's approval. And friendship. But Dane had always sought Dad's approval and had tried to get Rafe to fall in line. Rafe knew now it was because Dane was just trying to make things easier on all of them, but when Rafe was younger, he had felt it was a betrayal.

After almost a year away, he now had more perspective, and he realized his brother had always been looking out for him, in his own way.

"Well, I'm here now and I'd like to jump back into things, if that's okay with you."

Dane smiled broadly. "That's better than okay. I'm off on a trip to Chicago for the rest of the week, but we can meet when I get back to see what you want to take on. This week, Melanie can ensure you get up to speed on what's been going on."

He watched as Dane swirled his glass again.

"I know that look," Rafe said. "What's on your mind?"

"This thing with you and Jessica. I'm just wondering what your intent is."

"My intent? You sound like her father."

"Did he ask you that, too?"

Rafe chuckled. "Not in so many words, but the way he'd look at me . . . I doubt he wanted his daughter falling for a tattooed musician."

That's why it had surprised him so much when her dad had spilled the beans about where she'd gone.

Dane chuckled, too. "I wonder what his attitude would be if he found out you were a billionaire entrepreneur."

Rafe shrugged. "It probably wouldn't have changed. He clearly loves his daughter and wants her to be happy. That's why he didn't toss me out on my duff when we were together. Because she was happy."

Rafe wished he had experienced that kind of love from his own father. He set his glass on the table. "And I intend to ensure she's happy again."

Jessica glanced up as soon as she felt his presence. Not Dane. Storm. Or rather, Rafe. Damn, she'd never get used to thinking of him as Rafe Ranier.

She remembered her brother telling her that Storm had gotten that name because when he played guitar, he took the audience by storm. The moniker suited him so well, she couldn't imagine him by any other name.

As she stared at him standing in her doorway, dressed in an expensive suit, looking way more like Dane than she ever would have imagined, her heart stammered.

He was Storm, with his gentle eyes and the slight curl to his lips as he watched her, yet he was a stranger.

"What is it?" she finally asked, since he seemed determined to just stand there.

"I'd like to talk to you."

She pushed her keyboard tray under the desk and sat back in her chair. "Okay, go ahead."

He crossed his arms. "Not here. My office would be more private."

She frowned. "What if I don't want to be somewhere private with you?"

He compressed his lips. "You do realize I'm your boss, right?"

She frowned. "Actually, Dane's my boss."

He raised his eyebrows. "Dane? You call him by his first name?"

Damn, she hadn't meant to do that.

"No, I call him Mr. Ranier, but his first name is Dane and that's the only way to differentiate the two of you."

He gazed at her speculatively, then continued. "Dane and I both own the company, so I qualify as your boss, too, even if you don't report directly to me."

She stared at him defiantly.

"Miss Long, I want you in my office now."

His words sent a quiver through her . . . of anxiety, but also of excitement. He was more like Dane than she'd thought, especially when he pulled that commanding boss thing on her.

She pushed herself to her feet, then followed him to his office. When he closed the door behind them, she felt another shiver. Other than their short interaction in Dane's office yesterday, she hadn't been alone with him since the time he'd walked out on her. But she'd dreamed of him. Longed to be with him.

But he'd broken her heart and she didn't want that kind of pain again. Not only that, he'd lied about who he was.

He stepped behind her and as soon as she felt his hand on

her shoulder, she shot forward a step, her heart racing. She reached for the stone in her pocket and stroked it.

He walked toward his desk, then turned to face her.

"Jess, we have a lot to talk about. I know you probably don't want to do it here in the office, so I want you to come to my place for dinner this evening. We can discuss what happened and I'll answer all your questions."

"I can't. You had your opportunity and you broke my heart. You can't just waltz back here and expect to pick up where we left off."

"Jess, come on. Give me a chance." He reached for her and stroked her hair behind her ear. The gentle touch sent tingles through her, and a dangerous desire to lean into his hand. To nuzzle his palm, then press her lips to his skin. "I made the biggest mistake of my life. Now let me spend the rest of it making up for it. I'm ready to be the man you deserve."

As if sensing her capitulation, he stepped closer and leaned toward her. He was going to kiss her. And she wanted him to. To feel his lips against hers again. His solid body pressed tight to hers.

The door opened.

"Jessica, we have to go. We have a plane to catch."

She jerked back from Storm, her gaze darting to Dane's. "Yes, Mr. Ranier."

She felt guilty having been caught almost kissing Storm. Even though Dane knew about their past, and her relationship with Dane was only physical. Still, she was with him, no matter how casual the relationship and she felt as if she'd almost cheated on him.

Storm's highly observant gaze locked on her and her heated

cheeks. Then he glanced at Dane. "Is there something going on between the two of you?"

"Right now what's going on is that I need my assistant to accompany me to the airport. I'm going to Chicago to close a deal—something you'd know if you'd been here where you should be."

"Is she accompanying you just to the airport, or to Chicago?"

"To Chicago, of course."

"And do you have separate rooms?" Storm's eyes flared with anger.

"That's none of your damn business," Dane retorted.

"Yes, they're separate rooms," Jessica snapped, then turned and left the office.

Jessica sat beside Dane on his private jet as it sped along the runway, then lifted off. The off-white leather seats were very comfortable and she settled back as they accelerated into the air.

"So, do you want to talk about you and Rafe?" Dane asked.

She pursed her lips and shrugged. "I don't know what to say. It was a shock to find out he wasn't who I thought he was, and the fact he's your brother is . . ."—she glanced at him—"really awkward."

"That's an understatement." He glanced out the window and asked casually, "Do you think you want to take up where you left off with him?"

"Where we left off was him walking out on me."

"But he's back now. When I met you, it was clear you were still in love with him."

She shook her head. "I was in love with Storm. I don't know who Rafe is. And Storm broke my heart."

Dane nodded, his expression giving away nothing.

Once the plane was in level flight, the steward brought them lunch and offered them a selection of drinks. When they arrived in Chicago, they would go straight to their first client meeting. Dane had told her it would probably take a couple of days to hammer out all the details of the contract before they could close the deal.

It wasn't a very long flight, so she ate quickly, but ever aware of Dane's powerful presence beside her. The steward cleared away their dishes and poured them coffee. Dane filled the time between them with conversation about their upcoming meeting.

Once the steward disappeared, she glanced at Dane's profile as he stared at his tablet, going over some of her notes for the meeting. If Storm hadn't walked back into her life, she and Dane would probably not just be sitting here. They were high above the air in a luxurious private jet. It would be exhilarating to take advantage of this exciting situation.

She gazed at his handsome profile and imagined unfastening her seat belt and lowering to the floor, then stroking his crotch. She could imagine him quickly rising to attention. Would he then decide to punish her, or order her to unzip him then bring him to climax?

He glanced toward her, catching her staring at him.

She smiled. "Is there anything you'd like me to do for you, Mr. Ranier?"

"No. Just relax until we get there," he said with a deadpan expression. "It will be a busy afternoon."

Was he just focused on the important meetings to come, or did he have an issue with the fact she used to be his brother's lover?

She needed to talk to him about it but before she could

find the words to start, the pilot announced that they were approaching Chicago and they should fasten their seatbelts.

She would have to bring it up later.

The afternoon rushed by in a flurry of meetings, followed by dinner with the key players at Bright Lights, a company that did research into green technologies.

By the time the day ended, and she and Dane walked down the hotel hallway to their rooms, she was dragging her heels.

"Get a good night's sleep," Dane said as they reached her doorway, then he continued on to his suite next door.

"But—"

"Goodnight," he said as he opened his door, then disappeared inside.

She sighed and stepped inside. Their luggage had already been delivered to their rooms and her bed was turned down and was oh, so inviting.

Even more inviting was the thought of sliding into Dane's bed, naked and ready for him.

But she knew deep inside that what she was really looking for was a distraction from thoughts of Storm and what his return meant to her. How would it change things?

Was she still in love with him?

Rafe tried to get work done, but he found himself just staring at the document on his screen, one of the many Melanie had gathered together for him to summarize what had been going on at Ranier Industries in his absence.

Thoughts of Jessica kept pushing through every effort he made to concentrate on work. She'd been gone a day and wouldn't be back in the office until Monday. Not that he'd wait until he saw her in the office. He would fly to Chicago right now if he didn't think that course of action would cause more problems than it solved.

Damn it, he just didn't know if he'd been imagining something between Jessica and his brother. When she'd used Dane's first name rather than calling him Mr. Ranier, as Dane would expect of any of his employees, it threw him. She'd claimed to use his first name to differentiate between him and Dane, but he had his doubts. Then her cheeks had flushed when Dane came into the office, as if she'd been caught cheating on him.

He pushed his chair back from the desk and stood up, then paced across the office. He was probably reading way too much into the incidents. Old fears rising. There was not substantial evidence that Dane was stealing Jessica from him. His lips compressed. Maybe it was time to let go of the past and move on.

Jessica walked through the small boutique looking for an unusual nail polish to bring back for Melanie, but it was difficult to find something that her friend didn't already have. She considered the bottle of blue polish with gold and purple flakes which the clerk told her was brand new, but Melanie tended to order a lot online and often before they were available in the stores.

Finally, she decided on a designer brand name, remembering that Melanie hardly ever indulged in the expensive brands. It was only fifteen dollars, but for an avid collector like Melanie, that amount for a bottle of polish added up fast.

Her phone chimed and she pulled it out and read the text message.

Need you back at four.

It was the second day of their trip, and they had started

early and had been in meetings all day. After lunch, Dane had given her a break and told her to go see the city while he met one-on-one with the president of Bright Lights.

She located the higher-end polishes and found one in her price range—a pretty shimmery lilac—made her purchase, then headed back to the client's office.

When she walked into the office, Dane sent her a broad smile, telling her all had gone well.

Then they met with the senior staff and Dane answered some of their concerns, but it seemed merely a formality. Afterward, the president invited them to join him and a few others from his team for champagne and hors d'oeuvres in the swanky restaurant in their hotel.

Jessica allowed herself only one glass. This was still a business meeting and she wanted to stay sharp. After about an hour and a half, the others excused themselves and soon she found herself alone with Dane.

He poured her another glass of champagne. "This is cause for celebration. I've been working on buying this company for six months now."

"Congratulations," she said, lifting her glass.

He tapped his tall flute against hers, then they drank.

"You were a part of making this happen, so congratulations to you, too."

She smiled impishly, feeling the warmth of the bubbly alcohol washing through her. "So do I get rewarded for my diligence?"

His eyebrows arched as he sat back in his chair. "Are you angling for a bonus?"

"I guess I am, but I'm not thinking money." She slipped off her shoe and with a boldness she didn't know she possessed, she slid her foot forward until she felt his shoe, then glided up his leg. As her toes ran along his inner thigh, he coughed.

"This is highly inappropriate," he said.

"I thought you sometimes enjoyed inappropriate."

He stilled her foot with his hand, but she pushed past and found his crotch, then stroked him, feeling his shaft harden immediately. Tremors of awareness rippled through her at the feel of his solid column.

"Jessica, you have to deal with the fact that Rafe has dropped back into your life. You were in love with him—maybe still are. You need to figure that out before we can continue with whatever it is we have between us."

"Why? What we have is just physical, remember?" She pressed her foot against his erect cock, longing to hold it in her hands, then lifted her other foot and squeezed him between both of them. He looked in pain.

"Mr. Ranier, you don't look well. I think we should get you up to your room."

As she slid her feet away, she tortured him with a long, firm stroke.

Fire burned in his eyes, but not the kind she'd hoped for.

"You require some severe disciplining, Miss. Long," he growled under his breath.

His menacing expression unnerved her.

"Yes, sir."

"Stand up and give me my jacket." Even though he spoke quietly, his tone vibrated with authority.

She stood up and grabbed the jacket that he'd draped over the back of a neighboring chair earlier, then handed it to him. He'd need it to hide the erection that would be all too visible when he stood up.

He snatched it from her as he stood up, then carried the jacket draped in front of him as they walked. Barely suppressed anger emanated from him.

There were people with them in the elevator on the way up, then she followed him down the hall to his suite.

He jabbed his keycard into the slot, then unlocked the door.

"Get inside," he commanded.

She skittered through the doorway, barely able to catch her breath. She had never seen him so angry and she wondered what he intended to do. The air around her seemed to vibrate with his authoritative presence.

And a shiver of anticipation danced along her spine.

Despite her nerves, her eyes widened at his suite. Her room was nice, but this was impressive, and gorgeous. Huge. Open and bright, with floor-to-ceiling windows overlooking the city. And the air was sweet with the fragrance of flowers from the fresh cut arrangement on the table.

"Oh, it's lovely."

"Never mind that," he snapped. "Get over here."

At the stormy expression in his eyes, she wondered if she'd pushed things too far. Warily, she walked toward him. He grasped her shoulders and turned her around, then took her arm and gruffly walked her across the room. Was he going to throw her out?

But she found herself facing the window, then being bent over the back of the couch. Her hands flattened against the fabric to steady herself, then she felt Dane's hand smack across her rear.

"Oh," she exclaimed in surprise.

"You were very bad. Now you'll have to accept your punishment."

"Yes, sir."

The feel of his hand smacking across her clothed behind was titillating, but not enough.

Then she felt her skirt shift. His hand glided up the back of her thigh, then across her naked buttocks. She still wore a garter belt and thong every day as instructed by him. The feel of his warm hand on her flesh sent heat coursing through her.

His other hand found the button of her skirt and released the zipper. Her skirt slipped to the floor, leaving her ass naked to him. He smacked her, then again. Her flesh tingled. He smacked again and she moaned.

She felt herself twirled around, then his arms wrapped around her and his mouth covered hers. His tongue delved between her lips in a full assault and she melted against him.

Then he tore his mouth away. "Fuck, Jessica, I was trying to be sensitive to the fact you'd need time. I knew you might want to call it off between us. I didn't want to mention it yet, because I thought it would just pressure you."

She cupped his crotch, then stroked up the length of his cock and squeezed. "Then *I* pressured *you*."

"God damn it, woman." He stepped back, out of her reach, his hot, gaze searing her.

His loud, ragged breath filled the room and she wasn't sure whether to stand there, or flee to her room while he collected himself.

Then he drew in a deep breath and his body relaxed as he regained complete control. But the fire remained in his eyes.

"Strip. Now," he commanded.

Her eyes widened, then she worked hard to suppress a smile as she unbuttoned her blouse and slipped it from her shoulders. When she reached behind her to unhook her bra, he stopped her.

"Let me." He stepped toward her and she turned around. His fingers played along her skin, sending electricity along her nerve endings, then her bra loosened. He dropped each strap from her shoulders.

"Turn around."

She turned to face him and he reached for the lacy bra and drew it from her body, then dropped his heated gaze to her naked breasts. Immediately, her nipples puckered. He cupped her breasts and lifted, then caressed them. She sighed at the feel of his big hands covering her.

Then he stepped back and she shed her thong.

"The rest can stay," he said as she stood in only her stockings, garter belt, and black high-heeled pumps. "Now,"—he unzipped his pants and pulled out his big cock, swollen and in need of attention—"you caused this. I think you should deal with it."

She stepped toward him. "Yes, Mr. Ranier." She wrapped her hand around the kid leather–soft skin surrounding a rock-hard core, and squeezed.

He rested his hand on her head and pressed down, so she sank to her knees. The plush carpet was soft on her knees as she settled in front of him. She stroked him several times, then brought his tip to her mouth and licked him. He groaned as she wrapped her lips around him and drew his plum-size head into her mouth. She licked and sucked a little, then took him deep. He twined his fingers through her hair and pulled her deeper still, then guided her head forward and back.

"Oh, fuck." He stiffened and hot liquid gushed into her mouth.

She continued to suck until the flow stopped, amazed at how quick it had been to bring him release.

Now would he send her away? Not that he'd ever left her

unsatisfied before, but this time she really had defied his wishes and manipulated him into this.

But he grasped her shoulders and pressed her backward as he lowered himself to the floor. She found herself on her back with him sliding his arms under her thighs and lifting her pelvis.

"I did promise you foreplay." Then his mouth covered her and she moaned.

He licked the length of her slick slit, then pushed his tongue inside. As heat washed through her, she felt his fingers slip into her, too. Then his tongue found her clit. Wild sensations fluttered through her as he licked and stroked her.

"Oh, Mr. Ranier, that feels so good." Her fingers glided through his hair, then she clutched his head to her as he sucked her clit. Waves of pleasure swelled through her and she moaned as he propelled her to ecstasy.

She arched against him and rode the wave to heaven.

When she finally collapsed on the floor, he swept her up and carried her to his bedroom, then placed her on the big bed. She watched him strip off his clothes, then he prowled over her, and she felt his hot, hard cock pressing against her.

"God, I want to fuck you so badly." Then he thrust forward, filling her with his huge erection.

"Oh, yes." She clung to his shoulders, loving the feel of his hard shaft inside her. "Please fuck me, Mr. Ranier. Make me come."

He groaned and thrust into her. Again and again. His big cock stroked her with his length each time he drew back, then propeled forward again. She gasped as he drove deeper still. Her breathing accelerated.

He nuzzled her neck. "Are you close?"

She nodded, then knowing he liked her to say it, found her

words. "Yes, sir. I'm,"—she gasped at another deep thrust—"very . . . ah . . . close."

He nipped her earlobe, sending her close to the point of no return, then murmured in her ear, "Tell me when you come. And use my name. Call me Dane."

Then he thrust deep again, just as his finger found her clit.

"Oh, I'm coming." Pleasure swamped her senses. "Dane. You're. Making. Me." She moaned. "Come!"

He drove deep and she felt his liquid heat gush inside her.

He kept thrusting, building her pleasure even more. Her orgasm went on and on, then he spiraled inside her.

"Oh, Dane." She gasped and wrapped her arms tighter around him. "Oh, yes." She nearly fainted at the exquisite pleasure he gave her.

Finally, it ebbed and she sucked in air as she collapsed against the bed.

"Oh, my God, that was,"—she pushed her hair back from her face—"sensational."

His lips found hers and the passion of the kiss surprised her. His tongue stroked deeply as his hand caressed her face. He rolled her onto her side, then drew her close to his body. Her head rested against his muscular chest, his heart thumping under her ear.

She was tired, and she'd had a little too much champagne, and she definitely didn't want to think about what all this meant, so she just nuzzled against him and allowed herself to relax until soon sleep took her.

Dane woke up and instantly knew he was in trouble. Jessica's face was pressed against his chest, her soft breath caressing his skin, her warm naked body so close, acting like an aphrodisiac.

Damn it, he couldn't be falling in love with the woman his brother loved. It was idiocy. It would ruin everything he'd done to mend fences with Rafe.

He could tell the instant she woke up . . . and stiffened in his arms.

"Good morning, Jessica." His lips brushed the top of her head.

"Good morning, Mr. Ranier."

Dane's arm tightened around Jessica's waist and she felt herself rolled back, then she gazed up at Dane Ranier, him gazing down at her in turn, his large, masculine body covering hers.

"Not Mr. Ranier. Call me Dane." His deep blue eyes bored into her, demanding acquiescence.

Her breath caught and she nodded. "Dane," she said breathlessly.

Then his lips brushed hers. Coaxingly. Until, with her heart pumping erratically, hers moved, too, as she was swept away by his sublime tenderness. His tongue swept into her mouth and she opened, welcoming him. Wanting him to devour her in this loving onslaught.

He deepened his kiss and her arms slid around him, pulling him closer, wanting to eliminate any distance between them, wanting to absorb him into her body. Her need for him grew so intense, she thought she'd die from the ache in her heart.

Then his lips slipped away and she wanted to protest, but he kissed along her cheek, then nuzzled the base of her neck, sending tingles of joy flooding through her.

He eased back and gazed at her body. Her breasts swelled and her nipples elongated. He smiled and stroked a finger down the middle her chest, between her breasts, then over one mound to the tight nipple at its peak. When he touched it, ever so gently, she gasped. He leaned forward and licked the hard nub, then gently took it in his mouth and drew on it lightly. The exquisiteness of his touch made her want to weep. His tongue swirled over it and she arched forward, needing to be even closer to him. Needing to be completely possessed by him.

"Oh, Dane. I need you."

He drew back his head and his simmering navy eyes caught on hers. She could see a depth of longing there she'd never seen before.

"I need you, too," he murmured.

His hand stroked down her belly toward his swollen, rock-hard cock, then she felt his hardness press against her. She widened her legs, opening for him. His mesmerizing gaze holding hers captive, he pressed into her. His masculine member, so thick and hard, filled her in an exquisitely slow glide forward. Her body opened for him, welcoming him.

Once he totally filled her, she clung to him, holding him close, nearly gasping for air.

This felt so right. It was nothing like the thrilling, highly erotic lovemaking they usually enjoyed. This was deep and poignant. Leaving her vulnerable and open.

With his gaze still holding her captive, he began to move, his big member sliding back, then slowly propelling forward again. Filling her with his thick, hard length. Filling her with a joy that threatened to overwhelm her. She could feel tears well in her eyes.

She said nothing, but she knew her eyes laid bare her soul. Oh, God, she loved this man. He had to see it.

She moaned and her eyelids fluttered closed as he glided

deep. She squeezed him as he withdrew and then he pushed inside again. Her whole body thrummed with vibrant pleasure.

"Dane, yes." She tightened her arms around him as he drove into her a little faster, but still excruciatingly slower than she wanted. Until the buildup started, and the pleasure turned to joy. Then blissful sensations shuddered through her.

She sucked in a breath, hovering on the edge. "Dane, I'm going to—"

But his lips covered hers, preventing the words, as he thrust again, flinging her to ecstasy. She moaned into his mouth and it was as if he swallowed her joy, then jerked tight against her, groaning his own release.

But he kept driving into her, faster now, driving her pleasure higher. Extending her orgasm until she lost track of time. With a sense of wonder, she rode the wave of sensation, gasping and moaning until reality faded away.

Dane stared at the prone, still body of Jessica below him. The woman had fainted in his arms. He'd heard of such a thing, but never experienced it before.

His cock was still deep inside her and he so wanted to stay that way with her snuggled close against him, but it didn't seem right. He drew away, his member sliding from the warmth and comfort of her body, and he sat on the bed beside her and stroked her cheek.

"Jessica, are you all right?"

Her eyelids fluttered open and she gazed at him. Oh, God, the warmth in those eyes—that was there now and had been during their intense lovemaking—told him more than he wanted to know. More than he could allow.

Those open, expressive green eyes of hers radiated with love. A love he felt burning in his own chest.

A love he couldn't allow.

As soon as Jessica woke up, she felt the absence of Dane's body next to hers. After their poignant lovemaking earlier this morning—when she'd fainted, no less—Dane had wrapped her in his arms until she'd fallen asleep again, cozy in the protective cocoon of his embrace.

Her stomach quivered at the thought of what had happened between them. Could it be that Dane was falling in love with her? Was she falling in love with him? But this wasn't supposed to happen. She'd only wanted a physical thing. No commitments. No feelings getting in the way.

After what Storm had put her through, she wasn't ready to get involved again so soon. And, oh, God, she still had to deal with Storm when she got home. He seemed to want to pick up where they'd left off and she couldn't just ignore him. How was he going to react when he found out she was involved with Dane?

She pushed aside the covers and stood up, then showered and towel dried her hair. After brushing it out, she slipped on the terry cloth robe the hotel supplied and walked from the bedroom to the main area of the suite. Dane sat at the table reading a newspaper, a thermos jug of coffee in front of him.

Even though she couldn't see his face, the sight of him set her heart thumping. Maybe she hadn't wanted to fall in love with him, but this morning had been wonderful. She'd felt so cherished and . . . loved. Maybe this wasn't a bad thing after all.

"Good morning, Dane."

He lowered his newspaper and folded it, then set it on the table. "What happened to calling me Mr. Ranier?"

She smiled. "Yes, Mr. Ranier."

She gazed at him, remembering the warmth of his arms around her, the passion of his kisses this morning, and she wanted to leap into his arms again.

He sat there impeccably dressed in his suit and tie, and she wore only the terry cloth robe, with nothing underneath. She could just open this robe and stand before him, and he would doubtlessly order her to her knees to take care of his body's natural reaction.

She walked to his side and rested her hand on his shoulder, needing to touch him.

"Maybe we should talk about what happened this morning," she ventured.

His gaze locked on hers, flat and expressionless. The way he'd look at an employee. In fact, with a harsh glint, as if she'd displeased him in some way.

She drew her hand away and walked around the table, then drew in a calming breath as she sat across the table from him.

He shrugged. "There's nothing to talk about."

She gazed at him over the thermal jug as she poured coffee into her cup. "What happened this morning was different than what we've done before. It was . . . I don't know . . . deeper. I think we should talk about how our relationship is changing."

He leaned forward. "Jessica, I'm your boss. You're my assistant. We have a sexual relationship but it's a no-strings-attached affair that either one of us can walk away from any time we wish. What more is there to discuss?"

Her heart stammered at his cold words.

"Unfortunately, the change of setting seems to have blurred the line for you, but let me remind you what *you* originally proposed. This is a physical relationship only." His gaze slid down her body and lingered at the tie at her waist. "If you'd like to drop that robe and fuck right now, I'm happy to oblige, but don't read anything more into it than shared sexual release."

Her hand slipped to the front of her robe and she had to stop herself from pulling it tighter around her.

He glanced at his watch. "In fact, we're running short of time. Go to your room and get packed, then meet me back here. You've got twenty minutes."

"Packed? But I thought we were here until the end of the week?"

Dane's lawyers were flying in today to join him while they finalized the details of the contract negotiations.

"I am. You, on the other hand, are going back to the office. I've arranged a driver to take you to the airport, then someone to meet you at the other end."

Jessica climbed aboard the private jet and slumped onto the buttery-soft leather seat. The steward helped her settle in by stowing her briefcase and purse in a compartment, and instructed her to buckle up once the pilot was ready to be underway.

She spent the flight staring at her tablet, trying to review her list of goals for the week and determine how to spend the rest of the day once she got back to the office, but her head ached with the effort. She knew that if she put it aside, however, thoughts of Dane and his rejection would overwhelm her.

"Would you like something to drink?" the friendly young steward asked.

She returned his warm smile. "It's tempting, but I have to go into the office when we land."

"That doesn't stop most of our passengers." His smile broadened.

"But most of them are executives."

"True, I guess they don't have to worry about their boss getting on their case."

She frowned at the reminder of her boss and how he'd rejected her.

"You know, a glass of wine won't hurt, and it might help that headache."

"How did you know?" She gazed at the young man and realized he was quite attractive. And he was flirting with her.

He shrugged. "You seem stressed and you were rubbing your temples."

"Well, maybe I'll just go directly after the problem and take a pain killer if you have one."

"Of course." He disappeared for a moment, then returned with two caplets in a small cup along with a glass of water.

She took the pills and spent the next hour chatting with him. Her headache diminished and his conversation helped the time speed by. When they finally landed, she said good-bye with a smile and headed across the tarmac to the terminal. Once inside, she glanced around, wondering where to find her ride.

"Welcome back."

She started at the sound of Storm's voice behind her. She turned to see his smiling face. She wasn't sure she'd ever get used to seeing him in a tailored suit rather than the tattered jeans and tank tops she was used to.

He took her briefcase and then pressed his hand to the small of her back. She had to remind herself this was not the Storm she knew. This was Rafe Ranier.

"This way." He guided her through the crowded airport terminal and then outside to the waiting limo.

"You're who Dane sent to pick me up?"

His eyebrow arched. Damn, she'd used his brother's first name again. What was wrong with her?

She settled into the cozy seat and Rafe settled in beside her. The limo moved into the airport traffic.

"Have a good flight?" Rafe asked.

"Fine." She glanced out the window, gazing at the sunlight glinting on the cars traveling beside them, her thumb gliding over the worry stone in her pocket.

She knew he would take this opportunity to open up their past and discuss why he'd left—he'd already tried to before she'd left for Chicago—but she wished he wouldn't do it right now.

"I'd like to talk to you about something important," he said.

"Please, not now," she said, continuing to stare out the window. But the quaver in her voice betrayed her.

"Jess, what's wrong?"

His gentle hand on her shoulder was her undoing. Tears welled in her eyes and she tried to blink them back, but didn't quite succeed.

"I'm so sorry, sweetheart. I know I let you down when I left—"

She waved him away. "It's not that. It's . . ."

He cupped her chin and turned her to face him. When he saw the two small tears that had escaped down her cheek, his face etched with concern.

"Did Dane do something? Did he make a pass at you?"

She shook her head. "No. It's just been a really exhausting trip, that's all. Just really exhausting."

Her throat closed up and she couldn't manage anything more. And she didn't know what she'd say if she could. What had Dane done, anyway? Reminded her what their relationship actually was. She was his employee and they shared a purely physical relationship. Exactly what she'd told him she wanted.

But now . . . what *did* she want?

"Come here." Rafe folded her into his arms and held her.

She rested her head against his broad chest and let the comfort of his arms lull her.

She knew she shouldn't be taking comfort from him. He was her ex-lover. The man who had broken her heart. But despite that, he was a good man, and right now, she needed this.

He stroked her hair and she closed her eyes, letting the warmth and protectiveness of his body, paired with the relaxing motion of the vehicle, calm her.

She felt his lips on her forehead.

"Jess, we're here."

She opened her eyes and realized she'd dozed off. Self-consciously, she drew away from him. The driver opened her door, and she stepped out of the limo, and then glanced around at the unfamiliar surroundings.

"This isn't the office."

"That's true." Rafe pressed his hand to the small of her back again and guided her to the glass doors of the towering building in front of them.

Oh, damn, did he expect her to accompany him to a client meeting? He was her boss, too, and it was still workday hours. A doorman opened the door for them and as soon as she stepped inside, she could tell this was a residence. And a very posh one at that.

The lobby was light and airy, with leather couches and chairs forming sitting areas. Light filled the space, reflecting off cream-colored marble walls and floor. One section of the wall was covered in stacked slate, a nice contrast to the shiny surfaces. The ceilings were off-white, with crossed beams to give architectural detail and tall floral arrangements sat atop low cabinets in insets along the marble wall.

"Where are we?" she asked as Rafe guided her into the elevator.

"This is my place."

Her chest tightened and if the door hadn't already closed, she would have lurched forward.

"Do you mean you own the building?"

"I mean, this is where I live."

She shook her head. "Rafe, I—"

He gently grasped her shoulders. "Jess, I just want to talk to you, and this is not a conversation I want to have in the office." He tipped her chin up. "Okay?"

She stared at his intense, blue eyes and compressed her lips, then nodded.

The elevator doors opened, then they walked down a short hall and he unlocked an elegant mahogany door. She stepped out to a bright, spacious penthouse. The dark hardwood floors gleamed in the sunlight cascading in from the huge windows. His furniture was beige leather and dark wood. Bright accents of red, orange, and yellow threaded throughout the living area in the form of accent cushions, artwork and flowering plants, adding warmth and flare to the space.

"This is where you live?" It was huge and beautiful and clearly expensive.

She couldn't imagine the Storm she knew strolling in here in his jeans and worn leather jacket, tossing his backpack onto the entryway floor, then relaxing in one of the easy chairs. Before he'd moved in with her in Bakersfield, he'd been sharing a small apartment with another guy in the band. His room had had only a mattress on the floor, and they'd had a card table and folding chairs in the kitchen, and a secondhand couch and coffee table in the living room.

"I bought it three years ago, but I've been away for over a year." He shrugged. "But, yeah, this is home."

She nodded. "Why did you leave? To come to Bakersfield, I mean." She remembered Dane telling her that their relationship had always been strained after a falling out over a woman, but she wanted to hear Storm's interpretation for herself. "Why would anyone leave all this?"

He shrugged. "The question is, why I didn't leave sooner. My father was a controlling man. He controlled everyone and everything around him and I hated it. But that's also the reason I didn't leave." He paced across the room. "He programmed me to do as I was told. To live the life I was told to live. To follow someone else's dream. And if I tried to stand up to him . . ." His hands clenched into fists, his jaw tight. "When I was a kid, he beat me into submission. When I was older, he threatened me in other ways."

Shock vaulted through her at his admission. "That's awful." How could a father be so cruel?

He sat down on the leather couch facing a big fireplace and she settled beside him.

"After he died, I realized that I didn't have to do that anymore. There was no reason I couldn't be who *I* wanted to be."

"So you left and became Storm."

He nodded. "When I was a kid, a friend of mine had a guitar and he taught me a few chords. I asked my father if I could take guitar lessons and when he said no, I made an excuse to stay after school and took lessons anyway. But when my guitar teacher ran into my parents and told them I had talent, my father found where I'd hidden my guitar and nearly smashed my head in with it. Fortunately, I have good reflexes and it smashed against a wall instead. See, he didn't want me to let anything as trivial as music get in the way of the grand plans he had for me and Dane running Ranier Industries. Even simple guitar lessons set him off because they didn't have a place in his carefully laid plans."

"I take it you taught yourself."

"I figured out a way. I couldn't let him steal everything that mattered to me." He sighed. "But I didn't bring you here to talk about my childhood."

She nodded. "I know."

He wanted to tell her why he broke her heart.

"Jess, I'm sorry about what happened. I was living my dream, being free for the first time in my life. Answering to no one but myself."

"And you thought being with me took away that freedom?" She couldn't help the catch in her voice.

"No, that's not it at all." He turned toward her and took her hand. "When I realized how much you meant to me . . ." His gaze caught on hers, and held. "When I realized you might be starting to feel the same about me . . ." He shook his head, and gently squeezed her hand. "I realized I couldn't keep living a lie. Someone was going to get hurt, and I didn't want it to be you."

She drew her hand away. "But I did get hurt. I thought you loved me and when you walked out like that, acting as if what was between us was nothing . . . It broke my heart."

He ran his hand through his hair. "Damn it, I know. I just thought it would be worse later."

"Why didn't you just tell me who you are?"

"Tell you that I'd been lying to you? That I was someone totally different?" He shook his head. "I could only do that if I was totally ready to embrace our relationship and move forward. But that would mean deciding who I wanted to be: Storm or Rafe. If I wanted to build a future with you, Rafe seemed the better choice."

"Why?"

"Do you really see yourself wanting to join me on the road? Traveling from town to town. Living the life of a musician's wife. Or me traveling and you staying at home?"

"But you did leave me while you went on the road."

"And you didn't like it."

"Because I didn't know if you'd come back."

"Isn't that always going to be true? If I went on the road for months on end, wouldn't you always wonder?" He took her hand again. "The point is, I would want to offer you more stability than that. But, I wasn't ready to be Rafe again. I didn't know if I ever wanted to be Rafe."

"So you ran away from me, too."

"No. I just knew I had to take the time to go on the road. To see what it was like. And I didn't think it was fair to keep you on the hook."

"You say you cared about me, but you were willing to lose me."

"Because I really thought that was the best for you. I didn't think you should be saddled with a guy who didn't know what he wanted, or even who he should be. You deserved better than that and if I couldn't figure out my shit, then I didn't deserve you."

"Since you came back here, I assume that means you've decided to be Rafe," she said.

He sighed. "I hadn't been away from you for very long before I realized that whatever life I chose, I wanted you in it. That's why I went back to Bakersfield. I was going to tell you my whole story and convince you we had a future together. When your mother told me you'd moved away, and that you didn't want to see me again, I realized I'd lost you. At that point, my world came crashing down around me."

"Mom told me my dad gave you my number, but you didn't use it."

"I knew you were in Philly and I decided I'd come home and get my life together again, then I'd come looking for you." He smiled. "I didn't realize you'd be here waiting for me."

"So who do you want to be?"

"I want to be whoever it is that makes you happy." His thumb stroked the back of her hand and she shivered. "Whether it's Storm or Rafe, I'll be happy if you're by my side."

Her heart swelled at the warmth and passion in his sky blue eyes.

"That's why . . ." He slid from the couch and placed one knee on the floor, then kissed her hand. "I want to ask you something very important."

She shook her head. This couldn't be happening. He reached into his pocket and pulled out something. She realized it was a royal blue velvet box, which he opened to reveal a stunning ring with diamonds forming the shape of a butterfly. Or a moth.

"Will you marry me?"

Entangled

Jessica stared at him. Her heart clenched. A part of her wanted to fall into his arms and tell him yes, yes, yes! But the reasonable, *sane* part of her flared with anger.

"Are you kidding me?" She bolted to her feet, then across the room. "I don't even know who you are. Do you really expect me to marry a complete stranger?"

He stood up and closed the ring box, looking totally crestfallen. She felt cruel rejecting him like that but . . . it was crazy of him to put her on the spot like this. He'd dumped her, then waltzed back into her life and two seconds after explaining why he'd left . . . proposed!

And that ring. It was beautiful and expensive and exactly underscored the difference between Storm and Rafe. Storm could never afford something like that, whereas Rafe wouldn't even blink at the price tag, no matter how high it was.

Fuming, she turned her back on him and strode to the window, taking solace in the spectacular view of the city below.

Then she felt his hands on her shoulders.

"You *do* know me, Jess. I'm the same man you fell in love with."

"I did not fall in love—" she said as she spun around, but as soon as she faced him, he pulled her into his arms and captured her lips. At the gentle pressure of his tongue against her mouth, she opened, almost in a gasp of surprise. The passion of his kiss overwhelmed her and she melted against him. Oh, God, it felt so good to be in his arms. Warm and protected. And loved.

But none of it was true.

She stiffened and pressed against his shoulders. Reluctantly, he eased back.

"Jess, please. I love you."

"But I don't love you."

He stared deep into her eyes, reading all her secrets.

"I don't believe that."

She dodged around him, unable to bear his closeness any longer.

"Is this really about me," he asked, "or are you involved with someone else?"

Her eyes narrowed. "Why do you think I'm involved with someone else?"

His lips compressed. "You keep calling Dane by his first name."

"I've already told you—"

"And I get a certain vibe from the two of you. Is there something going on between you?"

She sucked in a breath, then walked across the room, needing to release some of her pent-up energy. Could she really tell him about Dane? It wasn't any of his business, but she didn't want to lie.

Even though telling him would surely cause problems between the brothers.

"There is something between us, but it's not romantic."

Anger flared in his sky blue eyes. "What is it then?"

She raised her head and met his harsh gaze. She had no reason to be embarrassed. What she shared with Dane was quite reasonable. They were just two consenting adults in a purely sexual relationship.

"It's just physical. Nothing more."

Maybe it would have been better to let him think there was a deeper relationship between her and Dane. Then it would be easier to keep him at a distance.

The problem was, now that he'd opened up to her, she wasn't sure if she wanted to keep him at a distance forever.

"So the two of you are having sex." His hands clenched into fists.

"Look, I know you and Dane have had problems over women before, and I don't want to be the cause of more friction between you."

The muscle in his jaw ticked, and he said, "Well, it seems you don't have any control over that."

She stepped toward him. "Please, don't let this come between the two of you."

But his closed expression told her that this had opened a can of worms between the brothers. Damn it, why hadn't she kept her mouth shut? She didn't have to lie, but she could have held her silence.

"Rafe, your brother—"

"I don't want to hear about my brother right now, especially from the woman I just proposed to who is turning me down because of him."

Anger flared in her again.

"That's not fair. It's not because of Dane. I only met him because you left me and broke my heart."

His eyes narrowed. "If I broke your heart, that means you were in love with me."

Her chest compressed. She sighed, gazing at this practical stranger in his expensive, tailored suit and designer silk tie. "I was in love with Storm. But he doesn't exist."

"Fuck that. I am who I have always been." He pulled off his suit jacket and tossed it across the room. "Don't let this suit confuse you."

Her eyes widened as he loosened his tie, then tugged open the buttons of his shirt, revealing his broad muscular chest. With a rapid jerk, he pulled the shirt over his head, tie and all, and tossed them aside. She couldn't help but gaze with longing at his perfect pecs and six-pack abs. Tattoos adorned his arms and shoulders. He'd gotten a few new ones on the road.

Then her gaze fell to the leopard moth on his left shoulder, near his heart.

He saw where she was looking and pointed at it. "I meant this, Jess. I got this to tell you I would always be there for you, and it's true."

He stepped toward her and she gazed at the warmth and sincerity in his sky blue eyes. In those eyes, she could see the glow of love. Her heart pounded and she felt light headed.

This man walking toward her, his muscular chest bare, covered with tattoos . . . *this* was Storm. This was the man she loved. He had walked out on her and broken her heart, but now he was back. And he still loved her.

Oh, God, all the love she'd felt for him . . . that she'd kept locked up inside her . . . came flooding back.

He must have sensed her surrender because he strode to her and pulled her into his arms. His lips meshed with hers and she knew she was lost.

The overwhelming passion of his kiss broke down the last of her defenses. Tears welled in her eyes as she clung to him.

"I was devastated when you left."

He gazed down at her. "I'm so sorry, baby." He wiped away her tears with a soft stroke of his thumb. "When I was out on the road, doing what I'd wanted to do all my life, all I could think of was you,"—he brushed her eyelids softly with his lips—"and what an idiot I'd been to leave you. I knew I had to make it up to you. To find you and explain everything. To convince you that we have a future together."

His lips found hers again for a sweet, tender kiss.

"When I left my life behind a year ago, I knew I was searching for something." He cupped her face and tipped it up. "I just didn't realize it was you."

The glow of warmth in his eyes, paired with intense longing, filled her with joy. Storm was back, and she was in his arms, being loved by him. She stroked his cheek, loving the slightly raspy feel under her fingertips. So masculine. So Storm.

"Oh, God, I've missed you," she murmured.

The world tipped sideways as he swept her into his arms and carried her across the room and into his bedroom. He set her on her feet, stepped back, and unfastened his pants, then pulled down the zipper. She watched, holding her breath, as he dropped his pants to the floor, then his boxers, revealing his long, hard, and oh-so-familiar cock.

He walked toward her, magnificent in his unabashed nakedness, and she reached for his thick shaft, longing to feel it again. To taste it. But he captured her hand and pressed it to his mouth. The delicate brush of his lips against her palm made her insides flutter.

"No, sweetheart. First you."

He nuzzled her neck, then she felt his fingers on her top

button. It released, then he moved to the next. Then the next. He gazed at her chest, a simmering heat in his eyes, as he continued to open her blouse, then he drew it wide and smiled.

"Beautiful."

She shrugged off her blazer, letting it fall to the floor, then he pushed her blouse from her shoulders. It fluttered to the ground, landing atop her jacket. She reached around behind her and unfastened her skirt. He smiled and drew it down her hips, slowly, then let it drop to the floor.

His smile turned to a broad grin as he stared at her garter belt. "Very sexy."

Guilt swept through her, since she wore the garter belt because of Dane's command, but Storm seemed too caught up in their current situation to think about that. Because if he did think about it, he would realize she'd worn it for Dane.

He scooped her up, then set her on the edge of the bed, and knelt in front of her. The feel of his fingertips grazing her feet as he slipped off her pumps sent quivers along her skin.

Then he cupped her head and drew her toward him for a deep, passionate kiss. His lips, so warm and firm on hers, sent her heart racing. She stroked her fingers through his dark hair, shorter than it had been before, as his mouth lingered on hers, then his tongue dipped inside. When he finally released her lips, she drew in a deep breath.

His hands glided down her shoulders. He leaned forward and nuzzled her neck. She drew in a slow breath as his mouth continued downward, then she felt the brush of his lips on the swell of her breast. His hands skimmed along her sides and she longed for him to pull down the cups of her bra to reveal her swelling nipples. As if reading her mind, he reached behind her and found the hooks, then unfastened them. The elastic of her bra released and he peeled the lacy garment from her.

He leaned back, gazing at her naked breasts with deep admiration in his eyes. The nipples hardened, peaking forward as if reaching out to him. Begging him to touch them. And he did. Lightly, he caressed her swollen, aching breasts, then ran his fingertips over her nipples reverently.

"I've missed your beautiful breasts."

She sucked in air as he lightly stroked her hard nubs.

He smiled. "I've missed how you react to my touch."

He leaned forward and his mouth covered one nipple. She grasped his head and held him to her as his tongue laved over her sensitive nub, then he suckled and she thought she'd faint from sheer pleasure.

He continued to suck and she moaned as her whole body quivered.

"Oh, Storm, I've missed you."

He gazed up at her, his eyes aglow with deep emotion. "You don't know how much it means to me to hear you say that."

He dipped his head and sucked deeply, sending her blood boiling. He eased her back onto the bed and caressed her breasts, stroking and squeezing as he lapped and suckled her nipples. She arched against him. A deep craving built within her.

She took his hand and glided it down her belly. "Please, Storm. I need you."

He chuckled and eased back, admiring her. He tucked his fingers under the elastic of her thong and slid it down. His gazed locked on her shaven folds as he stripped off the bit of satin and lace.

She opened her legs as he leaned toward her again, her insides quivering in anticipation. At the first touch of his lips on her sensitive inner thigh, she arched, but he merely teased her flesh, kissing lightly, then circling upward, past her aching, hot flesh, to her navel. He dipped his tongue inside and swirled. Then slowly . . . torturously slowly . . . he drifted down, nearing her throbbing sex.

When his mouth finally touched her intimate flesh, she moaned. He licked the length of her, his tongue gliding along her slick folds. She coiled her fingers in his hair, clutching his head to her. His chuckle rumbled through her.

Then he found her clit. His tongue nudged it, then swirled over it. Heat radiated from that one point, spreading wider and wider in an expanding well of joy. Her head fell back on the bed, her fingers loosening from his hair as she stroked his head absently, allowing his expert attention to sweep her away.

Fingers found her opening and slipped inside. One. Then two. He surged inside her as his tongue lavished her sensitive bud with rapt attention. She tightened inside, squeezing his welcome fingers, drawing them deeper. They thrust in and out as his tongue teased her clit.

"Yes. I'm so close."

He chuckled again, then sucked. Pleasure spiraled through her.

"Oh, Storm," she moaned. "You're making me come."

"Mmm. I like hearing that." His tongue swirled on her bud and his fingers thrust in and out.

She gasped, then plummeted over the edge. He stroked and licked as she rode the wave of bliss.

As she caught her breath, he smiled and reached up, pushing the hair from her face, then he sat on the bed beside her. She sat up and rested her hands flat on his solid chest. She stroked the hard wall of muscle, then slid to the moth tattoo on his shoulder and ran her finger around the outline.

He took her in his arms and kissed her tenderly. She could

taste herself on his lips. Now she wanted to taste him. Her fingers glided down his solid chest, over his rippled abs to the hard shaft pressed against her stomach. She wrapped her fingers around it. It felt like hot marble in her hand and her insides clenched in desire.

She kissed his neck, then trailed her lips down his chest. She licked his hard, beadlike nipple, then continued downward toward her goal. She slid off the bed, pulling him to a sitting position, and knelt in front of him, the dense carpet soft beneath her knees. She drew his cock forward, admiring its length and impressive girth.

She leaned forward and licked the mushroom-shape tip, swirling her tongue underneath, then she glided downward to the base. She tipped her head sideways and dragged her lips the length of his hot, dark red flesh. He twitched in her hand, the veins along the side pulsing with life.

She slid back down and continued past the base to his hairless sacs below, then licked them.

"Oh, baby. You know how I love that."

She smiled. She did know. She knew she could drive him crazy paying attention to his balls. That's why he'd always kept them shaved. To encourage her. She lapped one into her mouth and pressed gently with her tongue.

She released it, then drew the other into her mouth, giving it the same attention. His breathing increased as his excitement mounted. She stroked his big cock with her hand, then glided her lips upward along the shaft. When she reached the tip, she opened wide, taking his cockhead into her mouth. As she moved down, she had to strain her jaw to accommodate his size.

His fingers coiled in her hair as she pushed forward, taking him as deep as she could. She squeezed him, then drew back.

Then she moved forward again. She continued surging forward and back and soon his hand began to guide her to his preferred rhythm. His quick breathing told her that he was close. She caressed his balls with one hand and stroked his long shaft with the other.

"Oh, yeah, baby." Then he jerked forward and hot liquid erupted in her mouth.

She continued to suck until he'd finished, then she licked one last time before she released his deflating shaft.

He dragged her into his arms and kissed her, his tongue delving into her mouth. She sucked on it, eager for more. She desperately wanted this man inside her.

He stood up, taking her with him and sat in the armchair beside the bed. He guided her around to sit on his lap, facing away from him. He tightened his powerful inked arms around her waist and held her tight to him.

"Do you remember our four month anniversary? When you wanted to do something to make the night memorable?"

Of course she remembered. She laughed as his hands stroked up her ribs, then over her breasts. She settled on his cock and glided back, stroking his shaft with her slickness.

"You like it when your own private stripper gives you a lap dance?" she asked, recreating the moment that had driven him absolutely wild.

He groaned. "You bet I do."

She gyrated her hips, feeling his cock harden beneath her. She leaned back against him, allowing his erection to push upward in front of her, then she grasped it with both hands and stroked lovingly. She pushed his now rock-hard cock against her and rocked her pelvis up and down. As it stroked her sensitive flesh, excitement quivered through her, and she longed to feel it caress her intimate passage.

He teased her hard nipples with his fingertips as he nuzzled her neck, sending tingles dancing along her spine.

"Baby, what you're doing feels so good," he murmured against her ear. "You've got me so hard."

"I know, big guy." That's what she'd teasingly called him that night. "And I'm soaking wet for you." She squeezed him in her hands and stroked. "I need it so bad," she murmured in a throaty voice.

Suddenly, he pressed her forward onto her feet, took two steps toward the bed, then leaned her over it. The cool fabric brushed against her nipples as she dropped onto the firm mattress. She turned her head sideways as his hands pushed her legs wide. His cock pressed against her dripping folds and excitement shot through her. The big head nudged, then slowly glided inside.

She drew in a deep breath. "Oh, yes. That feels so good."

His erection caressed her opening as it slid deeper and she moaned at the welcome feel of his invasion.

Once he was fully sheathed, he leaned over her, his chest against her back, and nuzzled her neck.

"I've wanted to be inside you again for so long," he murmured against her ear.

His hands skimmed along her sides and she trembled.

"I've missed this, too," she whispered.

She squeezed him as he drew back and when he slid forward again, she moaned at the exquisite pleasure. He drew back again, then forward.

"That's so good." But she wanted more. She wanted him deeper.

His hands slid under her body and cupped her breasts as he propelled into her again. And again.

She sucked in a breath as he thrust even deeper. "Oh, Storm, yes." Delight flared through her.

He squeezed her breasts tighter as he thrust faster, with long, smooth strokes, driving her pleasure higher and higher.

"God . . . I've . . . missed . . . you . . . so . . . much," she panted as pleasure blossomed within her.

He surged deep on his next thrust and she gasped, then her moan turned guttural as he drove harder and harder, filling her with his impossibly thick shaft.

"I've missed you, too, baby." His lips caressed her temple. "You have no idea how much."

Then he reached around and found her clit, then stroked it lightly.

That did it. She flew over the edge, moaning long and loud.

He nuzzled her neck. "God, I love hearing you come."

Her mind blasted into a state of euphoric bliss, echoes of joy cascading through her.

He thrust again and again as she wailed in ecstasy. Then he groaned and held her tight as his body shuddered against her. Through her haze of expanding pleasure, she felt him erupt inside her, his hot seed spilling deep.

They seemed poised like that for several long moments. Their bodies joined in exquisite bliss. Then he collapsed on top of her, sucking in air in panting breaths.

He rolled onto his back, taking her with him, and she found herself lying on top of him, his arms tight around her. She gazed at the ceiling as they lay sprawled on the bed, their legs dangling over the edge.

"I could fall asleep right here," he murmured, sounding very sated.

"Mmm." She rolled her head sideways and nuzzled his neck. "I have a nice, comfy mattress right here." In actuality, his solid body was all hard muscle, but she didn't mind. He was also warm and his arms curled protectively around her.

He chuckled, then rolled sideways, spilling her onto the bed. He pulled back the covers, then swept her into his arms and placed her on the soft gray sheets, then climbed in behind her. The pillow was soft against her head and his body was hard and solid against her back. With his arms around her, she felt so warm and cozy that she drifted off to sleep.

Jessica awoke to find herself alone in the bed. The comfort of Storm's solid body against her was gone. She bolted to a sitting position, wondering if the wonderful lovemaking with Storm had been a dream, like so many dreams she'd had over the past months.

But she was in his bedroom. His luxurious bedroom. In his king-size bed with satiny-soft gray sheets, surrounded by his solid teak furniture, and a huge window overlooking the city. In his expensive penthouse.

But where was Storm?

The aroma of freshly brewed coffee answered her question. He was probably in the kitchen whipping up a batch of his wonderful blueberry pancakes, or maybe his special bit-of-everything omelet, as he used to call it.

Sunlight shone through the large window. She stood up, grabbing the sheet to wrap around her, and stared through the glass at the glorious view of the city below. Stunning.

She glanced around the room for something to cover herself and saw Storm's white shirt on the chair. He'd shed it in the living room but it was now lying beside her suit and blouse on the armchair beside the bed. She grabbed his shirt and pulled it on. It was like being surrounded by him, with his scent filling her nostrils.

She wrapped her arms around herself in a hug, imagining him holding her. But why imagine, when she could just scoot to the kitchen and have the real thing? She fastened a couple of buttons and headed out the door and into the living room. She turned and sauntered into the kitchen to see Storm standing at the stove, wearing only a pair of boxer briefs that were molded to his perfect body.

All that male skin was a delight to behold.

"Good morning." She walked toward him and ran her hand along his back, feeling the hard muscle beneath her fingertips. She traced the intricate pattern of a tribal tattoo banding one bicep.

He flipped the four pieces of cinnamon swirl French toast he had in the pan, then turned to her. His arms swept around her and he kissed her, leaning her back in a deep dip. His lips moved on hers with a passionate hunger and she slid her tongue into his mouth, tasting coffee. When he returned her to her feet, she was breathless.

"Good morning to you, too." He grinned. "It was an even better evening last night." He gazed down at her body. "My shirt is very becoming on you."

"Thank you." She strolled to the coffeemaker and poured herself a cup. "Can I help with breakfast?"

"No, just sit and I'll bring it out. It's ready anyway."

She sat down in the bright sitting area in the kitchen and sipped her coffee. He had everything set up, with cutlery, napkins, and syrup already on the table. Even fresh flowers.

He placed a plate in front of her and sat down. She breathed in the sweet aroma, then began to eat. Oh, man, she had missed his wonderful cooking. As she sipped her coffee, she noticed the velvet ring box on the table, off to the side. Her chest compressed.

At her frown, Storm glanced at it. He picked it up and carried it to the desk off the side of the kitchen counter and slipped it into the drawer.

"Sorry."

They ate in silence for a few minutes. Then Storm put down his fork and gazed at her.

"So I just have to ask. Is it that you don't like the ring? Or is it just too extravagant?"

"The ring is beautiful. It's just that you sprang the whole proposal on me way too soon."

His eyebrows arched. "Too soon? So that means it's just a matter of time?"

"Um . . . I . . ." Oh, God, what could she say to that? "Storm, I really don't want to be pressured."

He raised his hands. "Okay, I get it. I thought, after last night . . ." He shrugged, trailing off.

Her lips tightened. She didn't want to think about this right now. They'd had a wonderful night together. "I just want to take it a day at a time. No commitments."

He frowned. "Is this about Dane?"

She put down her fork and stared at him, her stomach churning. "I really don't want to do this right now." She pushed her chair back and stood up.

But he grasped her hand. "No, Jess. Don't go. I'm sorry. We'll figure it out as we go. Okay?"

She sighed and sat down. "Okay."

He glanced at his watch. "Actually, I'll have to hurry. The driver is picking me up in twenty minutes."

"To go to the office?" She glanced at the clock on the wall. It was already after eight. "I'd better get cracking myself."

"It's okay. If you want to come in a bit later, it's no problem. I just have a meeting at nine o'clock I can't miss. I can send the driver back for you later."

"Oh, no, I can't just go in late."

He smiled. "You forget. I'm the boss."

Actually, she had forgotten. But now he'd reminded her. He was the boss. The man she knew—Storm—was just a role.

"I'm sorry," she said, "I'm not comfortable going in later. I'm supposed to be there at nine." She wiped her mouth with the napkin and stood up. "I need to shower. Do you need to go first?"

"There are two showers. Go ahead and use the one in my bedroom."

She nodded and walked away, then shot into the bathroom and took the fastest shower of her life. She pulled new clothes out of her suitcase and put on her makeup in record time. She was only a couple minutes late showing up at the front door.

He smiled. "You look beautiful."

"Thank you." She patted her still slightly damp, upswept hair, hoping it wouldn't come tumbling down, given that she'd pinned it in place at lightning speed.

He stood in front of her, in a tailored charcoal suit, the patterned blue tie matching his eyes. He looked so much like Dane. The perfectly attired, wealthy businessman. He strolled toward her, then took her in his arms and kissed her. She couldn't help stiffening in his embrace, and he released her and stepped back. Maybe it was the unfamiliar clothes, or the simple fact that she was still processing his new identity, but it felt odd to be held by him.

"We should be going." He opened the door and gestured for her to precede him out.

Jessica's heartbeat matched the blinking of the floors as the elevator carried her and Rafe up to the executive offices. The elevator doors opened and Rafe stepped out ahead of her.

"Rafe. Good morning." Melanie's eyes lit up at the sight of him.

"Good morning, Melanie. When Mr. Genese gets here, tell him to come right in."

"Of course." Then Melanie saw her. "Jessica." Her smile faded and her eyes lost their light.

Arriving at the same time had been a really stupid idea. Had Rafe thought of that when he'd suggested she come in a little later? No one would have thought anything of that given she'd just returned from Chicago.

Rafe had glanced at them before entering his office and noticed her expression. He smiled. "Don't worry, Jess. Melanie knows all about us. I told her our history."

Her gaze shot to Melanie and she didn't know if she imagined the accusation in her eyes or not. Her fingers found the worry stone in her pocket and stroked the smooth surface.

She wanted to take Melanie aside so she could talk to her. She didn't want to lose her friendship. She had to make this right somehow.

"Jess, since Dane is still out of town, why don't you join me in the meeting. You can take notes and update him when he gets back."

"Of course, Mr. Ranier."

He grinned. "You are not going to call me Mr. Ranier. Melanie calls me by my first name. You should, too."

"Yes . . . Rafe." It didn't even occur to her to call him Storm, since that's not who this man was.

But the name Rafe did not roll off her tongue and it must have sounded awkward to him. He glanced at her sharply and his gaze locked on her. Then he frowned.

She quickly strode to her office and put away her things, then grabbed her notepad and pen. She glanced up to see Melanie standing at her door.

"Here's the file for the meeting." Her expression was cool and her voice emotionless.

"Thanks, Melanie." She stepped across the room and took the file. "Look, I—"

"You should get in there. He's waiting for you."

Jessica pursed her lips and nodded.

Rafe's style at the meeting was different than Dane's. He was warmer, a little friendlier, and asked more questions, as opposed to Dane's no-nonsense, move-it-along style but, like his brother, he was exceedingly confident and very much in control.

After the meeting, he told her she'd done a great job, even though all she'd done was stay out of the way and take notes. After that, she'd left his office to leave him to his work.

She went back to her own office and dropped off her notebook, then walked to Melanie's desk.

"Melanie, here's the folder back."

Melanie was Rafe's secretary and would file it for him. Melanie just nodded and continued typing.

Jessica drew in a deep breath. "Can we get coffee together? I'd really like to talk."

Melanie's fingers stopped moving and her gaze turned to Jessica. Sparks of anger danced in her eyes.

"Melanie, you're my friend and I want it to stay that way. Please, can we talk about this?"

Melanie shrugged, then nodded. "I guess I could use a cup of coffee." She grabbed the phone and called for someone to take over answering her incoming calls, then she retrieved her purse from her desk drawer and stood up.

As they got on the elevator, Melanie said, "It's a nice day. Why don't we go down to the courtyard?"

A few minutes later, they stepped out the lobby door into the warm morning air and picked up a coffee at the coffee shop on the corner, then went down the steps to the courtyard next to the building and sat on one of the benches overlooking the large pots of brightly colored flowers.

Jessica turned to Melanie. "I'm really sorry things turned out like this. What did Rafe tell you about us?"

Melanie shrugged. "That he met you in Bakersfield. So I know he's your ex." She caught Jessica's gaze. "He's the man who broke your heart."

"That's true. And now he's back."

"And you slept with him last night." At Jessica's guilty expression, Melanie continued. "I made the arrangements for your trip home and I knew Rafe decided to pick you up. Then you didn't come back to the apartment last night and you both show up here together."

"Melanie, I know you have feelings for him. I would never have gotten involved with him in the first place if—"

"I know." Melanie stared at the coffee cup in her hand. "You were involved with him long before you met me. I get it. I'm sorry, it's just hard, that's all. You're one of my best friends and you're sleeping with the man I've wanted for such a long time. It just doesn't seem fair." She tipped her head sideways. "You do remember the part about him breaking your heart, right?"

Jessica's lips compressed. "How could I forget?"

Then, to her surprise, Melanie smiled.

"You know what's really not fair?"

"What?" Jessica asked.

"That you have not only one, but two Ranier men who want you. I'd kill for just Rafe. So what about Mr. Ranier? I mean Dane?"

Jessica sighed. "It's pretty clear he wants it to end between us. He doesn't want to do anything to ruin his relationship with his brother."

Melanie nodded. "He has missed Rafe. He's changing the business in ways that Rafe had suggested in the past." She toyed with the lid on her coffee cup. "So are you going back to Rafe?"

Jessica sucked in a breath, debating whether she should tell Melanie about yesterday. Then she decided secrets would only be a threat to their friendship.

"Actually, Rafe proposed to me."

Melanie's fingers tightened on her cup. "Oh. I see." She glanced at Jessica's left hand. "Are you holding off on wearing the ring until you have a chance to talk to Dane?"

Jessica shook her head. "I didn't accept."

Her friend's eyes widened. "What? Are you crazy? How could you possibly turn down Rafe? He's handsome, kind, sexy, rich, and . . . did I mention sexy?"

Jessica grinned. "So now you're trying to talk me into marrying him? I thought you wanted him for yourself."

"Yeah, that would be nice. But let's face it, he's my boss and it's obvious he just doesn't see me that way. I'm not going to cross the line and embarrass myself and risk my job for a guy who doesn't even notice me. It's different for you. You met him before you started working for this company. Same with Mr. Ranier. Although I admit I don't really get what you're doing with Mr. Ranier. The just physical thing, I mean. But you lived with Rafe. You're in love with him."

"Yeah, I'm in love with him," Jessica echoed.

"You don't sound very convincing."

"I know. I'm just . . . confused. Rafe is not the same as Storm. Storm was a free-spirited guy who played guitar for a local rock band. Rafe is a suave, rich business tycoon."

"But he's still the same guy."

Jessica sipped her coffee. "I'm not sure that's true. Even if it is, I'll have to get used to the differences. Get to know him all over again."

Melanie covered Jessica's hand with hers. "Whatever those differences are, it's worth getting past them. Rafe is a wonderful guy. Don't let him slip away."

Jessica shook her head. "How do you do that? Here I am, with the man you want, but you're taking it all in stride and actually trying to talk me into marrying him."

Melanie bit her lip. "I'd be lying if I told you I wasn't jealous. But it's clear that he doesn't want me, and,"—she gazed at Jessica—"when Rafe told me about the two of you . . . when he looked at me with those gorgeous blue eyes of his while he talked about what the two of you had . . . I could see he's in love with you." She sighed, her green eyes turning misty. "I just want to see him happy." She patted Jessica's hand. "You, too."

Jessica squeezed Melanie's fingers. "You're a good friend, Melanie. To me, and to Rafe. Thank you."

Melanie nodded. "Sure. Now, tell me about the ring. Was it gorgeous?"

Jessica smiled. "I have to admit, it was stunning. It was the shape of a moth outlined in diamonds."

"Oh, my God, that man is so romantic."

That evening, Jessica turned Rafe down when he asked her to join him for dinner, telling him she needed a little space. She needed him not to rush her. Even when Melanie invited her to go out with friends, she declined. A quiet Friday night at home was just what she needed.

As she sat relaxing on the couch, watching an old sitcom on TV, the phone rang and she picked it up.

"Jessica, it's Dane. Can you meet me for a drink?"

Her heart thumped loudly. She knew he'd had meetings all day today in Chicago. He must have just returned from the airport.

She didn't want to deal with this right now, but how could she turn down her boss?

"Um . . . It's getting late. By the time I get a cab and—"

"I'm downstairs in the limo."

Damn.

"I'm not really dressed to go out."

"I'm sure you look fine. Jessica, I really need to talk to you."

She sighed. "Fine."

But it just didn't seem appropriate meeting a man who was in an expensive suit and riding in a limo while she was wearing jeans and a T-shirt. He might call the shots in the office, but this was her decision.

"But if I'm meeting you, then I'm changing first."

"Fine. Whatever you want. I'll wait."

She hung up the phone and headed to her bedroom, marveling that a powerful man like Mr. Dane Ranier had acquiesced to her demand, however small.

A few moments later, she rode the elevator downstairs, wearing a simple black dress with high heels and a gold locket around her neck. She'd pulled on a light black sweater for warmth, since the spring evenings were still cool.

As she walked out onto the street, the first thing she saw was the long black limousine parked in front of her building. Dane stood beside it, looking devastatingly handsome in his usual tailored suit, this one a light gray.

"Jessica. There you are." He opened the door and she climbed into the car. He settled in beside her.

The warmth of his body next to hers, and his strong, dominating presence, threw her off balance. Even though she'd slept with his brother less than twenty-four hours before, she could easily fall into Dane's arms and have hot, sweaty sex with him right now. Her attraction to the man was just that strong.

"How was your flight from Chicago?" she asked, hoping mundane conversation would keep her urges at bay.

"Fine," he said curtly.

She frowned, wondering if he was angry at her.

A dismal thought occurred to her. Could he be taking her out to fire her?

Certainly having her in the office under the current circumstances would make things awkward, but . . . she really didn't want to lose this job.

She could understand why he'd want to be rid of her, though. Her being around was putting a strain on his relationship with his brother. And after the last night she and Dane had spent together, things would be awkward between them, too.

"Are you going to fire me?" she asked, her fingers stroking the smooth stone in her sweater pocket.

His eyebrows rose. "Of course not. Why would you think that?"

She pursed her lips. "Well, you don't seem very happy with me. You sent me home in the middle of the business trip. And having me around now that your brother's back isn't really conducive to a comfortable work environment." Not only for Dane, but for Rafe, and Melanie, too. "And,"—she stared at her hands—"you seemed pretty uncomfortable around me after what happened between us in Chicago."

"And what do you believe happened in Chicago?"

Her gaze darted to his. "You tell me."

She believed he'd shown real feelings for her, and she definitely felt something deeper for him. Maybe even . . . love. But she'd be damned if she'd admit that first.

But his stony gaze told her nothing.

The limo pulled up to the entrance of the Ritz-Carlton and stopped in front of the door.

"Shall I leave the luggage with the concierge, Mr. Ranier?" asked the driver, "or send it up now?"

"The concierge. I'll call for it later."

A doorman hurried forward and opened the car door for her. She stepped out of the vehicle, followed by Dane.

"Good evening, Mr. Ranier," the doorman said.

"Good evening, Andre."

Andre opened the door for them and she stepped into a large lobby of glass and marble with a large red carpet over a dark tile floor, tall plants and a sitting area with off-white leather furniture. Dane led her to an elevator and they stepped inside.

"Why are you having your luggage sent in?" she asked. "Aren't you going home?"

"This is home. The Ritz-Carlton offers private residences as well as hotel rooms. I find it convenient."

"I guess you don't have to worry about hiring staff to cook and clean."

"True," he said as the elevator doors opened.

They walked down a hallway and he stopped at the first wooden door, then unlocked it. She stepped into a large apartment, easily bigger than Rafe's generously sized place. She could see the lights of the city beyond the large, wall-to-wall windows.

"This way." He gestured toward a couch and chairs overlooking the view.

She sat down in an easy chair, facing the couch.

"I called ahead to have a pitcher of white wine sangria sent up. If there's something else you'd rather have, I can call down for it."

"No, that will be fine, thanks."

He walked to a table along the wall where a frosty pitcher and two tall stemmed glasses stood. He filled them both, then handed her one and sat down on the couch.

"We were talking about what happened in Chicago." He sipped his drink then set it on the oval glass coffee table in front of them.

"Yes, we were." She sat, tight-lipped, waiting for his next move.

"Jessica, I'm sorry I sent you home early. As soon as I did it, I regretted it."

Her eyebrows arched. "Why?"

"Because I missed you. Because I wanted you with me." He sighed and locked gazes with her. "Because something special did happen that night, and it scared the hell out of me. Even if I hadn't found out Rafe was the man you'd fallen in love with, it would have been difficult. You've said all along that all you wanted was a physical relationship. And I agreed to that. But with Rafe in the picture . . ." He shrugged. "I didn't want a woman to come between us again. So I sent you back, knowing I was sending you back to Rafe."

She gripped her glass tightly. She'd already figured all this out and she was sure this wasn't the only reason Dane had called her tonight, so where was this going? Did he simply want to make it official that they would no longer be lovers?

"But after you left," he continued, "I realized that as much as I value my brother's happiness . . ." He gazed at her, his expression solemn. "Mine is important, too."

Her chest tightened.

"So I need to ask you a question."

She stared at him, breath held.

"Are you in love with Rafe?"

She put down her drink and stood up, then paced across the room. "That's not an easy question to answer."

"It should be."

She glanced toward him. "I loved Storm."

"Storm and Rafe are the same person."

"That's not exactly true. As Storm, he was this free-and-easy guitar player with tattoos and a motorcycle, but now he wears a business suit and helps run a major corporation. I feel like the man I was in love with didn't actually exist, and I'm still struggling to make sense of this new version of him and trying to make it fit with everything I thought I knew."

"I'm sure you'll adjust to the change. He can still play the guitar, and I'm sure his tattoos haven't gone anywhere." He stood up and stepped toward her. "You know, you're just kidding yourself if you think the difference in lifestyle makes him a different person. Rafe has always been free and easy. At least, as much as our father would allow. That's why he broke away from all this." He glanced around the room. "In his heart, I'm certain that he's the exact same person you came to know as Storm. In fact, you probably got to know the real Rafe better than anyone ever has because with you he was being who he truly wanted to be."

"So you're saying that if I don't love him as Rafe, I never really loved him as Storm."

He shrugged. "I can't know that. Maybe you do love him, but you're still running scared. He walked out on you once, maybe he'll do it again. You don't want to be hurt. That's why you insisted things be only physical between us. I understood that."

Oh, God. She didn't know how she felt about Rafe, but if she told Dane that, he might pursue her. A part of her was over the moon about that, but another part was scared stiff. She didn't know what she felt. For either man.

"Rafe proposed," she blurted.

His gaze darted to her left hand. "Did you accept?"

She folded her hands together, conscious of her naked ring finger. "No." At his smile, she added quickly, "He sprang it on me too fast. I need time to get used to the idea. I need time to—"

But he had closed the distance between them and pulled her into his arms. Her words were stopped by his tongue sliding into her mouth. Then his arms tightened around her and his lips moved on hers with passionate persuasion until she melted against him.

At the sound of the door opening and closing, she jerked back, her gaze darting to the intruder.

"Rafe, what the hell are you doing here?" Dane demanded.

Frowning, Rafe stepped toward them, his gaze shifting from her heated cheeks to Dane's intense gaze.

"I asked Andre to let me know when you arrived, because I wanted to come by and talk. There are some things we need to sort out. When he told me there was a young woman with you who matched the description of Jess, I decided I'd better rush right over."

His accusing gaze fell on Jessica and her back stiffened.

"Did she tell you I proposed?" Rafe asked.

"Yes," Dane responded. "She also told me she turned you down."

Her stomach tightened as they talked about her as if she wasn't even there.

"And did she tell you that afterward she spent the night?"

Dane's gaze shot to her in surprise.

Anger burst through her and her hands balled into fists. "That's right. I slept with both of you. This is a very confusing and emotional situation for me and I'm dealing with it as best I can. But I haven't lied about anything I've done, and I haven't agreed to a commitment with either one of you." She placed her hands on her hips. "And maybe I like it that way. It's not like you own me. Maybe I'll keep on sleeping with both of you." She glared at them. "If either one of you wants to stop, just say the word."

At their open-mouthed stares, she spun on her heels and headed for the elevator. She jabbed the Close button several times as they watched, stunned. Finally, the doors closed and she slumped against the side of the elevator as it began its descent.

At the knock on the door, Jessica put down the magazine she'd been reading and stood up. She'd been out late with Melanie yesterday and was now spending a quiet Sunday afternoon at home while Melanie was out shopping.

She pulled open the door and her heart skipped a beat when she saw Rafe standing there. He was the image of Storm, gut-wrenchingly handsome in his jeans and leather jacket.

"What are you doing here?" she asked. Thank heavens Melanie wasn't here. That would make this even more awkward.

"May I come in?" he asked.

"Um . . . yeah, sure." She stepped aside to let him enter.

He shrugged off his jacket and hung it on the coat tree inside the door. His black T-shirt hugged his broad chest snugly and tattoos flowed past his sleeves down his biceps. Reluctantly, she tore her gaze from his big, masculine body.

"Can I get you anything? I have coffee on."

"No, thanks." He sat down on the couch, right where she'd been sitting.

She sat down in the armchair.

"After you left Dane's place Friday night," he said, "I thought you could use a little time to cool off, so I waited until today to come by."

She nodded. "I guess I went a little off the deep end."

He leaned forward, resting his arms on his knees. "It's all right. You had a right to be upset. Dane and I were acting like kids fighting over a toy."

Her fingers curled tightly. "I don't want to be the cause of dissension between you. I know Dane missed you terribly when you were gone, and he's tried to change things in the company in ways that would make you proud. He's developing green technologies, he's looking into programs to improve employee health benefits, and—"

"I know. I've been brought up-to-date on those things by Melanie. Dane has done some outstanding things and I'm pleased to see it. That doesn't change the problem between the three of us, though."

He reached out and took her hand. The feel of his fingers around hers sent sparks dancing along her skin.

"Jess, I love you. And if your feelings for Dane interfere with that, there's going to be tension between him and me. There's nothing we can do about that."

"I guess. But I don't want you to blame him. Not like with your prom date."

Rafe's eyebrows arched. "He told you about that?"

She nodded. "It was before we knew you and Storm were the same person. We were just getting to know each other. I was telling him about my ex—you—and he told me about his brother."

"Why would you tell him about me?"

She glanced at him. "Actually, you were the reason we met. I was eating breakfast at a restaurant before going to the career fair and I saw him outside. At first, I thought he was you."

"Did you just walk up to him?"

She smiled. "I followed him into Starbucks and walked over to him, then got embarrassed when I realized my mistake."

"And he used that excuse to pick you up?"

"No, I left, but then he saw me standing in the rain trying to get a cab and he offered me a ride."

"So he became the knight in shining armor."

"Well, he got me to the job fair, and gave me some helpful advice along the way." She pulled out the worry stone from her pocket. "He also gave me this. It helped me to stay focused and calm at the career fair. I was a bit of a wreck having to cope with all the stress, but his advice helped."

He took the stone from her hand and stared at it. "My brother had a worry stone? That's hard to believe."

She nodded. "He was carrying it in his pocket." She gazed at the stone as his thumb stroked its smooth surface. "In fact, he told me he'd actually gotten it for you, but you'd left and he didn't get a chance to give it to you. He said he wanted to show you that he respected your beliefs, even though they are different from his."

"Really?" He looked at the stone with renewed interest.

"I think you should keep it."

He glanced at her. "You sure?"

"Of course. I think it's an important gesture on his part." She shrugged. "And I can always get another one."

"Thanks." He placed the stone in his jeans pocket. "So what did you tell him about me?"

She glanced down at her hands. "I told him about when you left, and how devastated I was." The pain still resonated inside her.

"He probably thought I was a jerk."

She didn't say anything.

"It's okay. I was a jerk. I never should have left. But it was the best I could do at the time." He took her hand in his. "You know I never meant to lie to you. I was just being who I wanted to be. Leaving my old identity behind. But when I met you, it became a lie and I didn't want to keep lying to you."

Her insides ached. "You could have told me the truth."

He nodded. "I know I made some major mistakes and totally screwed things up between us." His lips compressed. "But I know that now, and it made me realize how much I need you in my life."

He stood up and walked to the coat tree and reached in his jacket pocket, then returned with a small gift box. He handed it to her.

She gazed at him warily as she took it. "I hope this isn't another ring."

He chuckled. "God, no. I learned my lesson on that one. When . . ." He hesitated, his gaze locking on her, and he turned serious again. "If you finally say yes, we'll pick out the ring together."

A lump formed in her throat. She wanted to tell him the moth ring was perfect. It was so beautiful, both in form and concept, but its dazzling beauty and high price had emphasized the difference between the Storm she thought she'd known, and Rafe. But she loved the ring and everything it said about him.

He gestured toward the gift box still in her hand. "I wanted to get you something special, but this time I kept it simple. Open it."

She pulled on the thin, curled ribbon and the simple bow pulled loose. She tore away the gift wrap and revealed a small box inside. She opened it and amidst some pink, glittery tissue paper was a bottle of nail polish. She lifted the small, cylindrical bottle from the wrapping. It was white with small black speckles.

"Look at the name." He pointed to the side of the bottle and in tiny gold letters it said *Leopard Moth*.

She grinned at him. "You're kidding. How did you find it?"

He shrugged. "I had a little help from Melanie."

Of course. And the fact that Melanie had helped him . . . maybe that meant she was really okay with Rafe and her being together.

"This is very nice. It looks like a designer brand."

"No, that's the thing. It's a kind you get in a drugstore."

She stared at the brand name—Accessorize—which she didn't recognize. "I've never seen this brand, and believe me, I've been shopping enough with Melanie to know them all."

He smiled sheepishly. "Okay. The drugstore is in England, but it's just an inexpensive bottle of nail lacquer, as they call it. Melanie saw it on one of the blogs she follows and she thought it would be a perfect gift for you."

"And it probably cost you ten times the price in shipping."

"Don't blow it out of proportion. It's no big deal." He took her hand again and squeezed. "It's just a token, Jess. Please don't turn it down. Even with shipping it was far less than the ring."

She smiled. "It would have to be, wouldn't it?"

"And if it makes you feel better, I also got Melanie the whole collection of those speckled polishes to thank her for listening to me ramble on about my love life and offering a woman's perspective, so you see, your bottle just hitched a ride with her gift."

She laughed and then gazed at the bottle, admiring it. "I love it. It was very thoughtful of you. Thank you."

He was so sweet, getting Melanie some of the polishes, too. She'd be thrilled at getting the exotic polishes, for sure, but the fact they came from Rafe meant that she would treasure them even more. And it made her feel good to know that Rafe had confided in Melanie about everything going on between them. Jessica still worried that her friend's feeling were hurt, but knowing that she and Rafe were strengthening their friendship was a good sign that Melanie had moved on.

She squeezed his hand and they both stood up.

"I'd better get going." But he didn't turn to leave.

She stepped close to him and put her hands on his shoulders, raising her lips to his in invitation. He swooped down and kissed her, his mouth moving on hers with passion. She melted against him, loving the feel of his big, hard body against hers, and the feel of his strong arms around her. His tongue danced with hers and her hormones spiked. His hands gripped her hips and he pulled her tight to him. A hard bulge pressed against her and she drew back.

"Rafe, I can't." There was no way she wanted to wind up with him in her bed. Not here. It would be awkward, and totally unfair to Melanie, if she had to skulk out of her bedroom with Rafe in tow.

He nodded. "I know. I didn't mean to pressure you." He stroked her hair behind her ear. "Would you like to go for dinner?"

"No. Not tonight." She knew dinner would lead to sleeping together, and she still needed to figure things out.

"Okay." He walked to the entrance and pulled on his leather jacket, but he didn't turn to leave.

"Jess, I know you need time and I'm willing to wait, but . . ."

The silence that fell between them made her heart ache. "But what?"

"I need to know. What are your feelings for my brother?"

"Oh, Rafe." How could she tell him when she wasn't even sure herself?

"You said it was just a physical relationship, but that's not you. I can't imagine you giving yourself to a man if you don't feel something for him." He took her hand and pressed it to his mouth. The sweet brush of his lips sent tingles dancing along her arm.

"I won't ask if you love him, but do you have feelings for him?"

She dragged her gaze away from him. "I never meant for it to happen. I just wanted something physical to keep my mind off my pain at losing you."

"Ah, fuck."

"I'd come from a small town to a big city. Everything was new and different. And a little overwhelming. Your brother helped me feel like I belong here."

He gripped her hand. "Just tell me. Do I still have a chance with you?"

She sighed and gazed straight into his sky blue eyes. "I don't know what to say. I'm really not sure what I feel about either of you right now. I just know you're both very important to me." She frowned. "I wish I didn't have to choose."

He tugged her into his arms and his mouth devoured hers, his arms so tight around her she could barely catch her breath.

As his tongue dove into her and caressed with sweet strokes, thoughts of his hands roaming over her body, his lips exploring her most intimate places washed through her. If this kept on, she'd be dragging him back to her bedroom post haste.

But then he released her and turned to the door. As he shut it behind him, she stood staring at it, sucking in air.

Oh, God, how would she cope at the office tomorrow?

The next few days at work weren't as bad as she'd feared. She'd barely spent any time alone with Dane and he kept everything on a business level. Rafe was out of the office most of the time at meetings.

Things between her and Melanie were back to normal. When Melanie had arrived home on Sunday night, Jessica showed her the nail polish Rafe had given her, and thanked Melanie for her part in it. Melanie had hugged her and then insisted that Jessica put on the polish right away.

She glanced at the trendy, speckled polish on her fingernails and smiled. Last night, Melanie had insisted on touching up her manicure with black tips which, paired with the white polish with black speckles, gave her nails an edgy, designer look. She even added a pearl accent on each tip. It was funny that Melanie would insist on such a dramatic look for Jessica in the office, when she would only wear subtle, neutral tones herself.

Melanie's plain Jane office attire was such a contrast to the bright colors and trendy clothing that she wore on her off time. She seemed to have a real need to conform when she was at the office. And rules meant everything to her.

Jessica remembered how she used to be before she'd met Storm. She'd been far more uptight back then, but her heated relationship with the badass musician had freed something inside her, and she hoped Melanie would learn to loosen up someday. Life was too short to play by other people's rules.

"Fancy manicure. Melanie's doing?"

She glanced up at Dane's voice and nodded. He looked spectacular standing there in her doorway. His tailored charcoal suit accentuated his broad shoulders, and the hint of a shadow on his square jaw enhanced his natural masculinity.

"Do you need me?" she asked.

His lips turned up in a smile and he stepped into her office. "Now there's an understatement."

Her eyes widened at the unexpected sexual innuendo. Her body heated as she thought about him calling her into his office, then closing the door and commanding her to strip down to nothing.

There was no doubt about it, spending the past several nights alone after the constant attention of two sexy men had left her more than a little hot and bothered. She wanted nothing more than to race into his office and be dominated by him, his deep voice commanding her to do dirty, sexy things to him, then his hard body satisfying the deep craving within her.

Oh, God, why had Storm turned out to be Dane's brother? And why had he returned and complicated things so dramatically?

"Don't worry, I'm not going to suggest we do anything about it. Right now. But I would like you to come to my place after work. We need to talk."

Jessica stepped out of the limousine and walked toward the entrance of the Ritz-Carlton. A doorman opened the door for her.

"Mr. Ranier will be down in a moment. You can wait in the lobby." He gestured to a sitting area with an off-white leather sofa and chairs and a square, light wood coffee table.

"No need. I'm here."

Dane stepped toward her, smiling. She followed him to the elevator and soon they were entering his luxurious apartment. She crossed the elegant living room to the couch and sat down. He poured a glass of white wine and handed it to her, then sat across from her.

"So you said we need to talk," she began, holding the tall stem glass in her hand.

She wasn't sure how he intended to tackle the issues between the three of them, but he was a problem solver and always took charge. He must have something in mind.

"That's right. The current situation is intolerable. I don't want to compete for you, especially with my brother."

Did this mean he was giving up on her? But his gaze drifted down her body and she shivered at the possessive look in his eye.

"We need to find a way to satisfy everyone involved."

At the sight of his heated gaze, images flashed through her brain of him dragging her into his arms to satisfy his needs.

"And how do we do that?" she asked.

"You said the other day that neither of us owns you."

She frowned, wondering where he was going with this. "Right."

"That's not entirely true."

Her eyebrows arched. "What do you mean?"

He walked to the executive leather chair he had by a cherry wood desk in the corner and turned it to face her, then sat down. "Come over here."

At his authoritative tone, she immediately stood up, set her glass on the table and walked toward him.

"Stand in front of me."

She stood three feet in front of him, his sharp gaze gliding the length of her body, sending heat humming through her.

"If I order you to do something, you'll do it, correct?"

At his firm, demanding tone, she nodded.

"Yes, sir."

"So in a way, I am your master." He smiled. "So I own you."

"That's not really true, I—"

"Silence."

She shivered. If he wanted it, he had full control over her. She knew it. And he knew it.

It would be a scary thought if she didn't trust him as much as she did, but in reality he always put her pleasure first, so it was an extreme turn-on. Desire washed through her and she longed for him to order her to kneel in front of him and unzip his pants and then tell her to draw out his big, swollen cock, proof that the situation turned him on just as much as it did her.

"Now, unbutton your blouse and step closer."

"Yes, Mr. Ranier." She unfastened the buttons quickly as she stepped toward him.

He drew her blouse apart and his gaze fastened on her lacy bra. His finger stroked over the swell of her breasts and tingles danced across her flesh.

"Now I want you to go into the bedroom and put this on."

He picked up a black bag from his desk and drew out a thin black leather strap with silver studs. He held it up and she realized it was actually a harness with silver chains dangling from it. And it would cover absolutely nothing. He handed it to her and then pulled a couple scraps of black leather from the bag. "Put these on, too."

She took them. A black leather bra and skimpy panties. She walked to the bedroom, anticipation quivering through her. With one command from Dane, this had gone from being a discussion to a sexual tryst. She should think of Rafe and stop this right now, but she didn't want to. She wanted to be with Dane. To feel his hands on her. She wanted to touch his body. To watch him come, knowing it was his desire for her that gave him so much pleasure.

Quickly, she stripped off her clothes and pulled on the bra and panties, then arranged the harness on her body. The straps surrounded her breasts and the chains cascaded in rows down the front of her midriff. She turned her back to the mirror and glanced around at her reflection. From the back, she might as well be naked.

She walked into the living room again, loving the heat in Dane's eyes as he watched her walk toward him.

"Over to the pillars." He pointed toward the dining room.

There were two architectural columns framing the large opening between the living room and dining room. He had wrapped two leather straps, with chains attached, around each column. He fastened a leather band around each of her wrists, then fastened the chain from the column to the ring on one wrist band with a carabiner clip. He took her other arm and drew it sideways until her arms were stretched apart, then fastened her other wrist in the same manner.

He did the same with her ankles, drawing her legs apart as he fastened the chains.

He stepped back and smiled as he admired his work. She stood spread-eagled in front of him and her core ached with need. Soon he would touch her and as soon as he did, she would go up in flames.

"There was another thing you said the other night. Do you remember?"

It was hard to think with his hot, blue gaze gliding up and down her body.

"I'm not sure."

"You said that maybe you'd continue sleeping with both Rafe and me. Did you mean it?"

Oh, God. "I don't know. I said it because I was angry. And I don't want to choose between the two of you."

He stepped close. She could feel his heat behind her and his breath on her ear.

"Tell me. Wouldn't you find it exciting if both Rafe and I made love to you at the same time?"

She hadn't meant at the same time, but his words elicited enticing images of both Dane and Rafe caressing her body. Their hands gliding over her naked flesh. Their lips nuzzling private, intimate places.

Her breathing accelerated.

His cheek brushed her temple and she shivered.

"So,"—he murmured softly in her ear, his breath sending wisps of hair caressing her cheek—"the question is, if you had the opportunity . . ." his lips brushed her neck and she sucked in a breath. "Would you have sex with both of us at the same time?"

"This is crazy. There's no way Rafe would agree to that."

"But Storm would." At the sound of Rafe's voice, her gaze shot across the room to where he stood watching her, his gaze unreadable.

Forever

Jessica sucked in a breath as she stared at Storm leaning against the doorway, exceptionally sexy in jeans and a T-shirt stretched across his broad chest, his tattoos spilling from the sleeves. Was he really here for a threesome with her and Dane? Or had Storm just walked in on them and she hadn't really understood his words?

"What are you doing here?" she asked breathlessly, intensely aware of her skimpy, leather attire, and Dane's hard body close behind her.

Storm pushed away from the doorframe and stepped toward her.

"I thought I'd made that clear." At his deep, edgy tone, shivers danced along her spine. "I'm here to bring your deepest fantasy to life."

Oh, God. Images from the past fluttered through her brain.

She'd once told him he was her fantasy come true—a badass rock musician with a fetish for wild adventures. He'd then asked her what other fantasies she had. Other, even more interesting sexual adventures he could bring to life for her. After a lot of prodding, she had finally admitted her deepest, most secret fantasy of having a threesome with two men. But she'd also told him she'd never consider doing it in real life. That night, he'd insisted they role-play it, though. He'd blindfolded her and told her another man was touching her. He'd even used a vibrator to give her the experience of double penetration.

It had been one of the most intense sexual experiences of her life.

But could she really do it with Dane and Storm?

"Why do you want to do this?" she asked.

He stepped close and stroked her cheek. "Because, baby, I want to prove to you that I really am that adventurous, badass, rock musician you fell in love with. You asked me once if I would ever turn down a challenge."

"And you said only one." And they'd both known he'd been referring to her fantasy, because he would never share her with another man.

"And you said you'd never actually live out your fantasy," he said. "But things have changed. Since you're already sleeping with both of us,"—he shrugged—"why not go all the way?"

He was trying to prove he was still the same man she'd fallen in love with. Be the man he thought she wanted him to be.

"Rafe, you don't have to do this to prove—"

He cupped her breast, and stroked over her leather-covered nipple, stealing the breath from her lungs. Then he leaned close to her ear.

"Admit it, baby. You want to do this."

Dane's hand stroked over her naked ass, then his finger slid along the soft leather crotch of her thong.

She ached inside, wanting both of them so bad her sex clenched painfully.

Her gaze locked on Storm's sky blue eyes, and she drew in a deep breath.

"Dane, why are you doing this?" she asked.

His arm slipped around her waist and he pulled her tight against him. The hard bulge in his pants pressed into her.

"Besides the fact I'm totally turned on?" He nuzzled her neck. "I think Rafe should see how much you like to be dominated in bed. Plus, the idea of watching you come while another man fucks you is extremely hot."

"Even if it's Rafe?" She couldn't stop the tremor in her voice at the images his words evoked.

"Since my brother is in love with you, too, he is the best possible choice. There's no one else I'd want to share you with."

"I don't know what to say."

Dane cupped her breasts, then dragged his fingers over her hard, aching nipples. "Don't say anything. Just do as I tell you."

At that, Dane ripped open the leather bra, the Velcro fastening at the front giving away with a loud, tearing sound. Storm's eyes darkened as he stared at her naked breasts, the distended nipples peaking forward. Dane tore the bra straps free and then tossed it aside.

Storm covered both her breasts and caressed them. Her insides fluttered with need.

Dane tore away the leather panties, leaving her naked except for the harness.

"Rafe, lick her pussy."

Storm dipped his head down and licked her nipple, then crouched in front of her. Her legs were held wide by the chains fastening her ankles and wrists to the pillars. His fingers trailed lightly down her stomach, then stopped just short of her clean-shaven folds. Then he leaned forward and she groaned as his tongue touched her slick flesh. He licked the length of her slit.

"Not too much." Dane's hands covered her breasts and he squeezed lightly. "We don't want her to come too soon."

Storm licked again and grinned. "I'm sure we can make her come again."

Dane laughed. "Of course, but let's keep her motivated."

Dane unfastened the chains from her wrists, and Storm released her ankles.

"Get Rafe and me a beer from the bar fridge," Dane commanded.

On shaky legs, she walked behind the bar and opened the small fridge, then pulled out two bottles of imported beer. She poured them into tall glasses while Storm sat on the couch and Dane settled in the chair facing him.

She handed a glass to Dane, then to Storm. His heated gaze settled on her naked body again.

"Jessica, kneel in front of Rafe."

At his command, she immediately knelt down.

"Open his pants and pull out his cock, then stroke it."

She pulled down the zipper of his pants, feeling the swollen ridge beneath her fingertips, then unfastened the button. She slipped her hand inside and found his hard, hot flesh, then drew it out. The veins pulsed on his red, engorged shaft. She stroked her hand the length of him, loving the feel, like solid iron covered in silk.

She continued stroking, longing to feel him in her mouth. His eyelids fell closed as he enjoyed her touch.

"Now treat him to your luscious, talented mouth."

She leaned forward and touched her lips to the tip of him, then pressed her tongue to his hot flesh and swirled, tasting a salty drop of pre-cum. She pushed down further, his cockhead filling her mouth. She squeezed it as her hand continued to stroke his shaft.

His fingers coiled in her hair as she took him deeper, then glided back.

"Swallow his whole cock while you stroke his balls."

She relaxed her throat and slid as deep as she could, her hand sliding under his balls. She cradled them gently in her palm as she tried to take his cock deeper still.

She glided back, then Storm guided her forward and back again. She followed the rhythm he established.

"Baby, that feels so good," he murmured.

His cock throbbed in her mouth and she could feel his body tensing. She slipped off the end, still holding his cock in her hand.

She turned her head to gaze at Dane. "May I make him come?"

Dane nodded curtly.

Then she turned back to see Storm frowning, but she took him in her mouth again and swallowed his cock whole. As she moved up and down, squeezing and sucking, his eyelids fell closed again and he moaned.

She stroked his balls and he tensed, then he shot hot liquid into her mouth. Still she squeezed and sucked until he was drained completely. She drew back and licked her lips.

He opened his arms to her. "Fuck, baby, come here."

Her glance darted to Dane and he nodded, then she surged into Storm's arms. He held her tight, stroking her naked back.

"Now come here, Jessica," Dane commanded.

Immediately, she drew away from Storm and stood up, then walked to Dane.

"Suck my cock until its rock hard."

She knelt in front of him, conscious of Storm's intense gaze watching her. She unfastened Dane's pants and drew out his erection.

"It's already hard, sir."

He grasped her shoulders and dragged her across his lap. Her face rested against the couch cushion while her ass arched upward.

"Don't question my commands."

His hand landed on her bare ass with a loud smack, followed by stinging heat where his hand had landed. Then he smacked her again. Excitement careened through her.

Her gaze shifted to Storm, who seemed to be restraining himself from coming to her aid.

"My brother seems concerned. Tell us how much you like this."

"Yes, sir. I like this very much, sir. Please punish me again."

He smacked her again and she shifted on his lap, her slit slick with need.

"Tell us how much this turns you on."

"Yes, Mr. Ranier. This makes me wet with need."

"And what would you like me to do now?"

"I want you to drive your cock into me and make me come."

He swatted her ass again. "I thought you wanted me to punish you more."

"Yes, of course. Please smack my ass again."

He smacked her again and her heated cheeks burned with pleasure.

Dane pulled her to a sitting position on his lap, facing away from him, his hard cock pressing against the length of her slick folds.

"Do you really like this, Jess?" Storm asked with concern.

Her cheeks heated a little at his question.

"Yes," she answered timidly.

Dane whispered some instructions into her ear.

She obeyed, cupping her breasts and, as she stroked them, said to Storm, "Why don't you take off your clothes now?" Then in a throaty voice, "I want to see you naked."

Storm stood up and started peeling off his clothes. She watched in anticipation as he grabbed the hem of his T-shirt and pulled it over his head, revealing his sculpted chest. Then he dropped his jeans and boxers to the floor and stepped out of them. The sight of his muscular, tattooed torso sent chills through her, and her insides clenched at the sight of his enormous cock, already swelling again to a full-sized erection.

"Stand up and entertain Storm for a moment," Dane said.

She stood and walked toward Storm, then ran her hands over his chest. He enfolded her in an embrace, his lips finding hers. At the feel of her soft breasts crushed against his hard, naked chest, her knees went weak. He held her tighter as his tongue explored her mouth tenderly.

"Jessica, turn around," Dane instructed.

She drew her mouth from Storm's and his sky blue gaze seemed to challenge her to defy Dane's command. But she pulled herself from his embrace and turned to face Dane. He now stood, his beautiful, sculpted body totally naked, his enormous, purple-headed cock jutting straight up.

"Lean over the back of the chair."

She walked to the nearby armchair and leaned over, opening her legs in anticipation.

She felt Dane step behind her, then his hard cockhead stroked her slick slit. She drew in a breath as his cock stilled against her, then he slowly pressed his tip inside her, stretching her. He drew out, then slipped inside, a little deeper. Then out again.

This time, she felt the pressure of his hard flesh against her back opening. He eased forward and her narrow passage stretched for him, allowing his hard flesh to slide inside. Very slowly. She forced herself to relax while he pressed deeper. She pushed her muscles against him, allowing him easier entry.

His cockhead was now fully inside her and he pushed deeper still. Once he was all the way in, he wrapped his arms around her waist and held her tight to him. He eased their bodies around and perched against a tall stool he must have brought in earlier from the kitchen. He lifted her legs until her knees rested on his thighs, her legs spread wide.

The feel of his enormous cock inside her felt incredible. She gazed at Storm, who'd been watching them, his cock at full attention, and she longed to feel him inside her, too.

"Now's the time to fulfill her fantasy, Rafe."

The turbulent expression on Storm's face seemed to conflict with the glint of lust in his eyes. He strode toward her, his hand wrapping around his cock, then he pressed it to her opening and thrust forward. She gasped at the feel of his huge erection driving into her.

"Do you like that?" Storm demanded, almost savagely.

The intense sensation of being sandwiched between their two hot, muscular bodies, and filled by their two huge cocks sent her senses reeling. It was strange and exciting and extremely wild.

"Oh, yes, sir."

Storm's eyes grew darker still and he cupped her face and

kissed her, his tongue driving into her with power and authority. He released her mouth, his expression fierce, and he grasped her hips and thrust forward, driving Dane's cock further into her, too.

She cried out at the intense pleasure of both cocks filling her so deeply.

Dane grabbed her hair and coiled it around his hand, pulling her head back against his shoulder. "Do you like both our cocks inside you?"

"Oh, God, yes, Mr. Ranier."

"You heard her, brother. Now fuck her hard."

Storm thrust forward and she gasped. Wild sensations rippled along her nerve endings. The two men found a rhythm, Storm driving forward, Dane thrusting upward. Her arms wrapped around Storm and she clung to him as pleasure swept through her, higher and higher with each thrust of their bodies.

"Oh, yes." After uttering the tremulous words, she whimpered, her whole body trembling.

Both cocks drove deep again and she cried out.

"Please . . . Oh, God, I'm so close."

Pleasure spiraled and she felt faint yet enlivened. Surely she would soon implode.

Storm's fingers stroked her face and her eyelids popped open. His lips grazed her cheek.

"Come for me, baby," he murmured.

His cock filled her, moving in rhythm with Dane's and pleasure exploded through her. She wailed as her body burst into pure sensation, ecstasy vibrating through her entire being.

"That's right." Storm's fingers glided along her cheek as his cock drove in and out.

Her wail intensified to a shriek of pure delight.

Dane groaned and arched upward, his cock drilling deep before hot liquid filled her. Then Storm's powerful body jerked forward and his cock pulsed inside her and then erupted. She squeezed him as his hot seed flooded her insides. His mouth captured hers as his body continued to shudder against her.

Finally, Rafe drew back, his dark gaze locked on her face. "Was that worthy of your fantasy?"

She smiled. "Totally blew it out of the water."

Jessica awoke to darkness. She stroked her hand along the strong back she leaned against. Dane. After the incredible sexual adventure she'd shared with both Dane and Storm, the three of them had wound up on Dane's bed and fallen asleep. She rolled onto her back and reached for Storm . . . but he wasn't there.

She lifted her head and glanced around. He wasn't in the room. She slipped from the bed and walked to the dresser where Dane had piled their clothes. She found one of Dane's shirts and pulled it on, then fastened several buttons, loving the feel of the fine silk against her body. She opened the bedroom door and walked down the hall.

There were no lights on, but the moonlight silhouetted Storm sitting on the living room couch, nursing a drink. He wore his faded jeans, but no shirt. She turned on a table lamp and he glanced at her.

"Hi," she said softly.

He just nodded. She sat down on the chair and leaned toward him.

"What's wrong?"

He shook his head and shrugged, then took another drink. She eased onto the couch beside him and took his hand.

"Tell me," she insisted softly.

His blue gaze turned on her, and she could see the turmoil plaguing him.

"Is that really what you like?" Rafe demanded. "Being ordered around?"

She shrugged, trying to make light of it. "Yeah. It's sexy to be dominated by a strong man. But it's all just a role."

"Is it?" he demanded. He pushed himself to his feet, drink still in his hand, and paced. "And what about the *punishment*? That seemed real enough." He stopped walking and tipped back his drink, then his gaze pierced her. "Do you like pain?"

"No, it's not that. When Dane smacks me, it's not all that hard. It's more stimulating than painful. My skin gets all tingly and sensitive. Then he strokes it and . . . I don't know. It's just exciting."

His eyes narrowed. "So you'd like it if I dominated you?"

Her heartbeat fluttered and she nodded.

He set his drink on the table and stepped toward her, then grabbed her shoulders and pulled her to her feet. His lips met hers in a hard, demanding kiss. His arm wrapped around her waist and he crushed her body to his as he assaulted her mouth with his tongue. She could taste Scotch. Her breathing became labored as excitement rushed through her.

Then he released her.

"Strip off your fucking clothes," he demanded.

She fumbled with the top button, but finally got it released, then gasped as Storm impatiently tore open the shirt. He pushed it from her shoulders and stared at her naked breasts. The nipples immediately peaked.

"You are so fucking beautiful." He grabbed her shoulders and turned her around, then marched her around the couch. "And I want to fuck you so bad."

He pushed her forward to lean over the back of the couch and she grasped the upholstery to steady herself. She heard a zipper, then his jeans hit the floor with a *thunk*.

"I'm going to fuck you now. How do I command that? *Be* fucked?"

Clearly, he'd had a little too much to drink, but she could feel that his big cock was hard and ready to go as he pressed it between her thighs, and stroked her slick flesh.

"You are fucking wet, so obviously this is turning you on." He pressed his cockhead to her opening.

She gasped as he drove in hard and deep.

"Fuck, you okay?" he asked.

"Yes," she assured and squeezed him inside her. "I love the way you feel inside me."

"Yeah? Tell me more. Like when you're being a slave."

He drew back and thrust again.

"Yes, Mr. Ranier. Please fuck me hard."

He drew back and smacked her ass. "Don't fucking call me *Mr. Ranier*." He drove into her, then drew back and smacked again. "Understand?"

"Yes, sir."

He thrust and smacked, then again. His strikes were harder than Dane's and her ass was burning with heat.

He thrust faster and harder, and with every thrust, he smacked her ass, alternating sides. Her ass burned painfully, but her pleasure rose as his cock stroked her passage. She squeezed him and he groaned, then shuddered against her as his cock exploded inside her.

His arm curled around her waist as he leaned against her back, holding her close to him. She could smell the Scotch on his breath as he pressed his face into her hair.

Finally, he eased back, then stiffened.

"Ah, fuck." His fingertips stroked over her stinging ass. "I'm an asshole. Look what I've done."

She turned around and at the sight of his pained expression, she stroked his cheek. "No, sweetheart, it's okay. I liked it."

"Your ass is dark red. Clearly, I hurt you," he insisted.

It had hurt a little more than she liked, but that didn't matter. She'd still enjoyed it.

"It's all right." She stroked his whisker-roughened cheek again and smiled. "It was really sexy."

He dragged her against him and kissed her, his tongue exploring her mouth gently this time. She responded with light sweeps of her tongue.

"Oh, fuck, Jess. I never want to hurt you again." In his eyes, she could see that he didn't just mean the spanking.

She stroked his tousled hair from his eyes. "I know, sweetheart." She kissed his neck. "I know."

He kissed her again with passion. "I love you, Jess."

"Me, too." She sighed and snuggled in his arms, sleep threatening to overcome her. She smiled and took his hand.

"Come back to bed. Sleep with me."

He followed her to the bedroom and climbed in bed behind her, draping his arm around her waist. Thankfully, Dane was still asleep.

Dane lay quietly in the bed as Jessica led Rafe into the room, then climbed into bed behind him. He hoped she wouldn't notice his rapid heartbeat.

Dane had seen the whole thing in the living room. He'd heard Jessica leave the room and he'd glanced around to see that Rafe was gone, too. He'd silently followed her into the living room in time to see her coax Rafe to talk about what had happened between the three of them. Dane had stayed in the shadows, not wanting to disturb them. He should have come back to bed, but he'd needed to know what Rafe's feelings were. How he had coped with the dominance. And especially the punishment.

With Rafe's history with Dad—with the beatings—Dane really didn't know if it had been a good idea or not to punish Jessica in front of him. He'd hoped it would be, to help Rafe get past his own traumas.

Seeing his brother on the couch, clearly a little drunk, his heart had sunk, believing he'd done him a disservice, but Jessica had masterfully handled the situation with her loving encouragement. When Rafe had actually punished Jessica with harsh blows to her ass, Dane had had to stop himself from coming to Jessica's rescue. But he was sure that if she had told Rafe to stop, he would have. So Dane had just watched, letting the scene play out.

He knew the blows must have hurt her, but she'd taken them stoically. Then Rafe had apologized, and they'd shared a tender moment. Dane's heart ached at the memory. Rafe loved Jessica, that was so clear.

Dane loved Jessica, too, and ordinarily he would have let nothing stand in the way of possessing her, but it was also clear that Jessica loved Rafe. And she was good for him. With her by his side, Dane believed that his brother might finally get past their father's brutal treatment of him and maybe even come to accept himself for the wonderful human being he was.

Damn it, he knew in his heart that Rafe and Jessica should be together.

Dane woke up with Jessica pressed tight against his back, her naked breasts warm and delightfully soft against him. His groin tightened. If he lay here for another few moments, he would wind up rolling her over and gliding his rising cock into her.

And he didn't want to do that.

Right now, he needed distance, and time to think.

He slipped out of bed, careful not to wake her. A quick glance across the bed told him Rafe had already left.

Smart. Neither one of them wanted a face-to-face this morning.

Dane grabbed a set of clothes and headed to the guest room so he could shower and dress without waking Jessica. Fifteen minutes later, he left a note for her on the kitchen counter, then headed down to the lobby. The limo was waiting for him when he stepped outside.

As the driver negotiated the morning traffic, Dane's thoughts turned to Jessica, his heart aching at the thought of losing her. Jessica had told Dane early on that she didn't want a romantic relationship, because she didn't want to be hurt again. Because Rafe had hurt her badly when he'd left her. That was why she'd hesitated to accept Rafe's marriage proposal once he'd returned, or even commit to a romantic relationship with Rafe.

Even after last night, Dane was worried that she might use her relationship with him to avoid moving forward with Rafe.

The limo pulled up in front of his building and he went inside and rode the crowded elevator to the executive floor. When the doors opened, he noticed Melanie sitting at her desk. It was early for her to be here.

"Good morning, Melanie," he said as he walked by her desk.

"Good morning, Mr. Ranier."

He went into his office and closed the door, then started up his computer, intent on keeping his mind busy. He'd just opened his e-mail when he heard a tap on the door. He frowned. Melanie never interrupted him when his door was closed.

"Come in," he said.

The door opened and Melanie peeked inside. "I'm sorry to bother you, Mr. Ranier, but . . ." She hesitated and drew in a breath. "May I talk to you for a moment?"

He glanced at the clock on his computer screen. He had an hour before his first meeting.

"Of course. Come in."

She closed the door and walked across the room, clearly nervous, then sat in the guest chair facing his desk.

"I know you're not going to want to hear this, but . . ."

Jessica awoke to bright sunshine across her face. She murmured, unwilling to open her eyes yet, still captivated by sexy images of last night's exhilarating activities. Her body felt well used and sensitive, but heat coiled through her at the memories of the way she had used, and been used by, her two sexy lovers last night.

She opened her eyes, expecting to see Dane lying by her side. But he was gone. She rolled over. Storm was gone, too.

She glanced at the clock. Damn, it was after nine o'clock. She was late for work.

She pushed herself to her feet and raced to the shower. Twenty minutes later, she trotted into the kitchen, the aroma of coffee encouraging. There was half a pot in the coffeemaker, so she poured herself a cup and, spotting a note on the counter, sat on one of the stools and sipped her coffee while she read it.

It was from Dane, telling her the limo would be waiting for her whenever she was ready.

She knew she should hurry, she was already quite late, but

clearly Dane wouldn't be angry with her. She rested her chin on her hand, staring at the note. Although she'd woken up in the warm, cozy bed still enamored of the previous night's adventure, now sitting at this cold granite counter facing a note from one of the men who'd fled her bed, she felt a shiver crawl the length of her spine.

Being with both of them last night had been beyond anything she'd experienced before. It had been exhilarating and potently erotic. But it had also been taboo. Two men, let alone two brothers, making love to her at the same time. Especially these two brothers, with their history.

What had she been thinking?

Well, that's just it. She hadn't been thinking.

Her cheeks heated. Both men had rushed off so . . . what must they think of her?

Sure, they had arranged the adventure, but based on *her* fantasy. Clearly, in the cold light of day, faced with the result of their act, they hadn't been happy. Otherwise, wouldn't they have waited around to enjoy more of the same? At least, that was the way it always happened in her fantasies.

Fool. The two men probably didn't even want to look each other in the face.

So she'd made an already complex and uncomfortable situation even worse.

She sighed and finished her coffee, then called to tell the limo driver she'd be down in five minutes.

She'd just have to steel herself and face whatever awaited her at the office.

The elevator doors opened and Jessica walked out expecting to see Melanie sitting at her desk, but she was nowhere to be seen. She was probably off running a quick errand for Dane, and would be back shortly, but the phone on her desk was ringing so Jessica rushed over to pick it up.

She jotted a note on the small pad of paper Melanie kept by the phone, then hung up. She stared at Dane's office door, which was closed. Was Rafe already here, too?

If she was lucky, maybe both of them would be too busy today to even see her. More likely, they'd avoid her, which would give her some time to come to terms with what had happened. Or at least, for the sting of their abandonment this morning to wane a little.

Dane's office door opened. No such luck.

But she glanced up to see Melanie exiting the office and . . . she looked upset.

Melanie walked toward her desk, not seeming to notice Jessica. Her cheeks were flushed and she brushed her face with her hand. Suddenly, Jessica realized she was wiping away a tear. She bolted to her feet and rushed toward her friend.

"Melanie, what's wrong?"

Melanie glanced at her in a daze.

"I . . ." She drew in a breath and shook her head. "I . . ." Her voice cracked and then tears spilled from her eyes. "I don't work here anymore."

"What?" Shock rippled through Jessica.

Melanie grabbed her purse from her desk and hurried toward the elevator. Jessica followed on her heels. Melanie stabbed at the Down button.

"What happened? Did you quit?" Jessica asked.

Melanie shook her head.

The elevator doors opened and Melanie bolted inside. Jessica followed her, but Melanie shook her head.

"No, Jessica. I don't want to talk right now."

Jessica backed off and watched the doors close. What could possibly have happened? Melanie was the best secretary Dane could ever hope for.

She jerked her head around and glared at Dane's office, the door still open after Melanie's hasty retreat. She turned and marched into his office. He glanced up as she entered.

"Melanie just told me she's not working here anymore."

His lips compressed. "That's true."

"Did you fire her?" she demanded.

He was silent for a moment, watching her intently. Then he calmly answered. "Yes."

Her hands clenched into fists and she sucked in a breath, trying to calm the raging flood of adrenaline. "Why?"

He shook his head. "That's between me, Melanie, and Human Resources."

She scowled, anger surging through her. "How could you possibly fire her? It's wrong."

He sighed. "Calm down, Jessica."

She paced toward his desk, her heart thundering. "Don't you tell me to calm down."

"Then sit."

She sat, automatically acquiescing to that damnable authoritative tone of his.

He stood up and walked around to the front of his desk and sat on the edge. "You may have forgotten that this is a business. Sometimes people get fired."

"Not Melanie. It doesn't make sense."

"Only because you don't know the whole story, and that's not up to me to tell." He sighed. "Look, Jessica. It seems that our *arrangement* is blurring the line between our business and personal relationship. Not only that, it's causing unnecessary complications. With Rafe. And with Melanie."

"Clearly you solved the latter," she said with gritted teeth.

He raised an eyebrow and nodded. "And I intend to solve the former." He pushed himself to his feet. "Our arrangement ends now. From here on forward, you will be my personal assistant. That's all. If you prefer not to keep working directly for me, you could take over Melanie's role as Rafe's secretary. Or become his personal assistant. I'm sure he'd be willing to take an office on another floor if you'd like more distance from me."

Shock vaulted through her. She bolted to her feet and glared at him. "Oh, my God. Did you fire Melanie to open up the position for me? Were you tired of me so you wanted to push me into another job?" She planted her hands on her hips. "Or was that Rafe's idea?"

Annoyance flared in his eyes. "No. Rafe had nothing to do with this."

"Fine. You want me out of here. I'm gone." She turned and stormed out of his office.

Her stomach clenching, she headed straight for the elevator. She stabbed the Down button, but couldn't handle waiting for it to arrive, so she headed for the stairs.

Her heart raced as she realized she'd just quit her job.

But worse, Dane had ended their relationship. She was sure, deep down inside, that he had some good reason for firing Melanie, though she couldn't imagine what. But he'd offered no explanation. Even if he couldn't tell her why, to keep Melanie's privacy, he could have given her some hint that he hadn't wanted to do it.

But he hadn't. She never would have believed the man she'd fallen in love with could be so coldhearted; firing Melanie and then discarding Jessica as if she were nothing to him.

She sucked back a sob. In spite of everything, the finality of this moment, knowing that her relationship with Dane was well and truly over, made her ache inside.

Rafe dragged his hand through his hair as he stared out over the city skyline from his apartment window. Having a threesome with Dane and Jess had been an insane idea, but he'd been desperate to find a way to win her back, and somehow that had seemed like the best option.

Of course, the idea had turned him on. It had always turned him on, but he hadn't thought she'd go for it in the past. She'd even said as much. And he'd had a long way to go to get past his jealousy of another man touching her. But when they'd found themselves in this situation, where she was already sleeping with Dane, and didn't seem inclined to stop, even after Rafe had proposed, then he'd known he had to do something drastic. He'd been so sure that when she compared the two of them side-by-side, that she'd know in her heart that it was Rafe she loved.

Watching Dane punish her had been hard, but at the same time, it had turned him on immensely. So much so, that when she'd come to talk to him in the middle of the night, and he had taken control, he'd actually beaten her. His hands clenched into fists. He'd been a fucking idiot. Acting on hormones rather than compassion. As much as she said she'd liked it, he knew he'd gotten carried away. The angry redness of her skin had shocked him back to reality. How could he have allowed himself to hurt her like that?

His cell phone buzzed and he pulled it from his pocket.

"There is a Ms. Jessica Long here to see you, Mr. Ranier. Shall I send her up?"

Fuck. He really didn't want to face her right now.

"Yeah, Benjamin. Go ahead."

He walked to the bedroom and grabbed a T-shirt from his dresser drawer and pulled it on. His jeans were worn and thread-bare in places, but they were comfortable and he knew she was used to seeing him dressed this way. In fact, she preferred it to his more expensive in-line-with-their-family-status clothing he now typically wore. At least, as Rafe Ranier. As Storm, he wore whatever the hell he wanted and didn't give a shit what anyone else thought.

A knock sounded at the door, so he headed toward it and pulled it open.

The sight of Jess standing there, her pretty face drawn into a tight expression, clearly distraught, was like a punch in the gut.

Was she upset that he'd walked out this morning? Or was it about their midnight dominance session?

"Come in."

She followed him into the living room, and they sat down on the couch together.

"What's wrong, Jess?"

She gazed at him and he could see the turmoil in her eyes. "I quit my job."

He frowned. "But I thought you loved working for Dane." Ah, fuck. "Is this about last night? Did our . . . escapade make things too awkward in the office?"

"No. Nothing like that. It's because . . ." She sucked in a breath. "Dane fired Melanie."

Shock careened through him. "What? Why?"

She shook her head. "I don't know. He wouldn't tell me."

Rafe understood that. The reason an employee was fired was a privacy issue. But what possible grounds could Dane have for firing Melanie? She was an exceptional secretary.

"Don't worry. I'll talk to him. I'm sure we can get this all sorted out."

"I don't know. It's a pretty big mess." She folded her hands in her lap. "I hope you can get Melanie's job back, but mine . . ." She shook her head. "I don't think that will work."

"Why? What else is going on, Jess?"

"I just . . ." She sucked in a breath. "I couldn't believe Dane would do this. And when I confronted him, he broke it off between the two of us. He said our physical relationship was interfering with business."

She and Dane had broken up? He knew he should be happy about that, but he wasn't. Probably because deep inside he knew how much she loved Dane. Even while Dane took charge of her in the bedroom, there was a tenderness in his eyes when he looked at her. Rafe had no doubt that his brother was in love with this woman.

He rested his hand on her arm. "Jess, I'm sorry."

She shook her head. "No, it's good. It's better I find out now that he's a heartless bastard." She drew in a breath that he was sure was staving off a sob. "And that I'm nothing more to him than a lay."

Rafe stroked her cheek. "I'm sure that isn't true."

"I don't want to talk about Dane right now." She took his hand. "I think we should talk about last night. Since you were gone before I woke up this morning, I assume you had a problem with what happened. Were you jealous of me with Dane? Or,"—she gazed at him questioningly—"were you judging me for the fact I enjoyed being dominated and punished?"

Her words were like a kick in the gut.

"I wasn't judging you. It's just that . . ." Damn it. He pushed himself to his feet and paced. "It made me damned uncomfortable." He turned to face her. "My father was a real ass. He wasn't just authoritative, he was abusive. He beat me regularly."

Her eyes widened. "Oh, my God. That's awful."

He nodded as he continued to pace. "Not Dane, though. Dane was more the son the old man wanted." He shrugged. "Maybe part of it was, he had no use for a second son. Dane could take over the business, and I . . ." He shrugged again. "I was just more effort. If he could have found a way to send me off to foster care without it reflecting badly on the family, he probably would have done it. Instead, he kept me around, but made it clear to me that I'd better not embarrass the family by not being a Ranier. I had better fall in line and be an appropriate partner in the family business."

"I'm so sorry, Rafe." She stood up and wrapped her arms around him.

He enjoyed the warmth and acceptance of her embrace. She always made him feel loved, something he'd never really had before. He realized that that's why he'd run away from their relationship to go on tour. Because it scared him. And that's also why he'd run back. Because he didn't want to be without it.

She raised her lips to his and kissed him, her mouth soft and inviting. He felt her fingertips gliding under his T-shirt and over his abs. She started to pull the fabric up and his body ached for the intimacy her actions promised, but he grasped her hands to stop her.

"No, I can't," he said.

She gazed at him in shock. "Why not?"

"Because. It's not fair to you."

"What do you mean?"

He drew away from her warm, inviting body. "I can't do this because I know there's no future for us. I was wrong. We aren't meant to be together."

"Because I like to be dominated?"

"That's part of it. Dane can give you what you want in that department, but I can't."

"Rafe, that doesn't matter." She tried to touch him again but he stepped out of reach.

"It *does* matter. I can't allow myself to open that door. My dad was an abuser and . . ." He shrugged. "I can't go down that path. Dane has a lot of control, but I . . . I don't trust what might happen."

She shook her head. "No. You would never go too far."

"Do you think my father logically thought, 'Ah, I'm going to beat my son today'? Or do you think he just lost control and did it?" He stepped toward her and her eyes widened. With anger fuming through him, she must feel intimidated. "Like I did last night."

"No, you had just—"

"Had a drink? My father was often drunk when he beat me."

"I think your father was a monster and I know you *aren't*. You would never really hurt me."

He compressed his lips. "Well, that's where you're wrong. Because what I'm about to do will probably hurt quite a bit."

She gazed at him in shock.

"Because right now I'm telling you that we're through. I realized that I'm not really in love with you." He paced across the room. "I haven't had a lot of affection or love in my life, and when you showed me so much love,"—he shrugged—"I cherished it. Then when I lost it, I realized I couldn't bear my life without it." He patted his chest. "It filled a hole deep in here. But I realize, now, that it wasn't love. Let's face it. Neither of us really knew each other. You only knew a small part of who I am. And I had no idea that you liked to be dominated in the bedroom. And don't tell me it's not important to you because I know it is. But it makes us . . . incompatible." He sighed. "I don't want to hurt you. But just like last time, if I don't take action now, it'll only hurt more when we finally both discover that we're just not right for each other."

He took her hand, his heart aching at the tears swelling in her eyes. "Besides, I know that you love Dane."

Anger flashed in her eyes, and she tugged her hand free. "No, I don't." She glared at him. "If you want to break up with me, at least be man enough to do it without trying to look like you're doing me a favor. You don't love me. I get it."

She turned and strode toward the entrance.

"Jess, wait."

But she disappeared out the door. Damn, that hadn't gone well.

Jessica marched through the lobby and the doorman pulled open the door for her.

"Ms. Long," he said as she exited the building, "Mr. Ranier called down and asked me to arrange a ride for you. His limo is waiting just over there."

She glanced to where he pointed to see the familiar long, black car. It had only taken her five minutes to get down here. Did this guy just drive around waiting for one of the Ranier brothers to call?

The driver opened the door for her and she hesitated only a moment before she got in.

"I'm heading home," she said.

He knew the address. She settled into the comfortable seat as the car moved into traffic, then her tears started to flow. She'd been rejected by two men today. Both of whom had proclaimed their love in the past. And she had no job. Her closest friend had shut her out. Her whole life was crumbling around her.

When they arrived at her apartment, the driver opened her door, then hurried ahead of her and opened the door to the building.

"Thank you," she said, aware of her tearstained cheeks.

He nodded. "Of course, Ms. Long."

The compassion in his warm smile boosted her spirits a little and she walked to the elevator. She sucked in a breath as she rode upstairs, trying to regain her composure. Melanie had been fired today and now was the time to focus on getting her friend to open up so she could help her, not wallowing in her own problems.

She opened the door to their apartment, not sure what to expect on the other side. Certainly not what she saw. Melanie sat on the couch with nail polishes laid out on the table in front of her, mostly in bright, fluorescent colors. She had her nails partially painted with three vertical stripes of different colors and she was currently using a striping brush to add a vivid orange stripe to each nail.

"Just Give Me a Reason" by Pink was playing in the background. The phrase "nothing is as bad as it seems" echoed through their cozy little apartment and boosted her spirits the slightest bit.

Melanie glanced up. "Oh, hi. You're home early."

Jessica did not want to explain that she'd quit. Not yet.

"I wanted to check on you."

On the end table beside Melanie was a tall glass of cola and an open box.

"Donuts, Melanie?"

Melanie grabbed one and waved it at Jessica. "Don't judge me."

"Judge you?" She walked toward the box and grabbed one of the chocolate glazed donuts. "I want to join you."

Melanie laughed and set the donut on the table, then continued painting the stripes on her nails. Jessica took a bite of her donut and enjoyed the rich burst of chocolate flavor. Then she hummed along to the song, something about not being broken, just bent, and learning to love again. It spoke to her current situation perfectly.

"That's some manicure you've got going there," Jessica said as Melanie added a startling yellow stripe to her nails.

Melanie grinned. "It's not finished yet." Then she picked up a bottle of black polish and rolled it between her hands. Melanie had once told her that shaking a polish could introduce bubbles, so it was better to roll it like that. "Now I'm going to put a black crackle on top. I think it'll look quite dramatic." She nodded toward the bottles. "Grab some polish and do yours, too."

"Nope." Jessica settled back, donut in hand. "I'm just going to relax."

Melanie had applied the black polish to four nails so far and faint cracks were already appearing on some of them.

"So, Melanie, what happened this morning? Why did Dane fire you?"

Melanie inspected the hand she'd just finished and then started on the other one.

"I mean, I know he has no grounds on which to fire you," Jessica continued, "so we must be able to fight it."

Melanie frowned and for the first time, Jessica wondered if she was wrong. Had Melanie done something? Everyone made mistakes sometimes, but Jessica couldn't possibly figure out what Melanie could have done to deserve firing.

"I don't want to fight it."

"I know it would be awkward coming back to work for Dane," Jessica said, "but Ranier Industries is a big company. I'm sure they could find something else for you so you wouldn't have to work for him directly."

Melanie sighed and put a last swipe of polish on her nails, then put the cap back on the polish bottle.

"Dane already suggested that. I said no."

"What? I don't understand."

Melanie settled back on the couch. "This morning, I went into Dane's office to quit."

"Why did you want to quit?" As soon as she'd asked the question, Jessica wished she could take it back. It had to be because of the relationship between Rafe and Jessica.

Melanie frowned. "You know I don't begrudge you the fact that you and Rafe fell in love, but . . ."—she glanced down at her hands—"it's hard to watch. I'm happy for you and all, and when you get married, I still want to be your friend, but . . ." She gazed Jessica's way again. "I guess I always held hope that Rafe would eventually notice me and that we could somehow get past the whole boss-secretary thing and . . . I don't know . . . maybe my dream would come true. But I know now that it will never happen, and I don't want to hang around and watch that dream being torn away from me."

Jessica placed her hand over her heart. "I'm so sorry, Melanie. I knew—"

"*Please* don't be." Melanie smiled. "I didn't say it was logical, and I don't blame you for any of this. In fact, I didn't even realize I was harboring such insane feelings, but when I saw that you had won Rafe's heart and I didn't stand a chance, I realized I'd been letting that subconscious hope stop me from moving on with my life."

"How did that all translate to Dane firing you?"

"It turns out he already knew I had feelings for Rafe. Did you tell him?"

"No, I would never do that."

Melanie nodded. "Anyway, we both knew that no matter what I told Rafe about why I was leaving, he'd do everything he could to talk me into staying. He'd probably better any offer I might have received elsewhere and I'd find myself in an awkward position. Dane suggested that he'd just tell Rafe he laid me off. I wasn't comfortable with that, because you know that would cause huge problems between them, but . . . damn it, I was upset and things were complicated, and so Dane told me not to worry about it and to just go home and we'd figure it out. But I know I can't let him do that. It would cause too many problems. I'll just have to figure something else out."

Jessica bit her lip. "It's too late."

Melanie stared at her. "What do you mean?"

"I've already told Rafe. I confronted Dane right after you left and asked if he fired you, and he said he did. I then went over to Rafe's, hoping he could get your job back."

Her eyes widened. "Oh, no. I'll have to call and talk to him. Straighten this out. But what do I say?"

Jessica shook her head. "No, it's not your fault this all blew up. I'll talk to Rafe about this. I think I can fix it." She gazed at her friend. "I need to ask, though. If Rafe and I weren't involved, would it make a difference?"

"No. I'd just wind up back where I was before, wishing for something I can't have. I really need to move forward."

Jessica nodded. She stood up, and headed toward the door,

but then hesitated and turned around again. "Melanie, I know you don't want to hear it, but I'm sorry I caused you all this heartache. And even though it won't make a difference, I just want you to know that Rafe broke up with me."

Melanie's jaw dropped open. "Really? But he was so in love with you. Did it have anything to do with the threesome?"

Jessica's cheeks flushed. "You knew about that?"

"I wasn't supposed to, but Rafe's door was open when he and Mr. Ranier were talking yesterday afternoon and I heard just enough to get a gist of what they were planning. I also got the idea that you and Mr. Ranier do some dominance stuff." She smiled. "You know, sometimes I really wish I were you. Two hot guys ordering you to do unspeakably sexy things. I wish."

"Yeah, but Rafe didn't like the dominance and punishment. He's really uncomfortable with it."

Melanie nodded. "So is that why he broke it off?"

"That was part of it, but he also realized that he was never actually in love with me. I think he just wanted to be in love with someone, and I was there when he needed someone most. I also think he's a little lost right now and needs to figure himself out before he can really connect with someone else."

"I'm sorry, Jessica. I know it must hurt. But at least now you can focus on your relationship with Mr. Ranier. Maybe it will develop into something deeper."

Jessica shook her head. "Afraid not. Dane broke it off with me, too."

"Oh, my God, girl. Your day has been even worse than mine. Get over here. We're doing your nails."

Jessica stood in front of Rafe's apartment door for the second time today, her stomach fluttering. He opened the door, then tipped his head and smiled, showing his straight white teeth in a beaming smile. The one that always managed to melt her heart.

"I see you've decided to forgive me after all." He stood there looking exceptionally masculine, in his jeans, his chest bare and his hair damp. Whether he'd been for a swim or a late morning shower she didn't know.

She followed him into the living room and sat down.

"I'm glad you came back. I didn't want to leave things the way they were." He patted the moth tattoo on his shoulder. "I want you to understand that this still means something. I will always be there for you. I know you're mad at Dane right now, and frankly, so am I, but I'll sort this mess out with Melanie."

"I'm not mad at him."

His eyebrows arched. "You aren't? What changed?"

"I had a long talk with Melanie. It turns out Dane didn't fire her after all. Not exactly."

His brows furrowed. "What do you mean not exactly?"

She leaned forward. "Okay, I need you to listen to what I say and just accept it. No questions asked. You trust me, right?"

"Of course, I trust you."

"Then can you do that?"

He stared at her for a moment, then nodded. "Shoot."

"Melanie quit."

"Why would she—?"

"No questions, remember? And I mean don't go asking Melanie, either. Or Dane. Got it?"

"Sure, but why?"

"That's a question." At his pursed lips, she continued, "But I'll answer it. Because Melanie doesn't want you to ask her. That's what this is all about. She wanted to leave, but didn't want to have to face you and the fact you'd try to talk her into staying. She went to Dane and he said he'd take the hit and tell you he fired her."

"All this because Melanie wants to leave and she doesn't want me to know why?"

"Just respect her privacy, okay?"

He frowned. "I thought Melanie was happy working for me. Did I do something or say something to upset her?"

"See, you're still asking questions." But she smiled and leaned forward. "But I will tell you she loved working for you. Just accept that it's time for her to move on."

He sat back and sighed. "Okay. I'll miss her though." He glanced toward her. "So what about you? Is it time for you to move on? Or can I talk you into staying?"

She had quit her job, but only because she thought Dane had unfairly fired Melanie. She leaned back, crossing her arms in front of her.

"I don't know if Dane will want me back."

A pounding on the door startled her and she turned around.

"What the hell is going on?" Rafe stood up and walked to the computer on his desk and tapped on the keyboard. An image of the hallway right outside the door appeared on his screen. "It's Dane."

Dane pounded on the door again, and kept on pounding. He'd rushed past the doorman, who'd been busy helping another tenant, and raced up here. He'd gone to Jessica's place first, and Melanie had told him she'd come here. Of course, what else would he expect?

The door opened.

"What the hell are you doing?" Rafe demanded, but Dane pushed past him, his gaze scanning the room for Jessica.

Then he saw her and his heart skipped a beat. God damn, but the woman had him fully and completely under her spell.

"Jessica, I need to talk to you."

"Uh . . . do you want me to leave?" Rafe asked, closing the door.

"Yes, but you'd better stay." He shot Rafe a glance. "I need to straighten some things out with you, too, and you're not going to like what I have to say." Dane's gut clenched, knowing this would drive a huge wedge between him and Rafe, but maybe with time Rafe would forgive him.

"What is it, Dane?" Jessica asked, looking at him with her big, green eyes full of concern.

"It's about you." He frowned. "Damn it, I am not going to accept your resignation. I don't want to lose you." His hands clenched into fists. "This thing with Melanie, I . . ." He glanced at Rafe and his mouth compressed.

"It's okay," Jessica said. "I talked to her. She explained that she really wanted to quit." As his gaze shot uncomfortably to Rafe, she added, "And I explained to Rafe that he has to respect her privacy and not ask her about it."

Rafe nodded and Dane returned his gaze to her. "Jessica, I know you love Rafe and I know he loves you. And I know I should just walk away and let the two of you be happy together, but . . ." He strode toward her and clasped her shoulders, his touch sending tremors through her. "I can't. Because I'm in love with you, too."

At his impassioned words, her eyes widened.

"If you tell me your choice is Rafe, I'll understand, but I have to tell you how I feel."

He pulled her into his arms and captured her lips, driving his tongue inside and stroking with overwhelming possessiveness. She clung to his shoulders and melted against him.

When he finally released her mouth, she gazed up at him and smiled. "Oh, Dane." She stroked his cheek, her green eyes glowing. "I love you, too."

At first he was confused, then joy surged through him. His lips turned up in a crooked smile. "Really? But, what about Rafe?"

"So you finally remembered me?" Rafe said in a deadpan tone, his arms folded over his chest.

Dane drew away from her reluctantly. Fuck, now he had to explain to his brother why he'd stolen away his woman. Again.

"Rafe, I'm sorry. You're my brother and you're important to me, but I had to give Jessica all the facts."

"That's my brother, all facts and logic."

Jessica frowned. "Rafe, why are you arguing about this? We've already agreed things are over between us."

At those words, Dane's heart thundered in his chest. "You did?"

Rafe chuckled. "Because we're brothers, Jess. That's what brothers do." He walked forward and held out his hand to Dane. "Since I assume you're going to be my sister-in-law, you should get used to that."

Dane shook his hand. "You were just screwing with me?"

Rafe shrugged. "As I said, that's what brothers do."

Filled with elation, Dane grabbed Jessica again and tugged her into his arms. Her lips, so soft under his, sent his blood boiling. God, he wanted her, and he couldn't help thinking that another round with the three of them could do them all a world of good. And it would allow him to order his annoying younger brother around.

But first . . .

He took Jessica by the hand and led her to the couch, then tugged off his tie and began to unbutton his shirt. She watched enthralled as his shirt parted.

"You two want me to leave?" Rafe asked.

Dane chuckled. "You really want to run off, don't you?"

Jessica's eyes widened as she saw the decorative heart drawn on his chest, and the words written in script proclaiming his love for Jessica inside it. She reached out and stroked her fingertips over the heart.

"You got a tattoo?"

"It's temporary. Melanie drew it on. But if you want me to, I'll have it made permanent to show you how much I love you."

She laughed. "Dane, you don't have to be Rafe for me to love you." She stroked his cheek. "I love you exactly the way you are."

He knelt in front of her and pulled out the small box he'd put in the pocket by his heart, then held it out and opened it. She stared at the large diamond ring in the black velvet cushioned box and her eyes widened. When she gazed at him, he could see tears welling in her eyes and he braced himself for the rejection he felt sure was coming.

"Oh, Dane." Her voice broke and she wiped a tear from her eye. "It's beautiful."

"You have to actually ask her," Rafe said in a stage whisper.

Damn, he was being an idiot. The woman just befuddled him so much.

"Jessica, will you marry me?" Dane asked.

Her face beamed with her bright smile and she nodded,

wiping away another tear, then she threw her arms around his neck and held him tight. She found his lips and her passionate kiss sent his heart soaring.

He drew his mouth away and tugged the ring from the box, then took her hand and slid the ring on. A feeling of possessiveness and satisfaction that she was finally his swelled within him. He pulled her into another kiss, their lips meshing, then their mouths consuming each other with passion.

Rafe stood up and started toward the door. "I really do think I should leave you two alone."

"Brother, sit," Dane commanded. "You are going to help us celebrate."

"Exactly what did you have in mind?" Rafe asked.

Dane gazed into Jessica's eyes and raised his eyebrow questioningly. She grinned and nodded.

"Well, first I think Jessica should apologize for running away. Don't you agree, Jessica?"

She stood up and bowed her head. "Yes, Mr. Ranier. I am very sorry I ran away. Please forgive me."

"Good. Now strip off your blouse and skirt."

"Yes, sir."

She unfastened her buttons, slowly revealing the black, lacy bra beneath. His heart pounded as she revealed more flesh. Then she slipped the blouse from her shoulders and dropped it to the floor. Next, she shed her skirt. The sight of her black lace panties framed by her garter belt and dark stockings sent his pulse racing.

"Come here, Jessica," he commanded. "Then bend over my knee."

His cock throbbed as she walked toward him. She lowered in front of him, resting her hands on his thighs, then bent over his knee. He couldn't drag his gaze from her delightful, naked ass.

He smacked her behind, leaving a red mark.

"Thank you, sir," she said.

Dane's cock swelled.

"Rafe, don't you want to feel her soft, round ass? It's warm and flushed. Just begging for your touch."

Rafe grinned. "No, brother, I'll leave the punishment to you."

Dane drew back his hand and slapped her again.

"Oh, thank you, sir. Another, please."

At the next smack, the blush of her skin grew dark rose. His fingers glided over the silky skin, soothing.

"Another, sir?"

"No." He drew his hand from her round ass. "Kneel in front of me."

She obeyed, sinking to the floor in front of him.

"Now pull out my cock and suck it."

She glided her hands up his thighs, sending tremors through him, then she opened his button and drew down the zipper. His cock swelled at the feel of her touch through the fabric, then her fingers slid inside and curled around his hot, hard flesh. She drew him out and stared at his swollen shaft with such heat that he grew even harder.

"Your cock is so enormous, sir."

"Suck it," he commanded.

Her delicate tongue swirled over his tip, then her lips surrounded the bulbous head and he shuddered with need. She slid down a little, then back up, then glided even deeper. Her fingers found his balls and she gently cupped them.

Fuck, he wasn't going to last more than a few seconds at this rate.

"Now, I think Rafe deserves an apology, too, since the job you ran away from was at his company, too." He glanced toward Rafe, whose gaze was locked on Jessica's mouth gliding on Dane's cock. "Rafe, get over here and pull out your cock."

Rafe strode over and sat down beside Dane, then pulled out his cock.

"Suck us both," Dane commanded.

Her lips released Dane, and she turned her head toward Rafe. The cool air surrounding his cock calmed Dane's ardor enough to give him some breathing space. But watching her grasp Rafe's cock and take it in her mouth ramped it up again.

"Take him all the way," Dane commanded. "I want his cock down your throat."

She surged forward and back, deeper each time, until Rafe's whole cock disappeared inside her mouth.

Dane ached with need. He wanted so badly to drive into her.

"Keep him in your mouth and stand up."

She got to her feet and straightened her legs, so she was bent over, her naked ass exposed. He stroked her round ass, then glided his finger under the thong and along her folds. They were slick with moisture. He pushed inside her opening to find hot, wet velvet.

He needed to be inside her.

He stood up and stepped behind her, then hooked his fingers under the top of the thong and pulled it down. He pressed his cockhead to her opening and, answering the urgent demands of his body, pushed forward, driving his cock deep into her velvet depths.

"Make him come," Dane demanded as he stayed buried inside her, knowing if he moved, he would erupt.

She bobbed up and down on Rafe's erection, until Rafe stiffened and Dane knew he would blow at any time. Dane drew back and thrust forward. Jessica murmured and Rafe groaned, his whole body shuddering. Dane thrust again. Rafe's cock slid from her mouth and Jessica began to groan, her head cushioned against Rafe's stomach.

Pleasure swelled within him and after two more thrusts, he erupted inside her. She wailed in orgasm and he continued thrusting, trying to prolong it as much as possible. He drove in and out, until her wails slowed to moans, then finally she slumped against Rafe.

He drew in a deep breath, then withdrew from the warmth of her body.

She turned to him and stroked her nipples through the lace of her bra.

"Please, sir. I want more."

He sucked in a deep breath. "More fucking, or more punishment?"

She smiled. "Either."

Her eagerness sent blood to his groin all over again.

"Get your ass in the bedroom," he demanded, then gestured to Rafe to follow them.

She raced to the bedroom. Once in the room, he told Rafe to sit on the bed.

"Jessica, I want you to make him hard again, then take his cock up your ass."

"Yes, Mr. Ranier." She stripped off her bra and stroked her nipples, then stepped in front of Rafe and wrapped her hand around his semi-erect cock. She eased herself down, his thighs between her legs, and rubbed his cockhead against her folds. She pinched one nipple while she teased his cock with her slick flesh.

After a moment, his cock disappeared inside her and she moved up and down a few times, slowly. Dane could hardly wait to feel her warm opening surround him again.

She stood up and turned around, then eased back down, slowly taking Rafe's now fully erect cock into her ass.

"Fuck, that looks so sexy. How does it feel?"

"It's big and hard inside my ass, sir. Stretching me."

"Move back on the bed, Rafe."

Rafe slid his arm around her waist and moved farther onto the bed, taking Jessica with him, until only his feet were dangling over the edge. Dane prowled over their bodies, and pressed his aching cockhead to her wet opening.

"I'm going to drive into you now. Then both our cocks will be inside you again."

"Oh, yes, sir. Please."

At her trembling words, the fire inside him blazed even hotter.

He drove forward, loving the feel of her slick passage around him. Knowing Rafe's cock was also inside her sent adrenaline rushing through him. He drew back and thrust again. She moaned. He began thrusting deep and fast. Rafe groaned as her body rocked with Dane's thrusts.

"Oh, yes. That feels so good," she cried.

"I'm going to make you come with both of us inside you."

"Yes. Please, make me come."

He thrust deeper and harder.

"I'm . . ." She moaned, and sucked in air.

He drove in again.

"Coming." She threw her head back and wailed.

Rafe groaned beneath her and Dane felt the swell of oncoming release. Then he exploded inside her with a loud groan, filling her with his hot semen.

"Oh, yes," she whimpered, her hands clinging to his shoulders.

Her orgasm waned and she drew in a deep breath. She was so beautiful in her state of bliss. He couldn't resist. His lips found hers and their mouths joined. His tongue swirled inside her as he continued to pump into her steadily, keeping her orgasm simmering. He sped up as she exploded into another orgasm. Her mouth slipped away as she gasped for air, and he rode her to another climax, her face aglow with pleasure.

When she relaxed, he pulled her to his body and rolled onto his back, taking her with him. She rested her head on his chest and sighed. Rafe kissed her on the cheek and slipped from the bed. She drew open Dane's shirt and stroked his chest.

The door closed and Dane realized Rafe had finally succeeded in slipping away.

Now he was alone with the woman he loved, her naked body tight against his. He wanted to devour her. To possess her totally and completely.

He pulled off his shirt, then shed his pants. She smiled and pulled off his boxers, then lay back on the bed and opened her arms to him. He prowled over her. Even though she'd just emptied him of all he had, somehow his cock revived as he slid it over her slick folds.

She smiled as her fingertips outlined the heart shape of the tattoo Melanie had drawn on him.

"Tell me again that you love me." Her eyes glowed as she gazed at him.

"Of course I love you." Then he drove his aching cock into her.

Tears welled in her eyes as he thrust steadily.

"I love you, too." Then she moaned, her passage clenching around him. She clung to him and he watched her eyes as they glowed brighter while a beautiful, intense orgasm blossomed within her. Her breath caught, then she wailed her release.

As she bucked and trembled beneath him, to his total surprise, an orgasm rocked through him at the same time.

He collapsed on her, then rolled over, pulling her tight to his body. Joy swelled through him as he realized Jessica was his. Forever.

Even though both he and Rafe had been torn over their relationship with Jessica only days ago, now not only had the rift between him and Rafe been closed, he had won the woman of his dreams. Life would never be the same again.

He held her tight to his body, breathing in the heavenly scent of her, knowing he would never let her go.

Epilogue

Storm reached for Jessica, longing for her soft body next to his. He opened his eyes and, as the daze of sleep dissipated, realized that Jessica wasn't here.

Jessica was Dane's now.

He rolled over and groaned as the bright sunlight shone in his face. He glanced at the clock. His alarm wouldn't go off for another twenty minutes, but he was awake now, so he might as well get up.

He pushed the covers aside and stood up, then stretched.

After his shower, he returned to the bedroom and dressed. He gazed in the mirror as he adjusted his silk tie. The man who stared back at him in the impeccable charcoal suit, white shirt, and magenta tie was not Storm, the free-wheeling rock musician who hopped on his motorcycle and traveled wherever he wanted, whenever he wanted, on a moment's notice.

No, the man in the mirror was Rafe Ranier, an executive who helped run a huge corporation. A man who went to the office everyday, who attended meetings and made important decisions.

He frowned, not liking what he saw. He just wanted to be true to who he was deep inside, instead of being something his father had molded him into. He wanted to *like* who he was.

Jessica had loved Storm. She was the first person who had loved him exactly as he was. She'd even seen past the rock-star persona, seeing him more clearly than the fans, than his family. Even than himself.

He wanted that. He longed for a woman who knew *him* and wanted *him*.

He turned and strode to the door. Ten minutes later he got into the limo that was waiting for him outside the entrance of his apartment building. He checked his e-mail as the limo negotiated the city streets. Finally, it pulled up in front of the office building, and he went inside and headed across the lobby.

"Good morning, Mr. Ranier." Betty from Accounting smiled at him as he stepped into the elevator.

"Good morning, Betty."

Several other people stepped inside before the doors closed, then the elevator glided upward. The way people in the company acted around him, respectful and a little nervous, made him uncomfortable.

The doors opened on the executive floor and Rafe stepped out. A stranger sat at Melanie's desk. She was a lovely young woman with upswept, sandy brown hair and wide, hazel eyes. She smiled pleasantly as he walked by, and bid him a good morning, but he instantly resented her.

He knew he was being unreasonable, but she was sitting at *Melanie's* desk. He wanted *Melanie* to be sitting there. This woman reminded him that Melanie was gone. That she had left because of *him*. And, damn it, no one would tell him why.

As he walked into his office, his cell buzzed. He sat at his desk and pulled the phone from his pocket and glanced at it.

HEY, STRANGER. STILL IN PHILLY?
DOING A GIG THERE. INTERESTED?

It was from Travis, Jessica's brother and lead singer of Savage Kiss.

Storm smiled. He would love to play with the band again. He looked up Travis in his contacts list, then called him.

Travis's familiar voice answered. "Hey, man. What took you so long?"

Storm chuckled as he leaned back in his leather chair. "You texted me all of two seconds ago."

"So, you made up with my sister yet?"

Fuck. Storm gripped the phone tightly, leaning forward. Even though Travis had tried to play it cool, Storm knew Travis had been upset about Storm walking out on Jess. Storm had never revealed his alter ego to Travis, so he couldn't tell him he'd done it to avoid hurting her. Of course, he got a big fail on that one.

"No. It turns out she hooked up with another guy."

He knew Travis would find out eventually that Storm was really Rafe Ranier, a wealthy businessman, but he didn't want that to happen yet. Travis was his friend—Storm's friend—and Storm didn't want things to change between them.

"Too bad. Mom and Dad liked you, though *I* can't figure out why," Travis said.

"Gee, thanks."

"So what about the gig? You in?"

Storm asked details about where and when, and finally

agreed and then disconnected the call. Of course, he'd known all along he would. He practically salivated at the thought of getting back up on stage, even if just for a few days.

"Hi, do you have a minute?"

He glanced up to see Jessica standing in the doorway.

"Sure."

She came in and sat down. "A lot has happened over the last few days and I just wanted to make sure everything is okay between us. I mean, I know we discussed it, but now that Dane and I are together . . . I don't want things to be awkward between us."

"It'll be fine."

"Are you sure? Because Dane and I discussed it, and Dane said he could find a position for me somewhere else in the company, so you and I wouldn't have to see each other every day."

He frowned. "Are you having problems being around me?"

He'd already driven Melanie away. Would he be the cause of Jessica leaving her job, too?

She smiled, but sadness haunted her eyes. "No, of course not."

"Jess, I don't want you to quit your job. We've already lost Melanie."

She frowned. "Rafe, don't beat yourself up about that. I told you, it was just time for her to move on."

"If that was true, Dane wouldn't have tried to make me think she'd been fired. She wouldn't have avoided telling me why she wanted to leave."

Jessica's lips compressed. "She was just afraid you'd try and talk her into staying."

"In other words, she didn't trust that I'd want the best for her."

She leaned forward and placed her hand on his. "Please, Rafe. Just let it go. She's found another job and she seems to like it."

"Where?"

Jessica released his hand and toyed with a pen lying on his desk. "At Verve."

His eyebrow arched. "She's working at a coffee shop? Did she get a management position?"

Jessica's hesitation told him everything.

Why the hell would someone with Melanie's skill and experience take a minimum-wage job serving coffee?

"Which location is she at?"

Jessica shifted in her chair. "Look, I need to get back to work. Dane needs a report for his three o'clock meeting."

He pursed his lips. "Okay, but before you go, I just wanted to let you know I heard from Travis. He's coming to town."

She smiled brightly. "Yes, he called me last night. The band will be playing here for a few days, then he's going to visit for a couple of weeks before they continue their tour."

"You didn't tell him you and Dane are engaged?"

"No, I didn't want to tell him on the phone. I thought I'd wait until he gets here and meets Dane, then tell him."

Storm smiled at the thought of the laid-back Travis meeting no-nonsense Dane. The two were as different as night and day.

"Travis asked me to play with the band."

She gazed at him, her eyes wide. "What did you say?"

"I said yes."

"Oh."

The anxiety in her wide green eyes tore at his heart.

"You don't think I should play with them?" he asked.

"No, it's just . . . does this mean you're leaving?"

"No, nothing like that. I'm just joining them for the concert in Philadelphia."

"Oh, good. Dane is so happy to have you back, and I know it would hurt him to lose you again."

He shook his head. "I already left once. I won't do that to him again."

She smiled. "I think your playing with the band again will be good for you. And I'd love for Dane to see how talented you are."

He wondered what Dane would think, watching his younger brother strutting across the stage, whipping the audience into an exhilarated, screaming frenzy.

"Did I hear someone mention my name?" Dane said as he strode into the office.

"No, sir. We wouldn't dare talk about you when you aren't here." She winked at Rafe as she stood up.

"I didn't mean to interrupt your talk." He stepped to her side and kissed her cheek, though Rafe could tell his brother wanted to do far more than that. He could see the desire in his brother's eyes—not just lust but a deep need. He'd never seen his brother so demonstrative with a woman. So totally captivated.

He clearly loved her.

"I just wanted to let you know I'll need you to join me in my two o'clock meeting."

"Yes, sir." Jessica fell into the role of obedient assistant, showing no hint of the closeness they'd just shared. He watched her follow Dane from the office.

He knew she loved this role and she played it well. Being controlled by Dane turned her on immensely, and just thinking about it made him remember the domination scenario they'd played out the last time they were together. His groin tightened at the memory.

It made him wish he could call Melanie in here, close the door, and then play the role of aggressive boss to submissive secretary. The images playing through his mind, of Melanie stripping off her suit at his command, of her unfastening her bra and revealing her naked breasts, shocked him. He'd never thought of Melanie that way before. Melanie was his secretary and his friend.

He shook away the idea. It was probably just that Jessica and Dane were sending off pheromones.

Or was it more that it was starting to sink in that Melanie was really gone.

And the realization that since she no longer worked here, he would never see her again.

A deep emptiness gnawed at the pit of his stomach. She had been more than a secretary. He had been able to talk to her.

He missed that.

He leaned back in his chair. And damn it, the thought of Melanie working at some minimum-wage job disturbed him.

He didn't know why she'd left, and Jessica kept telling him to leave it alone, but he didn't want to.

Maybe he couldn't figure out his own problems, but somehow he would find a way to put things right. He'd talk to Melanie and see if he could convince her to come back to Ranier Industries where she belonged.

Rafe and Melanie's story continues in . . .

HIS TO CLAIM

Coming soon from St. Martin's Press
Visit www.opalcarew.com for the latest news